Don't miss these other exciting titles
Vickie McKeehan

The Pelican Pointe Series
PROMISE COVE
HIDDEN MOON BAY
DANCING TIDES
LIGHTHOUSE REEF
STARLIGHT DUNES
LAST CHANCE HARBOR
SEA GLASS COTTAGE
LAVENDER BEACH
SANDCASTLES UNDER THE CHRISTMAS MOON
BENEATH WINTER SAND
KEEPING CAPE SUMMER
A PELICAN POINTE CHRISTMAS
THE COAST ROAD HOME
THE BOATHOUSE

The Evil Secrets Trilogy
JUST EVIL Book One
DEEPER EVIL Book Two
ENDING EVIL Book Three
EVIL SECRETS TRILOGY BOXED SET

The Skye Cree Novels
THE BONES OF OTHERS
THE BONES WILL TELL
THE BOX OF BONES
HIS GARDEN OF BONES
TRUTH IN THE BONES
SEA OF BONES
FORGOTTEN BONES
DOWN AMONG THE BONES

The Indigo Brothers Trilogy
INDIGO FIRE
INDIGO HEAT
INDIGO JUSTICE
INDIGO BROTHERS TRILOGY BOXED SET

Coyote Wells Mysteries
MYSTIC FALLS
SHADOW CANYON
SPIRIT LAKE
FIRE MOUNTAIN
MOONLIGHT RIDGE

Moonlight Ridge

by

VICKIE McKEEHAN

Castletown Publishing

Copyright © 2020 Vickie McKeehan

MOONLIGHT RIDGE
A Coyote Wells Mystery
Published by Castletown Publishing
Copyright © 2020
Vickie McKeehan
All rights reserved.

Moonlight Ridge
A Coyote Wells Mystery
Copyright © 2020
Vickie McKeehan

All rights reserved. No part of this book may be reproduced, scanned, or distributed in any printed or electronic format without written permission. Please do not participate in or encourage piracy of copyrighted materials in violation of the author's rights. Purchase only authorized editions.

This book is a work of fiction. Names, characters, incidents, locales, and dialogue are drawn from the author's imagination and are not to be construed as real. Any resemblance to actual events or persons, living or dead, businesses or companies, is entirely coincidental.

Castletown Publishing
ISBN-10: 8574041215
ISBN-13: 9798574041215
Published by
Castletown Publishing
Printed in the USA
Titles Available at Amazon

Cover art by Vanessa Mendozzi
You can visit the author at:
www.vickiemckeehan.com
www.facebook.com/VickieMcKeehan
http://vickiemckeehan.wordpress.com/
www.twitter.com/VickieMcKeehan
https://www.instagram.com/vickie.mckeehan.author/

Moonlight Ridge

by

VICKIE McKEEHAN

Castletown Publishing

Copyright © 2020 Vickie McKeehan

1

Awash in spring-like temperatures, March arrived in Coyote Wells like a baby lamb, snuggled and wrapped in a soft pink blanket.

That wasn't the case the day before.

The last day of February went out like a roaring lion, packing a punch with a series of powerful storms that raged up and down the coast. High winds bashed and battered the shoreline for twenty-four solid hours, sending floodwaters thundering through the streets and spilling over the curb into the downtown businesses.

By morning, most of the water had receded. But the downtown area faced a daunting cleanup. As business owners greeted Monday morning, they cleared away their sandbags and began mopping up the damage.

One woman had been up all night.

Gemma Channing Bonner, owner of Coyote Chocolate Company, had opted to spend the night in her shop, doing her best to keep the water from seeping in and ruining the floors.

With mop in hand, her dark caramel-colored hair slipping out of its ponytail, Gemma surveyed the mess. It stretched from the counter to where she'd stacked the tables, one on top of the other.

She'd brought in huge fans to dry up the water. But the whole store still had that musty odor that lingered long after the rain had stopped.

To keep everything else dry, she'd stored away expensive supplies back in the pantry. Now, one by one, she brought everything back out, ready to start her day, ready to begin making chocolate again. It was the one bright spot she looked forward to in an otherwise depressing, stressful twenty-four hours.

After protecting and guarding what she owned from Mother Nature's wrath, she felt exhausted. Bringing her arm up to mop her brow, she noticed the rip in her new mint green sweater where a tear had frayed the sleeve. Letting out a low groan, she looked down at her stone-washed jeans only to see that she'd ripped the knee on her right leg. Little drops of blood had seeped out into the fabric.

She'd probably need to rub antiseptic cream on her kneecap. Later. For now, it would have to wait until the big fans completely dried the wet floors. Everything would have to wait until business got back to normal.

Out of the corner of her eye, she caught sight of Lianne Whittaker, her friend and now a business owner, standing inside the doorway that joined the chocolate shop to Lianne's new venture—Collette's Collectibles.

With Gemma's help and advice, Lianne had hired Billy Gafford to transform the old pizza place into a homage to Collette, Lianne's murdered sister. Collette had made plans before her death to turn the old pizzeria into a winetasting slash bookstore but never got the project off the ground. Lianne meant to change that. At the very least, turn the space into a viable retail outlet.

It hadn't been easy. The winetasting slash bookstore idea had fizzled for a variety of reasons.

After two years of changing her mind, Lianne had finally settled on what she hoped would work. This early in March, she had one goal in mind—the grand opening of the shop planned for Memorial Day weekend. By then, tourists would be flocking to the little coastal town in numbers that would double the population.

There was still a lot to get done. Lianne had crates to unpack and shelves to stock, which is why she worked at the chocolate store part-time. Helping Gemma balance mayoral duties while maintaining a brisk candy business kept Lianne on her toes.

"Hey, when did you get here?" Gemma called out.

"Just came in through the alleyway. Had to wait for the water to recede before my little Civic could make it downtown. Is it okay to come inside?" Lianne asked, looking out at the still-damp hardwood, then testing her foot on the slick floor. "How come this place got harder hit than..." She thumbed her fist back over her shoulder and pointed to the store behind her. "There's hardly any water at all in the shop. None of the inventory seems to have suffered damage. Although a few boxes got wet. But all the rest, especially those containing the books I got in on Friday, are dry."

"Maybe that's because you still have them in crates. Good call, by the way. I didn't understand at the time why you didn't get everything unpacked. You look like the genius now."

Lianne lifted a shoulder and studied the dining area and the counter, then sniffed the air. "Still smells like stale rainwater in here, but it'll dry out. We'll open both doors and let the breeze air it out. Everything will be okay. You'll see. But what a way to start the week, huh?"

"Tell me about it."

"Did you know there was a fire in the old mercantile building two doors down?"

"No, but I thought I smelled smoke earlier. And I heard sirens. But then I also thought I had all the water mopped up. How'd it catch on fire anyway? Lightning strike last night?"

"Don't know. But I saw Lando and Tully Beacham head into the building a few minutes ago. So, I would assume the fire had nothing to do with lightning."

"Lando was so busy answering calls he hasn't been to bed all night."

"I'd say the same could be said about you," Lianne decided, staring at the dark circles under Gemma's eyes. "How long have you been on your feet anyway?"

"Mopping up? I'd say practically all night. I was here at midnight to put sandbags out around the doors." She stretched her back. "What time is it anyway?"

"Almost seven-thirty. How did this side of the business get the worst of it? That's my question."

"We might be right next door to each other, but the chocolate shop is probably a foot lower and on a tilt. Be grateful Collette's is almost completely dry in there. You should be able to open on schedule."

"We," Lianne corrected. "Thanks to you, we were able to finally nail down an idea that works for the entire town, especially all the local artists, crafters, and writers. I'm excited to finally get this place up and running. It'll be an awesome shop to sell and showcase all kinds of arts and crafts created by a wide range of artisans from Crescent City to the Oregon border."

Amused at the enthusiasm in Lianne's voice, Gemma stoked the anticipation. "And featuring books from local writers who will stop in and do book signings now and then should boost our book club membership. It's all finally coming together, Lianne. A lot of hard work and tough decisions went into it. And I have to say Billy Gafford did a fantastic job."

"Well, he still has to finish painting the storeroom and put together the shelves for display. But yeah, I'm no longer worried about him completing the job on time. Told you so."

"Yes, you did. I had my doubts, but the guy came through like a workhorse."

When Gemma swayed on her feet, Lianne took notice. "Here, let me do that." She took out a white, starched apron from a drawer and tied it around her waist. "Sit down, get off your feet. You've got most of it already. One more swipe around the dining room, and the floor should be fine, especially with the fans. After we open both doors, front and back, the place will air dry, and in a few hours will be good as new. You'll see, we'll be ready when customers make their way downtown."

For the third time in as many hours, Gemma attempted to pull back her messy hair into a tight ponytail. "I'm not sure we'll get too many customers today. But just so they know we're here, I'll make us some coffee. I'll make it strong so that the aroma will waft out into the street. Let's hope it hides the musty smell."

"I wouldn't say no to an espresso. You look like you could use one, too. I've never seen so much rainfall in a twenty-four-hour period. Luke said it doesn't happen around here that often."

"The weatherman called it a one in a million freakish storm. Last time I heard, his forecast was for fifteen inches to fall within a few hours." She handed off her phone to Lianne. "Look at these pictures I took at two-thirty this morning. You can see how fast the water rose, moving up through the square from the ocean. Within twenty minutes, it became a deluge with high tide right outside the doorway. You couldn't even see the sidewalks. There was so much water I thought I might need a boat to get out of here. But then the rain stopped around five. I'm not afraid to admit, until then, I got plenty scared."

When she'd finished looking at all the photos, Lianne handed the phone back. "You should've called me. I would've come to help."

"And get you out of the house during a typhoon? Luke would've put his foot down." Gemma laughed at her own joke. "We should have named our typhoon. You know, like they do hurricanes. Last night with the wind, it felt like one. Hurricane Adam, first of its kind along the West Coast."

"I like that. Even though Luke reminded me why hurricanes don't happen here, something about warm water and ocean currents."

"That sounds like an opportunity to bring up Pacific hurricanes over a happy hour one day this week and argue about who's right. Over the years, there have been a few."

"No kidding? I can't wait to tell Luke that. Sometimes the doctor can be a real know-it-all."

"Uh-oh. I'm sensing trouble in paradise."

"Sometimes, that man can be so infuriating," Lianne confessed. "Just because Luke Bonner is a doctor doesn't make him smarter than me about everything."

Gemma thought of her brother-in-law and how much alike Luke was to Lando. "I agree. They are brothers, triplets at that, who shared a womb. It makes them more alike than they care to admit. What's my brother-in-law done now?"

"We got into an argument about, of all things, how to run the washer."

"You're fighting over laundry. That's never a good sign."

Lianne sputtered out a laugh. "Luke has this annoying habit of trying to tell me how to do stuff better, more efficiently."

"Like we don't know how to do laundry," Gemma grumbled with a roll of her eyes. "Men can be infuriating when they try to butt in and correct the way we've been doing something for years. All on our own. As if they willingly take our help when they're lost and need directions."

"Exactly. Like Luke trying to tell me how to load the dishwasher properly."

Running on fumes from the last several hours and stressed, a worn-out Gemma found that funny. She let out a string of giggles and didn't seem to be able to stop. For the first time in hours, she slid down into a chair and put her head on the table.

"I'm not sure you're laughing or crying," Lianne pointed out. "It wasn't that hilarious."

"I'm so tired I'm not sure either," Gemma said, turning her head to look at Lianne. "You and Luke aren't about to call off the wedding next month, are you?"

"No, it's not that bad. I don't think so anyway. But we are still wading through some personal issues. Day to day stuff that drives us both crazy and invariably leads to heated discussions, which, in turn, leads to little puddles of quicksand if we let them."

"I hate to tell you this, but minefields like quicksand are always gonna crop up no matter what you do about them."

"It's like whack-a-mole, isn't it? You knock down one issue, and another pops up."

"Exactly. A perfect analogy of married life. Whack-a-mole."

That got Lianne laughing.

At the back of the shop, the Westie named Rolo popped his head up out of a storage bin. Rolo whined as he nudged Rufus, the chocolate Labrador, into a standing position. The bigger dog stretched and yawned. With his nose, the Lab pushed Rolo toward the main room.

Still roaring with senseless laughter, Lianne turned her focus on the dogs. "They don't look too worse for wear. Did the thunder scare them?"

"Like two little babies, they were. Those two hid in the cupboards when the thunder and lightning showed up. To be honest, I would've crawled in there with them, but somebody had to stay out here and assess the water situation so we all wouldn't drown."

"Was it really that bad?"

"Felt like it," Gemma noted as she got to her feet again. She went over and scooped out dog food from a small emergency bag she kept under the back counter. "Now I know why our main street is named for water. Sometime during the last century, it had to overflow through downtown, and some genius decided to memorialize the event by naming it Water Street. We lost power around midnight. Telephones were still working, though, because people kept calling me to do something about it. I called the power company and they gave me a timeline as to how long the outage would last. Imagine my surprise when the electricity came back on about thirty minutes ago."

"It pays to be mayor."

Gemma grinned. "I guess it does."

After feeding the dogs and putting out fresh water, Gemma turned to load the coffeemaker with freshly ground beans. Instincts had her touching the pendant she wore around her neck. The silver chain held her four energy stones—turquoise, moonstone, lapis, and a smaller carnelian marble—joined together in an ornate, wire-encased amulet. Turquoise for protection. Moonstone for truth. Lapis for power. Carnelian for knowledge.

Still clutching her necklace with one hand, she used her other one to hit the brew button. As the coffee began its cycle, an odd feeling came over Gemma. Over the past year, she'd learned to listen to that little voice inside her head that often indicated something was wrong. "Oh, my God. I wonder if the electricity coming back on had anything to do with the fire three doors down. I better go check on Lando."

"Go on," Lianne urged, shooing the owner from behind the counter. "Do what you need to do. I've got this covered. Want me to start making the candy, too?"

"You know, we have cherry creams leftover from Friday, probably two dozen or so. When the rain hit, I started to toss them out. Glad I didn't. Why don't we see if those are still any good? I kept them in the commercial fridge. But the power did go out for almost five hours. If the candy is still okay, hand them out to the customers for free as a gesture to come back tomorrow. It'll probably take us that long to get back to normal. Then we'll pick up making the regular flavors Tuesday morning, use today to build our stock back up. That sound like a plan?"

"Perfect. That's why I came in to check and see how things were going. Monday's flavor is always hazelnut. Is it okay to go with that, or do you want something else?"

"Nope, hazelnut works for now. I am working on a new creation but I haven't finished it yet. We'll make a batch of those truffles with the strawberry filling and glaze on top. People seem to like those after stormy weather. I'll be back in twenty minutes to finish setting up."

"No need to hurry. Take your time."

As soon as Gemma stepped outside into warm sunshine, she spotted the fire trucks lined up in front of the old general store. But she didn't see anything on fire.

Approaching the front door, she poked her head inside only to see Payce Davis wave her back. "Hey, what's going on in here? Where's the fire?"

As the patrol officer in charge, Payce backed her out of the old building. "The fire was in the downstairs basement. Got us a murder on a Monday morning. A body. You know old Ben Zurcher?"

"The old postmaster? Sure. Everybody knows Ben." Gemma's eyes widened as the news began to sink in. "You're kidding? What was old Ben doing here in an empty shell of a building in the middle of a rainstorm?"

"Lando thinks maybe he was meeting someone, and they killed him, started a fire to cover their tracks, too."

"The killer tried to set him on fire. Ewww. What kind of person would do that to another human being? That's disgusting. That's insane. How? How did he die?"

Payce pointed to the back of his head. "Gunshot wound to the head. Do you remember how old Ben was?"

"I'd say probably around seventy-four or so. Why?"

A tired Lando appeared in the doorway. "Payce, go out front and see if you can locate the medical examiner. Find out what's taking Tuttle so long to get to the crime scene. Drag him in here if you have to. That's an order."

Payce gave a mock salute and started down the steps. "You want I should push him out of the interview he's giving?"

"What?" Lando muttered, storming outside and past Gemma. He spotted Jeff Tuttle across the street huddled with Tina Ashcomb, a staff reporter from the County newspaper. "How can he be giving an interview when he hasn't even set eyes on the victim yet? Get him over here, Payce. Now!"

Gemma found her lips curving into a smile. Watching Lando Bonner in his element always made her realize how lucky she was. She studied his dark hair, his dark eyes, the stubble on his face—and fell in love all over again.

He wore his hair longer these days, curling up just at the top of his leather bomber jacket. He wore his cowboy boots, a pair of dark indigo blue jeans, and a white button-down shirt that everyone called his Lando Bonner uniform. The outfit made him look delicious, good enough to eat for breakfast.

Tamping down one urge, she leaned over and pressed a kiss to his lips. "Bad morning?"

"Bad for Ben Zurcher. Someone shot him in the head, then rolled him up in a rug and tried to set it on fire. The carpeting didn't burn much." He lowered his voice and pulled her back into the building. "I found a partially burned note underneath Ben's body, though."

"And? You look upset. I'm guessing the note indicates it wasn't a suicide?"

"I am upset. The killer set fire to the note, hoping it would burn with the body."

"But it didn't."

"No, it didn't."

"Are you gonna tell me what the note said?"

"Do you remember the Copeland murders twenty years back?"

Lines formed across Gemma's forehead. "That family who lived out by the old highway, the one who got murdered on Friday the thirteenth? Sure. Who doesn't remember the County's most horrific unsolved crime? A mom and dad beat to death with a baseball bat along with their two kids. What does it have to do with Ben?"

"You're right about the date. Somebody murdered the Copelands on Friday, October 13, 2000. But the killer used a hammer, not a baseball bat. I already had Dale fact-check that. The note underneath Ben's body was all about the Copeland family. Imagine him holding on to that piece of paper clutched in his hand. I figure he had it there for a reason, trying to hide it from the killer. He'd scribbled the note himself. I recognized Ben's handwriting. It said he knew who killed the Copelands and why it happened."

"But if all this time Ben knew, why didn't he say something to you before now?"

"That's the question on my mind, too. Was old Ben involved in the murders? If so, what was his motive? Did the killer threaten him to keep his mouth shut? I mean, look where we are. Ben's dead, and someone shot him in the head during one of the worst storms in a decade. A lot of questions yet to answer."

When Tuttle stepped in, Lando glared at the coroner. "Took you long enough to get here. I saw you flirting with Tina."

Jeff Tuttle handled criticism the same way he viewed his job. He used humor and sarcastic wit to survive the never-ending stream of bodies that ended up in his morgue. "What's the rush? Has the victim got somewhere else to be?"

"I'd like you to do whatever it is you do here so I can get the asshole who did this. Is that too much to ask from a taxpayer?"

"Ah, so you're the impatient one. Got it."

"Could I get a little less attitude and more work? What else do *you* have to do?" Lando fired back. "My crew and I have been up all night. So excuse me if I'm not in the mood to stand around cracking jokes."

"Testy, aren't we? Fine. Show me what you've got."

Knowing there was a body in the basement—someone she had known—Gemma stiffened her spine and decided to tag along.

After thumbing on his flashlight, Lando led them down into a cavernous basement, once used for storing inventory. But now, the shelves were long bare, and the wood appeared to be rotting in places.

Gemma caught a whiff of decomposition. The unmistakable odor blended with the stale, musty air and the damp conditions in the cellar.

Tuttle went to the body, bent down over it for a few minutes, then straightened back up again. "He was shot right here. There's blood splatter on the rug. See?"

Lando nodded. "I figured that."

Tuttle pointed to a series of crimson red droplets still damp. Without waiting for anyone else's comments, the coroner moved to the side. "What that means is this. The rug was already down on the floor. The moment Ben got shot, he dropped right where he stood. That's when the killer wrapped the rug around him and tried his hand at arson, probably using an ordinary lighter to set fire to the inside of the carpet. Some of it burned. Most of it didn't. Not enough oxygen to fuel a little starter fire down here with all the damp floor conditions."

"Which means the killer was probably waiting down here for him, right? He already had the rug in place, and as soon as Ben was in position, he shoots him in the head."

"Sounds reasonable to me."

Since Lando had already bagged the note as evidence, he now handed it off to Tuttle to get his input. "I found this in Ben's hand. Partially burned. The best part, anyway."

Tuttle looked amused but read the letter before cutting his eyes back to Lando's. "Why, Chief? I do believe you might need to open up a cold-case murder investigation now. The bottom half of that note was burned right off before Ben named the killer."

"Bite me," Lando snapped. "Just give me the time of death, and you can get out of here."

"I'd say he's been here less than five hours. That would make it between two and three o'clock this morning."

Gemma stepped closer while still maintaining a respectable six feet from the corpse. "Worst of the storm happened right about that time. Just saying. Howling wind, rain gushing down in buckets. I remember the time because it was raining so hard that I thought the roof might blow off. Or at least the roof would start leaking. The dogs were going crazy."

"Did you hear a gunshot?" Lando wanted to know.

"I didn't hear anything but dogs making a fuss and the wind roaring and rain beating down so hard on the roof I thought it might give way."

Lando ran a free hand over his stubble. "Ben must've thought that meeting up with a killer was so important he had to do it during a bad storm. Weird."

"Maybe the killer was blackmailing Ben, or vice versa," she offered. "Maybe Ben's killer brought him money. Lots of people would go out in bad weather if it means adding to their bank account."

"I don't believe Ben would ever be involved in anything like that, though."

"Isn't it always the last person you'd suspect?"

"Maybe. Time to head over to Ben's place and check it out," Lando decided. "Jeff, you'll let me know when you finish the autopsy."

"Sure. If I find any surprises, I'll let you know that, too. But the GSW to the head is the reason he died."

Lando rolled his eyes. "Maybe you should do standup."

"Hey, I'm just trying to start my day in an upbeat manner. Sue me."

Gemma had a thought as she turned to face Jeff Tuttle. "If you're thinking of asking out Tina Ashcomb, you should really do it now before she decides to take that new job offer over in Crescent City."

Tuttle gave her a strange look before shaking his head. "I hate small towns. Does everybody have to know your business twenty-four-seven and then comment on it? Why don't I just put that I'm interested in Tina on social media?"

"Hey, it was a friendly tip, meant to give you a heads up if you're in stall-mode," Gemma explained. "If Tina has her sights set on moving somewhere else, you need to act now or be prepared to accept that you missed your chance when she moves away."

Tuttle gave her a sheepish look. "Okay, maybe I will ask her out. Do you think she'll take the job?"

"Crescent City isn't that much bigger than Coyote Wells. I think Tina will bide her time until something else even better comes along."

"Good to know," Tuttle muttered as he turned to go. "Do I need to hang around here while the techs from County finish taking pictures and evidence?"

"I guess not," Lando concluded. "Thanks again for dropping in when you did."

"Kiss my ass," Jeff stated. "I'm the only medical examiner for miles around here. I have things to do and places to go."

After Tuttle made his way back upstairs, Lando leaned into Gemma. "Are you picking up anything at all about why Ben was here?"

She shook her head. "All I know is that Ben Zurcher was a longtime friend of my grandparents. Marissa mentioned him often in her diaries. There's only a brief mention of the Copelands. And that's when she writes about the murders the day after it happened. If either Marissa or Jean-Luc had suspected Ben was part of any sinister plot to kill a family, she would've put it down in the journal. She didn't. That's significant to me."

"But hardly anything of real substance I could take to a jury down the road."

"True."

Disheartened, Lando tried to hide his disappointment. He planted a kiss on her brow.

In turn, she laid a hand on his cheek. "Look, I'm sorry. Maybe something will pop into my head later. I don't have much control over the ability to see the past. It just happens."

"What brought you down the street then?"

She lifted a shoulder. "Something felt off. I came to make sure you were all right."

He heard footsteps overhead and realized the crime scene techs were upstairs. "I better go point them in the right direction, else they'll be wandering around in the building looking for a clue."

Gemma clucked her tongue and patted his chest. "Let me know when you're heading home. I'll meet you there."

"Sounds like a plan, *Mayor*. How many disgruntled calls did you get when the power went out?"

She began to climb the stairs to the first floor. "I stopped counting at forty-seven. We have some angry people who live here just looking for a reason to complain. They should take a happy pill once in a while."

"Tell me about it."

"How many calls did you take last night?"

"Let's just say dispatch kept us busy. Turns out, Suzanne is good at handling unhappy people who think they need a cop for every little incident. She either works it out over the phone, or she de-escalates the situation. I'm telling you that having Suzanne on my team is like having another officer on patrol."

"Then maybe you should give her a raise."

"Is that in the budget? Better check, *Mayor*, before you go promising a raise to anybody."

"Duly noted."

"Although Suzanne probably does deserve one. After dealing with Louise for years, Suzanne is like a breath of fresh air. Besides, her presence at City Hall helps us both."

"I know that. Which is why I'm gonna check the budget to find the money for her a nice pay raise. I happen to know she could use it. And knowing how devoted she is to City Hall, she deserves one."

"She hasn't complained, not once, about the pay."

"No, Suzanne wouldn't. She loves her job."

After directing the crime techs down to the basement, Lando snatched her around the waist. "Why are you so feisty this morning? Shouldn't you be dragging after a night of no sleep?"

Her fingers crawled up his chest. "I've been up all night, same as you. Besides, you like me feisty. Now, if we could just get out of going to Leia's house tonight for dinner, we could get to bed early."

"Is that tonight? Who gives a dinner party on a Monday night? I thought we could just get takeout, then sleep for twenty hours or so."

"It's Leia's only night off. Oh, wow. Look at the time. I gotta go, Lando. I promised Anna Kate Baccarat I'd sit down with her this morning and talk about putting more money in the budget for more lifeguards on the beach this summer. She's my first appointment of the day. Darn. I had no idea I'd been gone this long. I promised Lianne I'd be back in twenty minutes."

"Anna Kate Baccarat? She was in the band, right? Little redhead? Didn't she marry Derrick Ross, a couple of years older than us?"

"She did, but it only lasted six years or so. They got divorced in Vegas. Or so I'm told. I plan on getting all the dirty deets after the meeting. Or maybe during."

"A mayor's job is never done."

She drilled a playful finger into his belly. "Hey, don't laugh. Since I took over this gig, I'm too busy to get into any trouble. And you haven't even noticed."

"Sure, I've noticed. But I didn't want to jinx it."

She swatted him on the arm. "Just for that, watch me round up my crew and see what trouble I can find."

2

Twenty years ago, the Copeland family murders had made national news. Not all that surprising when a quadruple homicide included an ordinary family of four, two of whom were children. The story became newsworthy because the callousness of the crime had all the elements of a whodunit. Each victim had suffered blunt trauma to the head, blows that far exceeded the definition of excessive force. Aside from the fact that the crime was horrific, senseless, and without motive, it came while the family slept. Each victim had been found still tucked in their beds.

The gruesome scene had put the entire Copeland family under a microscope. But what could an ordinary husband and wife have done to piss off a killer enough to kill the kids?

While sitting at his desk, Lando flipped through the pages of the fourth Copeland murder book—another fat blue binder that held valuable detective notes—and got reacquainted with the family's bio and the case.

Sandra had been a local girl from a well-to-do family named Trask. The Trasks owned a spread north of town. She'd met and married an eager entrepreneur named Todd Copeland, ten years older, who hailed from, of all places, New York City. After getting his business degree at Syracuse University, Todd moved out west, arriving in Coyote Wells in the early 1990s with a dream of living in a small town and starting his own business. Thanks to a loan from his father, a stockbroker on Wall Street, Todd began plans to re-open the general store that later became the Coyote Wells Mercantile.

Todd and Sandra settled down into married life, purchasing a house on forty acres next to Moonlight Ridge. When the kids started coming, Sandra became a stay-at-home mom to her two girls, Hallie and Julie. At the time of their murders, Hallie had just celebrated her seventh birthday, and Julie, barely five, had just started kindergarten. As for Todd, he'd spent the last several years trying to keep the Mercantile going.

Lando had just started laying out the crime scene photographs across his desk when Dale came strolling into his office.

"I can't find the fifth box," Dale announced.

"Fifth box of what?" Lando asked without looking up. Preoccupied with the task, he continued digging through the crime scene photos, trying to arrange them in some kind of order.

"The computer indicates there should be five boxes of evidence in storage, five murder books. One of five. Two of five. Three of five. Four of five. There's no five of five. I can only locate four, and you've already got Number Four."

That detail got Lando's attention. His head popped up. "Well, go look again. It has to be there."

Dale shook his head. "I've been down there in the basement since I got back from the Mercantile. I've rearranged boxes. I've re-stacked them. I've checked everywhere. I'm telling you that box is nowhere in the basement or on the premises. It's gone."

Lando pushed to his feet. "Keep looking. It's time to search Ben's house."

"But I want to go to Ben's with you. My time would be better spent there. I know the layout. I used to date his daughter, Carolyn before she married someone else and moved out of state."

"I know the layout as well as you do. But okay, just make sure you get Payce looking for that fifth box and ask anyone else who has time on their hands to help us out."

Dale took out his cell phone to text Payce, then angled toward Lando. "Something occurred to me while I was down in the basement. Ben is the one who wrote up the story the day the news broke about the Copeland murders. There's an old newspaper clipping in the second or third box with his byline. Did he pick up extra cash as a reporter back in those days?"

"Sure. Small town newspaper. Anybody could get their stories published back then if it was succinct and good enough. Elnora

Kidman used to write up the crimebeat column. Ansel Conover used to do a gardening piece every week. What's your point?"

"Well, if Ben had figured out who the killer was, say several years later, why would he keep quiet about it? I used to think Ben Zurcher was one of the good guys. But now I'm not so sure."

"I know. It's hard to imagine Ben keeping that kind of thing a secret. That wasn't the man I knew and respected. Something else bothers me, though. If Ben had been working on the Copeland murders long after he retired and thought he could solve it, why not give me a heads up about what he was doing? His house is right down the street from mine."

"You mean the bachelor pad you had on the beach."

"Yeah. I still own it. Anyway, the point is, I used to go by his house to check on him. He'd invite me in for coffee, and we'd sit there for an hour or so in his living room or at the kitchen table talking sports or politics. Ben never once brought up the Copeland case to me during all my visits, never once asked for my opinion. Not one time."

"See? It's weird."

"Weird enough that we'll just go tear the house apart," Lando concluded. When he got a wide-eyed look back from Dale, he added, "I'm serious. I want to know why the hell Ben kept a thing like that to himself."

Ben Zurcher's home was a brick and stucco mid-century modern located down the street from Lando's old beach house steps away from the shoreline.

Wearing latex gloves, Lando used the set of keys found on Ben's body to open the front door. He felt like an interloper spying on a friend as he stepped into the interior of the house. When he flipped on the lights, an energetic black and white cat jumped out from behind the drapes to greet him.

"Friend of yours?" Dale wanted to know.

"I've seen him around. His name's Orwell, as in the writer. I think Ben mentioned he was a fan."

"Orwell, huh?" Dale mumbled as he scooped up the kitty and held it close to his chest. "I'll go see if I can find him some food. He's bound to be hungry."

Jimmy stepped in behind Lando and bobbed his head toward the back of the house. "Nice wall of windows from floor to ceiling. These old houses seemed to have their own set of charm, don't they?"

"I guess," Lando said as he studied the open floor plan with new eyes. He'd never really noticed much about Ben's layout before now. But he could tell by the things left out that Ben had expected to return from his meeting alive. A TV guide was left open to Sunday night's schedule and a crossword puzzle with blocks yet to fill.

"Got the cat fed," Dale proclaimed. "Found one of those bags of dry cat food in the pantry. We'll have to call Inez LeMond to come and get him, though. She runs the only no-kill shelter around these parts for abandoned pets. Unless you know someone who wants a cat."

"Not me. You take care of contacting Inez," Lando told him, still looking around the house, assessing the best place to start their search. "Let's split up. Jimmy, you take Ben's bedroom. Dale, you take the living room. I'll start in Ben's office. We're looking for anything that links back to the Copeland murders, or anything that would tell us who might've killed Ben."

The men headed into different parts of the house, prepared to carry out a thorough search.

But it didn't take long for Lando to realize the task might be more daunting than he'd previously thought. He opened the door to the room that housed Ben's office, expecting a desk and some bookshelves, but what he discovered instead was an entire room dedicated to the Copeland murders. Their family pictures were plastered all over the walls, showing them in various stages of life. The other section of the wall held crime scene photographs depicting the family in death. He also spotted the missing fifth box sitting on the floor next to the desk, marked Five of Five.

He went over to the box, picked it up off the carpeting, and then slid it to a corner of Ben's desk. Easing off the lid, he peered inside only to discover the box was mostly empty. That's when he noticed the row of evidence bags laid out in order on the credenza. One bag held what looked like the murder weapon—the head of a hammer. *But where the hell was the handle?* Lando wondered as he started pawing his way through the other stuff on the desk.

After not finding the handle among any of the plastic baggies, he readjusted his focus to the pictures on the wall. He paced in front of what could only be described as Ben's shrine to the Copeland family. There were pictures of Sandra from high school tacked next to photos of Todd wearing his choir robe while singing in church. The photographs of the kids ranged from school pictures to snapshots taken in the couple's backyard.

Lando stood back and scratched his head, then yelled for the others. Jimmy appeared first, then Dale.

"Hey, that's the missing box," Dale exclaimed. "What the hell is this, Lando?"

"I have no idea what's going on, and because of that, here's what we're gonna do. Which one of you is the better photographer?"

Dale and Jimmy traded looks.

"That would be me," Jimmy offered.

"Fine. Then grab a camera, a quality one with a wide-angle lens. Purchase as much film as you can. I want every single angle of this wall photographed just as it is. Then, I want the entire room photographed, piece by piece, wall by wall. I want it all documented right down to each piece of paper, so we'll have a backup before we touch or remove anything."

"You do realize it will take days to get that done, right?" Jimmy clarified. "At the minimum three."

"That's okay. I don't care how long it takes. We're not in a hurry." He pivoted toward Dale. "I want you to set up a perimeter around the house, make sure one of us is on duty here twenty-four-seven to protect the integrity of the victim's house as we found it."

Jimmy walked around the room. "Why would Ben Zurcher have all this stuff here?"

Dale was just as puzzled, but he was upset. "Yeah, well, the bigger question is how he got his hands on that box of evidence. I wasted a couple of hours looking for that earlier. Did someone allow Ben to walk in there and just carry it out? How long has he had this stuff anyway? I mean, it looks like he's been at this since he retired."

"Maybe eight years. Can we all agree there is a multitude of questions and so far, no real answers to any of them?" Lando pointed out. "What we need now is to use this information to our advantage. Everything that's in here could be useful in catching Ben's killer and maybe solve a twenty-year-old cold case."

"I gotta say, Lando. It seems to me the Copeland murders are the backstory to this, the prelude," Dale said, scanning the wall again.

"I think he means the prologue," Jimmy decided. "Or what comes before. It's the reason *why* Ben was killed. He must've figured it out, then got too close, and the killer came for him, too."

Lando didn't like the sound of that, but he had a bigger issue he couldn't get past. "Why didn't he sit down with me and ask questions?"

"Maybe he didn't figure you were up to the task," Jimmy stated. "I'm serious. Taking evidence like this means he didn't trust anybody."

"There's truth to that," Lando agreed. "Hiding this from me is a slap in the face. I have to say it stings a little. You think you know somebody, and then you discover they've been keeping a secret." He stared at the wall again. "Everything we needed to get a conviction in the Copeland case was right here in Ben's house. I gotta say, ol' Ben might've been right to exclude me. Why didn't I know we were missing this much evidence? Think about it. Ben must've known we weren't actively working on it."

"Yeah. And started his own investigation," Dale concluded. "Don't be too upset. Because it got him murdered."

Gemma's meeting with Anna Kate Baccarat lasted forty-five minutes only because the two women tried catching each other up on everything that had happened to them since high school.

"So any kids?"

"Two boys. You?"

"Not yet." But Gemma could tell Anna Kate didn't want to talk about kids. The former classmate had other things on her mind.

"Is it true about Ben Zurcher?" Anna Kate wanted to know, lowering her voice to a whisper yet eager for all the juicy details. "Everyone is saying he met someone in that old mercantile last night and that someone bashed his head in just like what happened to the Copelands when they were murdered."

Gemma shuddered, remembering Ben's body lying in the basement on that filthy rug. She wasn't about to share information about one of Lando's cases, let alone mention the gunshot wound. Married to the top cop, she knew better than to spread those kinds of details to the general public. "I'm not sure how it happened. All I know is that Ben's dead, and it was a homicide."

Disappointed, Anna Kate narrowed her eyes. "But you were there. Tina Ashcomb said she saw you milling around the building. She said you must've seen the body."

"Well, yes, I did, but…"

"Who do you think killed him?"

"No idea."

"What about the note left with the body?"

"Who told you about that?" Gemma asked as she began to fidget in her chair. Feeling uncomfortable talking about the note with Anna Kate, she glanced up to find Leia listening at the doorway. Her sister-in-law looked radiant for a Monday morning. Wearing a dress in soft lilac that set off her dark Native American features, Leia cleared her throat. "Sorry, I didn't know you were busy.".

Thankful for the distraction from Anna Kate, Gemma scrambled to her feet and waved Leia into the room. "Hey, good to see you. What are you doing here? Look who's here, Anna Kate. You remember Leia Bonner, right?"

"Sure. Who could forget Lydia Bonner giving birth to triplets? How's Luke doing anyway? I had such a crush on him back in high school. Didn't you recently marry that tribal police guy last fall?"

Leia narrowed her eyes on Anna Kate. "His name is Zeb Longhorn. And yeah. We finally got married. What about you? How are things going with you and Darrell?"

"Derrick," Anna Kate corrected. "We're not together anymore."

Leia clucked her tongue. "Oh, no, what happened? Tell me everything. I want to hear it all."

For Gemma, watching the two women take turns verbally jabbing at each other made for an awkward moment. If she didn't know better, she'd actually believe Leia's empathy came from genuine concern. But she did know better.

While Anna Kate recounted the quickie divorce tale that ended up in Vegas because Derrick had fallen in love with another woman, Gemma tuned most of it out.

By the time Anna Kate had finished her story, Leia had somewhat softened. "Divorce is hard. But at least you found out what a jackass he was before you wasted any more time with him."

Anna Kate waved away the support. "What happened to me is all in the past. And I'm a lot happier without him than I was with him. Just a fact of life." She glanced over at Gemma as if remembering the woman was still in the room. "I was just about to mention to

Gemma the connection I have to the Copelands. My older sister, Laura Leigh, used to babysit for Sandra and Todd. So naturally, when the family was laid to rest, Laura Leigh was there at the funeral. But she also went to the graveside service. And what do you think she saw there?"

Without waiting for a reply from either woman, Anna Kate went on, "Sandra's sister, Jocelyn Trask, Jocelyn Williams now. She was there wearing Sandra's best dress. Must've taken it right out of her closet before the service."

"And you think Jocelyn wore that dress for spite?" Leia asked.

"Not me, but Laura Leigh did. She got the impression that Sandra and Jocelyn didn't get along at all. So, it's weird that Jocelyn would show up wearing Sandra's favorite dress. Laura Leigh always talked about that scene at the cemetery. Which is why I'd think Lando would want to talk to Jocelyn. You know, she still lives in town, over on Shell Bay, in that big house near the park. For a good ten years or so after the murders, Laura Leigh used to talk about her own theories about who killed them. She was always bringing it up."

Gemma's curiosity got the better of her. "Who did she think did it?"

"Laura Leigh? Oh, she was convinced that Jocelyn had something to do with it all along. Right up until the day she died, Laura Leigh believed that. Those poor little girls were such sweet little things."

Gemma frowned. "Wait. Your sister died? Laura Leigh died?"

"Oh, yeah. In a car accident out on the road leading to Moonlight Ridge."

"When?"

"Let's see. It'll be ten years this June."

Before Gemma could respond to the news, Anna Kate looked at her watch and grabbed her purse. "Girl, I gotta run. I have a million errands to do while the kids are in school. It was nice catching up. You guys should come over to the house one night for a girls' night out. We could fix mojitos and talk about the old days."

"That sounds great," Leia said and seemed to mean it. "Stop in at the restaurant any time, and I'll buy you a drink."

After Anna Kate had gone, Gemma turned to Leia. "What was all that about not knowing she'd broken up with Derrick? You're the one who told me about it when I came back to town."

"Oh, that. I just wanted to see her squirm a little because she couldn't remember Zeb's name. That was so fake. She knew all along who Zeb is because he arrested Derrick several years back on the Rez for public intoxication. Derrick had lost big at the tables and was wandering around the casino parking lot. The guy ended up falling into a ditch. He was that drunk. Zeb is the one who arrested him and made him sleep it off in a cell. Derrick threatened to sue. Some BS about a false arrest or something. Anyway, divorce or not, Anna Kate's probably still carrying around a grudge or two over the incident."

"It didn't look like that to me."

"Oh, it never does," Leia pointed out with a sigh. "You're always so ready to look the other way if I'm being dissed."

"Technically, Zeb's the one who got dissed. Instead of standing here arguing about something that happened to Derrick years ago, why don't you and I go out to the Copeland's old house, take a look around?"

Leia looked mortified. "What on earth for? Why would you want to go to that murder house?"

"Murder house? I haven't heard it called that in years. What could it hurt? I'd like to see where it happened."

"Oh, come on, you've been out there before—last time probably fifteen years ago on Halloween. Remember when Fleet Barkley turned it into a haunted house? He bought cases and cases of beer."

"I remember the party just getting started when Reiner Caulfield showed up and ran us all out of there."

"Exactly. So why would you want to go back now? That place is falling down. You know that sister never could sell it, right?"

"I remember something about that. But you just heard Anna Kate tell us her sister thought Jocelyn did it. And she's still living here in town."

"So what? That's ancient history." Leia recognized the look on Gemma's face, though. "Don't go sticking your nose into the past. Nothing good ever comes of it."

Since someone had already told Anna Kate about the note, Gemma decided it was no longer a state secret. "Ben Zurcher was carrying this piece of paper that said he knew who killed the Copelands. He must've mentioned what he knew to the wrong person. Now he's no longer walking around to tell anybody about who did it. I just want to go take a look inside the house, walk the floorplan, get the lay of the land, so to speak."

But something had just dawned on Leia. "By the wrong person, you mean the killer. The same guy who killed the family, killed Ben? That's what you're saying, isn't it?"

Gemma moved a shoulder and shrugged. "I believe so. But I'm not trying to step on Lando's toes or anything."

Leia lifted a brow. "Aren't you? Since when?"

"Okay. Maybe I am a tad curious. What would it hurt to look around, though?"

Not completely sold on the idea, Leia took a long look at Gemma. "Is this because you're bored with married life already?"

"What? No, of course not."

"Bored with your job then?"

"No!" But when Leia kept staring, waiting for a better explanation, Gemma let out a sigh. "Not married life so much as I'm tired of sitting behind this stupid desk for part of the day. Being mayor reminds me too much of my old way of life back in San Francisco. I hated practicing law. You know that."

"At last, honesty. So, you'd rather spend time at the murder house and piss off Lando than sit here and have a perfectly normal upstanding job as mayor." Leia shook her head. "Some days, I swear the world is upside-down, and I'm the only one with my head on straight. Okay, I'll go with you. Mainly because I haven't gotten under my brother's skin this year, and here it is March already. Although I don't like the idea of going out to Moonlight Ridge just the two of us."

Gemma bumped Leia's shoulder. "Moonlight Ridge. Another part of town no one thinks much about these days. Do kids still go out there to make out?"

"Don't ask me. I'm not in high school anymore. But from what I've heard, the place still makes for a great lover's lane."

"You've been out there with Zeb, haven't you?"

Leia's lips curved. "Maybe. But not since we stopped sneaking around behind everyone's back."

"Which was stupid. Anyway, we should stop and pick up Lianne. If we ruffle a few feathers, we should all go down for the crime."

"Sistas united. Sure. I like the sound of that."

3

From the top of Moonlight Ridge, Gemma could see the city of Coyote Wells stretched out all the way to the ocean. She took a gulp of air and set her sights on a small tract of homes that made up Oyster Landing, a subdivision sitting smack dab in the shadow of the ridge itself.

The area had never gained the same kind of successful tenancy as other neighborhoods. Most of the lots remained unsold. It was that fact that caused some people to refer to it as the ghost-town part of town. Gemma couldn't deny it gave off that kind of vibe. And after many years of not being able to sell lots here, the land had recently been repossessed by a major financial institution out of San Francisco, reinforcing the idea the area might be dying sooner rather than later.

But for the people who lived here, it was an affordable alternative to living along the coast, where prices tended to be more expensive and out of their reach. Even if homeowners had to settle for the rather haphazard range of styles and quirky designs, it was less expensive here. There were mobile homes on the same block as A-frames and custom-built cabins. With lot prices cheap, there was no shortage of neighbors.

Gemma kept that in mind from where she stood while studying the streets below and the town's layout. "Oh, look, I can see Gram's house from here."

"When are you gonna start calling it *your* house?" Lianne wanted to know.

"Old habits," Gemma muttered as she pivoted to face the Copeland farmhouse. This hundred-year-old homestead stood out for its weathered, enduring look, sort of like a sentinel protecting its younger counterpart, Oyster Landing, from the elements.

After twenty years of neglect, though, the damp, coastal weather had accelerated the aging process. The white paint had faded to a dull gray and long since peeled off in chunks or as small dust particles, carried on the wind, and likely blown out to sea. Seismic activity had shifted the foundation until it sat at a somewhat lopsided angle.

"Poor farmhouse," Gemma stated as she stared at the colonial structure, then took in the entrance to the driveway and its two fieldstone pillars, topped with lanterns. "This must've been some kind of house in its heyday. Wonder why the sister doesn't tear it down?"

Her friends weren't as impressed or interested in answering those questions.

"Are you sure you want to go in there?" Leia asked, clutching her cell phone. She'd been leaning against the side of Gemma's Volvo scanning the Internet, but now, she shoved off the car and stared at her companions. "I was just looking up the murders online. Gruesome is an understatement. What happened in that house was blatant excess. The killer beat each victim with a hammer. That took time. Back in the day, Chief Caulfield convinced himself that the killer was some random guy passing through town, carrying a hammer around with him to use as a weapon."

"The hammer came from the garage," Gemma corrected. "The killer used it to strike each one in the head while they slept. I think the killer knew the family, which means he was probably a local."

"A local? And could still live in the area?" Lianne uttered, swallowing her disgust. "So why am I here? The dogs and I could've stayed behind at the shop. I have work to do."

"You're here to provide support," Leia cracked, bobbing her head toward Gemma. "The psychic has an itch she needs to scratch."

Gemma cut her eyes back to the house. "I wouldn't use the term psychic so much as a seer into the past. Come on, let's get this over with and take a look inside."

"How do you intend to do that?" Lianne stated before taking a tentative step she didn't want to take toward the front door.

"The killer got in using the backdoor. We'll start there. The lock doesn't work."

Leia traded looks with Lianne. "Here we go down the rabbit hole again. We should probably go with her despite knowing better."

Gemma had already reached the corner of the house when the other two women caught up with her.

At the backdoor, she turned the knob and glanced back at her friends. "Here we go, ready or not."

Lianne shook her head. "Not. But how did you know about the lock?"

Gemma stood just inside the kitchen without answering the question, looking around at the empty room. "Does anyone know what happened to the furnishings?"

"Sandra's sister would probably know the answer to that," Leia said, running her fingers along the countertop, causing an inch or two of dust to flutter in the air.

As the dust scattered, Lianne sneezed in rapid succession. Reaching in her pocket for a tissue, she wiped her nose. When she looked up again, Gemma had disappeared down a hallway into another part of the house.

Lianne took Leia's arm. "I've never seen her like this before. Have you?"

"Not lately. Come on. We can head her off in the dining room." Leia burst into the room to see Gemma standing, arms crossed, looking out through the bay window into the backyard. "Are you feeling anything yet?"

"We're wasting time down here. All the murders happened upstairs," Gemma announced as she headed for the staircase.

Lianne and Leia exchanged looks again before Lianne lifted a shoulder. "She must be picking up something. She's on the move."

"I'll alert the media," Leia mumbled as the two women followed Gemma up the front staircase.

Once they reached the landing, it was clear to Lianne that Gemma had picked up on what happened that night. She could see the distress on Gemma's face. "What's going on right this minute? What do you see? Tell us."

Gemma sucked in a breath and spun toward the master bedroom. "The killer came up here carrying a hammer that he'd found in the laundry room."

"You said it came from the garage," Leia pointed out.

"I was wrong. The killer went in where Sandra and Todd were sleeping first. Up to that moment, the killer had been so quiet, so determined. He'd spent some of his time in the house searching for something, rummaging through drawers and closets. But he failed to locate whatever he was looking for. Then he abruptly stopped the search and went out to the garage through the laundry room. That's when he spotted the hammer laying out in plain sight on top of the washer. He picked it up and decided it would do the trick. But why a hammer? Why not use a knife? There were knives in the kitchen. Which begs the question, why didn't he come armed with his own weapons? The knives were out in plain sight, too. He'd walked past them to go into the laundry room. Why use the hammer from Todd's workbench?"

"That is weird," Lianne decided, beginning to feel spooked at the idea of standing on the very spot where the killer might've stood.

"What else?" Leia prompted. "His choice of murder weapons aside, why kill the little girls?"

Gemma turned her head to stare toward the other two bedrooms. "The five-year-old woke up. Julie recognized him. Now, he's in a tough spot. He has just a few seconds to make a decision. Does he leave witnesses behind?" She shook her head. "Nope, can't do that. He believes he doesn't have a choice. He leads Julie back into her bedroom, and when she turns her back to crawl into bed, he brings the hammer down, crushing her skull with the same instrument he used on her mom and dad. Then he went into the other bedroom and finished off Hallie."

Gemma snapped her fingers. "And just like that, four people are dead in under thirty minutes. No suspect in sight after all these years."

From the top of the stairs, Lando cleared his throat. "Any clue who this killer might be?"

Gemma jumped at the question. "Sorry. No. What are you doing here?"

"I should ask you that," Lando said, taking two steps toward his wife. He glanced from woman to woman until his eyes seared into Gemma's. "What gives? You really did bring your crew. What happened to the mayor staying out of police business?"

"Back at the office, after Anna Kate left, I got this overwhelming urge, this feeling that I could help out if I could just get inside the house and see where it happened. A feeling not altogether different from the one this morning when I wondered if you were in trouble."

"So you brought the whole gang with you for support? Who's running the grill at lunch?" Lando asked his sister.

Leia placed her hands on her hips. "It's my day off. I am allowed a day off once in a while."

"What's the big deal?" Lianne tossed out. "We're not bothering anyone. And it's long past an active crime scene here."

"You're trespassing," Lando fired back. "There's a caretaker that keeps an eye on this place. Bruce Barnhart. Bruce put in a call to Jocelyn Williams, who's owned this property since 2001 after it went through probate. I just got off the phone with her. Believe me when I say that she's not happy about anybody being here."

"Maybe you should ask her why she feels that way," Gemma stated. "Maybe she had a beef with her sister and—"

"Killed them all one night?" Lando finished for her. "I don't think so. Jocelyn Williams had an alibi for that night. She was away at college, San Francisco State, verified by at least six people who lived in the same apartment."

"Doesn't mean they aren't covering for her. It doesn't mean she didn't pay someone to get rid of her sister," Gemma pointed out. "What about a boyfriend? She could've sent him back here to do the deed. I think we should find out more about this Jocelyn Williams."

"We?" Lando proffered. "There is no 'we' on this investigation."

Lianne ignored that and lobbed back, "Or what about this caretaker? Where was he the night of the murders?"

"Let's just move along," Lando suggested. "We could stand here all day and name suspects."

"Really? There were that many suspects?" Gemma asked.

"We'll talk about this outside. For now, Mrs. Williams wants all of you out of her house."

Instead of arguing in front of everybody, Gemma decided to take a different tack. She looped her arm around her husband's. "No need to get in a snit. We're going peacefully. But just so you know, the four people who died here are counting on all of us to find answers anywhere we can get them. If that's uncomfortable for Jocelyn Williams, so be it."

"This entire discussion is gonna get lots of airtime tonight at dinner, isn't it?" Lando whispered in Gemma's ear as they left the landing.

"Oh, yeah. Count on it popping up."

For the rest of the day, the buzz at City Hall made clear that Ben Zurcher somehow managed to obtain access to the evidence room and get his hands on the Copeland murder files, files he had no business keeping in his possession.

Back in Lando's office, going over the evidence with Gemma, he kept trying to put the pieces of the puzzle together.

"I'm telling you he kept the entire contents of Box Number Five out in the open, just scattered around his office," Lando stated. "He'd covered the walls with Copeland photos. If that wasn't bad enough, Ben didn't even have the good sense to try to hide any of it."

"How is that possible?"

"I'm working on figuring that out. Do you have any idea how many times I stopped in to check on him? I was trying to be a good neighbor. I used to drop off food from the restaurant, little treats like homemade brownies, cakes, pies, whatever Mom had on hand. And all that time, Ben had this fixation on the Copeland case and never once said a word to me about it. Now I know why he never bothered to show me around the rest of his house."

Gemma's brows knitted together. "When was the last time anyone looked at the Copeland files, though? Didn't anyone notice a box of evidence was missing?"

"We did have a lag time after Louise left and Suzanne started her new job. Maybe Ben was able to get past the front desk and into—"

"A locked evidence room?" Gemma said, filling in the blanks. "I'll tell you what I think happened. At some point, before she was arrested, I think Louise Rawlins let Ben Zurcher in there to take whatever he wanted. It sounds exactly like something she would do to needle you. Louise always worked against you when you weren't looking. Don't deny it."

"Why would I do that when it's true? Sometimes right under my nose." He paced off a few steps and back again. "The how of it doesn't really matter, though, does it? Letting evidence walk out the front door reflects poorly on my oversight."

"How does that work exactly? You can't help it if Louise let him have access. I don't see how that's your fault. Someone obviously broke the law getting into an evidence locker and stealing what was there. How is that your fault?"

"It happened on my watch. Poor management on my part."

"Who's fixated on that besides you? Nobody."

Lando chewed the inside of his jaw. "Did you really see what happened out at the Copeland's farmhouse that night?"

"Why would I lie?"

"I'm not questioning that. It's just that your version pretty much lines up with the evidence."

Gemma tightened her jaw before looking away. "What I can't figure out is why the family was murdered in the first place? Are you sure Caulfield checked out every suspect he had and verified they had an alibi for that night? Caulfield wasn't exactly known for his due diligence."

Going on no sleep for the past sixteen hours, Lando worked out the kinks in the knotted muscles of his neck. "You know as well as I do, I can't be sure of anything Caulfield did. He wasn't exactly the epitome of efficiency. But like you said, Louise loved the guy. She was very loyal to Reiner. Maybe she did let Ben in to take whatever he wanted."

"That would explain a lot," Gemma pointed out. Arms crossed, she plopped down into a chair. "We might be looking at this all wrong. Why did Ben take Box Number Five and not all of the others?"

For the first time, Lando looked baffled. "Yeah. Good question. What was so special about Box Number Five?"

"Answer that, and you may unlock the entire mystery. What was in it anyway?"

"Mostly photos of the crime scene. A bunch of baggies filled with stuff found in the bedrooms that didn't seem to belong there. The items seemed out of place with what the Copeland girls had on hand."

"Really? Like what kind of stuff?"

Lando picked up a list of things Dale had compiled from Ben's house. "They found blue and red fibers that didn't match anything in the house. They found small plastic dolls that the girls didn't own, had never owned. And they found a pair of shoes that didn't fit anyone in the house."

"Interesting. That's almost as mysterious as why the killer kept looking around the house in search of something."

"Yeah. What could he have been looking for?"

"He or she," Gemma reminded him. "The killer could've been a woman."

Lando cocked a brow in her direction. "Are you seriously thinking the sister did it?"

"Who's to say Jocelyn didn't have a secret beef with her younger sister? It happens. Families don't always get along. The reality is they could've been at each other's throats and just pretended to get along."

"No, I get it."

"You know what that means, right?"

"I need to start the investigation from scratch, eliminate each suspect one by one, and then go back and check their alibis myself."

Gemma propped her feet up on another chair and let out a sigh. "I could curl up and sleep right here for an hour."

"You should go home, take a nap."

"Only if you go with me."

"You know I can't do that."

She grinned. "Then I won't do it either. Let's go get coffee. If we're lucky, we'll be able to make it through Leia's dinner party. I feel bad she's cooking for all of us on her day off."

"Are you serious? Zeb says she's been planning this for at least a month, looking for a reason to show off the house. She's excited to finally have everyone over."

"Which is why we don't dare disappoint her. Come on, let's get that shot of caffeine, maybe make it triple shots of espresso."

She looped her arm through Lando's. "What's wrong?"

"I wish we could go home right now and sleep for two days to recoup the sleep we lost."

"I'll have none of that talk," Gemma said, optimism in her tone. "Buck up. It's only eight more hours until the day is done."

4

Three long, difficult hours later, they made it home to get ready for Leia's dinner party.

A quick stop, a fast turnaround. They knew going in they had to head right back out.

But Gemma liked the idea of lingering at home for as long as she could.

Built on a cul-de-sac known as Peralta Circle, their home had started out as the town's first government offices. It was that old. The words "Coyote Wells 1908" had been carved into the stone above the front door.

The historical reference was a reminder that the one-story hacienda had once been the size of a postage stamp. At barely thirteen hundred square feet, her grandparents had added a series of additions to the main house over the years trying to make it function better as a residence. The renovations made for an interesting blend of architecture. Starting with the original Pueblo influence, they'd hired builders who couldn't quite pull off the same design. Happy to own a house at all, the Sarrazins had settled for a Spanish Colonial style that looked similar.

But no matter what, they kept the terracotta roof intact. That flair gave the one-story, ranch-style adobe all the charm made popular in California during the early 1900s. Thanks to its warm colors in golds and reds, its cobblestone driveway, the fountain in the middle of the courtyard, and its rounded archways, the building resembled an old mission right out of the eighteenth century.

Gemma loved the idea of living in a house steeped in such historical significance.

To give the place a little fancier upgrade, her grandparents had dreamed of having a solarium. At one end of the main house, they had added a room with a glass roof that let in light all day long. It was the one room where Gemma grew her fussiest, pickiest houseplants. Most anything thrived there in the warmth and sunshine. It was the one room where she felt Marissa and Jean-Luc Sarrazin's presence the strongest. Almost daily, she encountered some reminder of her grandparents there—a thimble, a book, the scent of a vanilla candle. Not even inhabiting the same master bedroom did she feel their spirit as vital and as strong as she did in the solarium.

But tonight, there was no time to dawdle there.

As she ran around the bedroom to get ready, she hurried to find a casual outfit that would keep her warm if Leia decided to serve appetizers outside, which she often did this time of year.

She settled on an oversized tan sweater with a pair of black pants. When it came to shoes, she bypassed heels, opting instead for comfort, slipping on a pair of black and white, low-cut Chuck Taylors.

Despite feeling sleepy enough to crawl between the covers, she put on fresh lipstick. But out of the corner of her eye, she longingly looked over at her bed. She would've loved nothing more than to curl up and sleep. That's when she realized how not in the mood to party she was.

When she finally went out to find Lando and tell him she was ready, she discovered he'd fallen asleep sitting upright in his favorite chair in front of the floor-to-ceiling kiva style fireplace.

At that moment, she would've loved nothing better than to kick off her shoes, get out of her clothes, and curl up next to him. Glancing over at the dogs sprawled out on the rug like they didn't intend to move for the next decade. She decided they were sacked out because they were happy to be home on a Monday evening. She so wanted to join them.

But it was not to be.

They were already running late when Gemma gripped Lando's shoulder to wake him up. "I'm sorry. You looked so peaceful and comfortable sleeping, but we have to go. Do you need more coffee to stay awake?"

Lando stretched out his long legs and scrubbed his hands down his face. "I couldn't drink another drop. Thanks, anyway. I'll be okay once I get moving."

She reached out a hand to help him get to his feet. "I wish we didn't have to go. But I've tried to think of a dozen excuses, none of which will work, none Leia will buy anyway."

"Same here."

Taking pity on him, she reached for his keys. "I'll drive. You still look wiped out."

"Maybe you should. I don't plan to argue."

The trip to Long Shadow Stables took under twenty minutes, but they were still running late. Gemma gunned the Volvo past the sign at the Longhorn property entrance, a ranching outfit located across from the Reservation. The family had owned the land for more than a hundred years. The compound stretched from the foothills of Fire Mountain to the walls of Shadow Canyon, where the Longhorns lived in several different homes, one of which belonged to Zeb, and now, Leia.

Gemma could see an anxious Leia standing on the porch, waiting for them.

"Sorry we're late. It's been a hectic day."

"I was beginning to think you guys weren't coming at all. I called you five times and left messages."

Gemma rolled her eyes as she wrapped an arm around her friend. "I didn't answer because I was rushing to get here. Cut me, *us*, some slack, will you? We're lucky to get here at all because Lando is dead on his feet. He's been up for twenty-four straight hours. He even fell asleep while I changed clothes. I almost took pity on him and left him there in his easy chair."

"What's to eat?" Lando wanted to know as he came around the other side to hug his sister. "I'm starving."

"Baked ham and scalloped potatoes. Help me set the table, and we can eat in five minutes."

"You got it."

The minute Lando stepped into the living room, Zeb slapped him on the back. "You get all the fascinating cases, don't you? While I get you a beer, why don't you tell me about Ben Zurcher's murder?"

Leia watched the men disappear into the kitchen before steering Gemma toward a sulking Lianne sitting across the room.

Leia lowered her voice. "She and Luke had a dust-up a few minutes ago. It looks like wedding jitters are getting to both of them."

"Is that why she looks like she lost her best friend?"

"Probably."

"What was the argument about?"

"Luke wants to push the wedding to June."

"Ouch. Did he tell her that in those exact words? Why would he do that?"

"He wants to go trout fishing next month."

"Trout fishing? That doesn't sound like Luke. Where is he?"

"He's been hiding in the kitchen, nursing a beer."

Gemma pushed up her sleeves and headed that direction. Once she reached the table where Luke sat, she grabbed his arm and yanked him out the backdoor. "I want a word with you, Mister."

"What'd I do now?"

Gemma waited until they were alone on the back deck, the shadow of Fire Mountain watching like a giant fortress in the background. The chilly night air didn't do much to cool off her temper. After several long minutes, staring out into the foothills, she whirled on her brother-in-law. "Why are you postponing the wedding?"

"Jeez, it's not like I'm backing out or anything. I just want to go fishing next month. Is that so hard to understand? It's *my* time off, and the only time I can take vacation this year. Sue me because I want to do something fun. For me. Besides, I thought all brides preferred June anyway."

"Don't be flip about this. Okay? Tell me the truth, Luke. You don't give a hang about getting married in June, and neither does Lianne. What happened to cause this?"

"I don't know. Maybe it's just not meant to be. Look, I've been having second thoughts lately. Okay? There I said it out loud. Lianne doesn't seem happy. And neither am I. Everything I do seems to piss her off. I can't say anything anymore that doesn't cause a fight. I don't want to live like that, and I don't think she does either. To me, it makes more sense to push the date back if we aren't getting along."

"So this is how you're calling off the wedding?"

"I guess. Yeah. I'm trying to talk Lando and Zeb into going fishing with me instead, taking some time off. Maybe the time

Lianne and I spend away from each other will do us both some good. God knows it couldn't hurt."

"Did you tell her this tonight? Here? At Leia's house? Why didn't you wait until the two of you were alone?"

"Because that's part of the problem. We're never alone. And when we are, we argue. We fight over any little thing. We haven't even had sex in six weeks. Instead of yelling at me, why don't you storm into the house and yell at her? Ask her what's going on in her world?"

"Good idea. I'll do that," Gemma said, brushing past him and back into the house. She marched past the kitchen and into the living room, plopped down on the sofa where Lianne sat, flipping through a magazine. "I've heard Luke's side. Your turn. Talk to me."

"What is there to talk about? The wedding's off."

"I'd say you're taking the news pretty well. What's wrong, Lianne? Are you having second thoughts, too?"

"Remember when we were worried that Zeb and Leia wouldn't make it to the big day? Who knew it would be Luke and me who'd decide to call it quits? This weekend I'm moving back into Collette's house. It's where I plan to sleep tonight. Want to help me move my stuff this Saturday?"

"Sure." Gemma noticed Lianne's left hand was already bare. "Did you give him back the engagement ring already?"

"Of course. Why on earth would I keep it if we aren't going through with it? And since he'd rather go fishing than get married, what was the point?"

"What happened, Lianne? I thought you guys were okay. Talk to me."

"Look, I hate to ask, but would you mind driving me home now? I mean, Luke's place, of course. I need to throw a few things together in a bag, just enough until I can pack up my other stuff. Right now, I just want to get out of there."

"Are you sure this is what you want?"

Leia came out of the kitchen, wiping her hands on a dishtowel. "Luke just dropped the bombshell. I'm so sorry."

"I'm the one who's sorry, sorry to ruin your dinner, but I think I'm just going to head out. I don't think I should stay."

"Head out? Where?"

"I was just telling Gemma that I'll spend the night over at Collette's old house."

Gemma looked over at Leia, her eyes filled with regret. "And I'm taking her back to Luke's to get her stuff and pick up her car. I'll be back to pick up Lando later."

Leia put her arms around Lianne. "Don't worry about it. I could make you a plate to go."

"No, no need to go to that trouble," Lianne said. "I'm not that hungry."

After the women left, Leia got everyone else to the table. But her festive mood had evaporated. She aimed her disappointment straight at Luke. "What were you thinking, telling her here at my house, waiting until tonight? It's like you planned to drop this on her for maximum effect."

"I did not plan it. It just sort of popped out of my mouth. We were bickering about where to go on the honeymoon."

"You wanted to go fishing?"

"Yeah. In Montana. What's wrong with that? It's better than some snobby, all-inclusive resort bumping elbows with people who would rather lay out by the pool. At least we'd be alone in Montana to work out our problems."

At the end of the table, Zeb cleared his throat. "Are we going to do this all through dinner?"

"I hope not," Luke muttered. "Because tension during a meal is the leading cause of indigestion."

"Oh, shut up," Leia chided. "You brought this on yourself. Who breaks up with a longtime girlfriend, let alone fiancée, on a Monday night at my house right before dinner? Who does that?"

"Leave the guy alone," Lando snapped. "It's done. Can't you see that it's for the best? He's not even that broken up about it."

"Well, sure, I'm disappointed. But it isn't like I didn't see it coming. We've been at odds with each other for two months now. So, if you're waiting for some huge emotion out of me, you're the one who won't be happy. Because I accepted the facts sometime back in January."

Lando traded looks around the table before landing his stare on his brother. "Okay, I'll bite. What happened in January?"

"You guys aren't willing to let this go, are you?"

"You're the one who brought it to our door," Leia reminded him. "It's your floor show. By all means, entertain us."

"Fine," Luke spat out, tossing his napkin on the table. "But just remember I didn't want to do this. Last January, Lianne seemed preoccupied a lot, obsessed with her phone. One day while she was in the shower, I discovered she was texting another guy. Happy now?"

Leia seemed stunned, speechless. After several long minutes, she glanced around the table. "Are you suggesting Lianne was cheating on you? Because there are other explanations."

"What else could it be? The number was from Portland, her hometown. We know most of the same people here. I didn't recognize the name or the number."

Lando shoved his plate aside. "Did you ask her about it?"

"Yes. That's when she denied ever getting the guy's texts."

"That's not good," Zeb said, picking up his beer. "Hard to imagine Lianne not owning up to it. What happened after her initial denial?"

"That's the interesting part. I think Lianne bought a burner phone and started using it instead of her main cell phone. The tension between us ramped up. It's been unbearable, especially lately. It's better this way."

Zeb glanced at his wife. "Happy now that you have all the gritty details?"

"Hey, don't look at me like that. I was hoping for a nice evening among friends. Look at us. Gemma and Lianne aren't even here. And if you ask me, things may never be the same again."

While those four sat around the table, kicking the story around, Gemma was still in the dark about the breakup. Five miles from the Longhorn house, she pulled her Volvo into the driveway of a cottage on Bar Harbor Lane. Luke's beach bungalow sat at the end of the block. Surrounded by dunes, beach grass, and stately sand reeds, the color scheme oozed a gray and blue palette of soft pastels.

Gemma turned off the engine and got a whiff of sea air. A brisk wind had turned the night chilly. She twisted in her seat to look at Lianne, who hadn't said a word on the drive here. Lianne had yet to shed a tear over the breakup. Her lack of emotion mystified Gemma. "Do you want to talk about it?"

"No, I really don't. I've got a splitting headache. I just want to toss a few things into a bag and get out of here, go to bed somewhere else." Lianne reached to open the door. "I don't plan to be here when Luke gets back. Thanks for dropping me off. I'll see you tomorrow."

"Lianne, you might not want to talk about it tonight, but just know that I'm always here for you when you're ready."

"Not sure how long that will last since Luke and I aren't together anymore. I mean, the guy is your brother-in-law."

"True. But you're my friend. Maybe my best friend."

"What about Leia?"

"Leia's my oldest friend. I can have more than one, you know."

"Maybe."

An awkward silence filled the interior of the car. "Want me to go inside with you while you get your things?"

"No. I'm okay. Thanks, Gemma. I'll see you tomorrow," Lianne repeated.

Gemma watched as Lianne took out a key and then disappeared inside the bungalow. She took out her cell phone and texted Lando.

Dropped off Lianne. Headed back now. Weird vibe. Lianne is acting really strange.

A few seconds later, Lando texted back. *You don't know the half of it. Tell you the rest when you get here.*

Leia had kept a plate of food warm for Gemma.

But Gemma was in no mood to eat. She studied the ham and potatoes in front of her and glared over at Luke. "Lianne is not having an affair. I don't care what you think you saw or heard. The idea is ridiculous."

"Then you tell me why she bought a burner phone?" Luke insisted. "Haven't you noticed how strange she's been acting lately, almost secretive, and at times, barely sociable?"

Gemma chewed a nail. "Maybe a little. She has been keeping to herself more than usual." She glanced over at Leia. "Have you noticed that about her? I just thought it was because I've been so busy. Between the shop and my mayoral duties, I might've neglected her a little bit in the friend department."

Leia topped off her wine glass. "All I know is that she's been scarce coming into the restaurant lately. She used to come in all the time. Remember, I brought it up around Valentine's Day. And then you guys opted to do something else rather than come into the grill for dinner."

"Uh, that's because we had a huge fight on Valentine's Day," Luke admitted. "I spent the night on the couch, and she got the bed."

Gemma tightened her jaw. "Okay, that is strange."

"But still," Leia began. "I'm having a hard time believing Lianne would cheat. She's not that kind of person."

"Yeah. Exactly. And who would she cheat with?" Gemma questioned. "Seriously. Think about it. We know every person in town. Who is this man she's been texting?"

"Luke thinks he's back in Portland," Leia reasoned. "Maybe someone there she used to date, an ex-boyfriend who got in touch with her recently."

Luke let out a sigh and looked at his watch. "When you guys figure it out, let me know, will you? How long should I give her to pack a bag before I head home? What's the protocol for that?"

"Don't be an ass," Gemma snapped. "That's the least of your problems right now. This isn't right, Luke. I won't accept that's she's been cheating. I won't. I'd know it if she were."

"Is that your psychic ability kicking in?" Lando proposed. "Because did you ever home in on what we're discussing here tonight? Six weeks before the wedding, did you pick up on the fact that there's trouble in paradise?"

"I told you, I've been busy," Gemma snapped. "But no, I never picked up on that kind of vibe. I never saw this coming."

"And here I thought we'd be discussing Zurcher's murder tonight," Zeb stated with a shake of his head. "It never occurred to me we'd be turning against Lianne tonight."

Gemma frowned. "Now, wait a minute, Lianne is my friend, a business partner. And until I know for sure she's cheating on Luke, until I see proof, I'm not turning on her."

"Same here," Leia added. "Lianne has been a good friend to me, to all of us. I'm with Gemma on this. Until I know what's what, I won't turn my back on her."

"Great, thanks for the support," Luke snarled, getting to his feet. "My own family thinks I made this up. Well, I know what I saw, what I read. For two months, she's acted like she didn't want to be around me. For two months, she's been somewhere else in her head. For two months, she's been messaging another man. So believe what you want. I'm out of here."

Lando followed him out the door. "Hold up. Just so you know, I'm not taking Lianne's side. For what it's worth, I think you did the right thing breaking it off."

"Thanks for that. What's wrong with them in there? Why don't they believe me?"

"Look, you've had two months to get used to this. We've all had two hours. Give Gemma and Leia some time, and they'll come around to see things your way."

"I don't know about that." Luke shifted his feet and combed his fingers through his dark hair. He faced going home alone. "Leia and Gemma seem unwavering in their support for Lianne. Did I screw this up or did I do the right thing calling off the wedding?"

Lando slapped his brother on the back. "You're not the bad guy here. In the final analysis, blood kin comes through for each other. Remember that."

5

Gemma woke to the smell of fresh-brewed coffee wafting into the bedroom. She reached across the covers for Lando, only to feel chilly air on his side of the empty bed. Not so different from how they had ended last night before crawling into the sack. She remembered their heated argument over Luke's revelation—Lando defending his brother, her defending Lianne.

Grabbing her robe, she headed down the hallway to the kitchen and saw Lando slipping Pop-Tarts into the toaster.

From behind, she slipped her arms around his waist. "I'm pretty sure I can do better than that. How about I scramble you some eggs?"

"That's okay. I need to run. Tuttle's meeting me at the morgue. He has some preliminary autopsy results on Ben he wants to talk about." He swung his arm around to wrap her up and kiss the top of her head. "About last night…I'm sorry."

"You beat me to it. I'm sorry for getting so upset. I thought I might spend this morning trying to get the truth out of Lianne."

"Good luck with that. Think about it. If she's so innocent, why didn't she just say so, protest or something?"

Gemma took his chin. "That's what I need to find out. She didn't exactly proclaim her innocence to me either last night because she refused to talk about it. After sleeping on it, Luke's probably right. Something serious is going on with her, and I intend to get to the bottom of it."

The flaps on the doggie door swished open, and the dogs trotted back in from their outside morning ritual, clamoring for food.

Gemma scooped out dog food into dishes just as the toaster gave up its two hot pastries.

Between fingers, Lando juggled the hot pieces before sliding them onto a paper plate. "I gotta go. If I'm late, Tuttle will use that as an excuse to send me packing and make me set up another meeting for this afternoon."

Gemma patted his chest. "Go on. I don't want you facing Tuttle's wrath. Let me know if I can help in any way."

"For starters, maybe stay away from the Copeland murder house."

"You know what bugs me about that case?"

"What?"

"There's no motive."

"Yeah. That we know about."

"Exactly. Sandra and Todd seem squeaky clean. But you know what they say about that. Sometimes squeaky clean is nothing but smoke and mirrors. One of them might be hiding a big ol' fat secret from their past. But if that's it, I don't understand why the kids had to die. Even if Julie did recognize him or her, why do that to a child? That's beyond crazy, beyond motivated."

"Maybe. How sure are you that little five-year-old Julie recognized the killer?"

"Good question. I'd say ninety percent."

"Okay. I'll keep that in mind as I reopen the case." He leaned down to plant a kiss on her lips. "I'll see you tonight. Hopefully, we're looking at a no-drama night."

She sputtered with laughter. "Yeah. Like that'll happen. There's always something beyond the norm going on around here."

An hour later, Gemma's insides gnawed with nerves as she waited for Lianne to arrive at work. She'd written down an index card full of questions, jotted down each one at breakfast so she wouldn't forget to ask about every detail.

Now she was in the process of memorizing what she wanted to say. She started a fresh batch of chocolate truffles, sprinkled them with chopped nuts to keep her mind occupied. But when nine-fifteen came and went, and there was still no sign of Lianne, Gemma finished the other batches of chocolate and sent a text to her friend.

Where are you?

No reply. She waited another ten minutes before sending another text—still silence.

"Come on, Lianne, there's no sense in acting like a child," Gemma muttered to herself as she kept one eye on her phone, hoping for an answer. When none came, she headed outside the store to wait.

Standing outside on the sidewalk, Gemma encountered the March wind. It howled and snapped as it blew in off the ocean making for a chilly morning. Gemma wrapped her sweater tighter and kept expecting to see Lianne's Honda make the turn onto Water Street.

But at nine-thirty, Gemma began to have doubts. Serious doubts. The woman was never late to work. Never. After another fifteen minutes, gnawing nerves turned to full-blown worry. She began to pace the concrete pavement, back and forth, to burn off energy.

At ten o'clock, she gave up and went back inside to get her purse and car keys. The only thing left to do was check on Lianne at her sister's house, property that rightfully belonged to Lianne, just as the old pizza shop did.

It took less than five minutes to reach the neighborhood. But as Gemma drove down the street, she realized Lianne's car was not in the driveway. She tried to recall if the garage had enough space for the Honda Civic and remembered it was full of furniture Lianne had brought with her from Portland.

It didn't deter Gemma that the car wasn't there. She got out anyway and went up to the front door to ring the bell. No answer. She knocked, calling out her friend's name. But there was no answer.

Deciding to go around back, she was determined to get in no matter what she had to do. She tromped into the backyard and was about to smash in a window when Enid Lloyd stopped her.

"Gemma Bonner, what on earth are you doing there? Are you trying to break into this house?"

Caught in the act, Gemma ignored the embarrassment and whirled around to see Lianne's petite, white-haired elderly neighbor glaring at her. "You startled me."

"I should hope so. If you want inside that house, all you need to do is ask. Lianne left me the spare key, told me to keep an eye on the place. Now I see why."

"When was this? When did you see Lianne last? When did she give you the extra key?"

Enid frowned and narrowed her eyes. "I thought you were her friend. When she moved in with Luke, of course, that was what? Ah, yes, last summer. Lianne comes by here though every week to water the flowers and run a dust rag over the furniture. She brings me chocolates, too. What's wrong? You look positively white as a ghost. What's the matter with you? Are you about to faint or what?"

"No, nothing like that. Lianne didn't show up for work this morning, and I'm worried."

"Well, maybe she's sick. Why don't you check with Luke?"

"I'll do that. In the meantime, could I just use your key to get inside and make sure she's not in there? Make sure she hasn't fallen in the shower or something."

"Sure. I guess it'd be all right. Have you tried calling her, though? Here at the house? I'm pretty sure the phone is still working."

"I'll do that."

"Good. You still want me to go get the key?"

"I do. Yeah. Please."

Gemma had to look up the number for Collette's old landline. It meant wading through her contact list and going back through two years' worth of phone calls. When she finally came across the right phone number, she punched it in and heard the wall phone ringing inside the kitchen.

But no one picked up.

Itching to get inside now more than ever, Gemma walked around to the front of the house. She stood on the porch to wait for Enid.

The older woman finally appeared, holding a housekey. "You let me have that back before you go, you hear?"

"Yes. Absolutely. Do you want to go in with me?"

Enid pursed her lips. "Do you really think something's wrong? Why would she be here and not with Luke?"

Gemma decided to level with the woman. "Okay. The truth is Luke called off the wedding. It happened last night. Lianne was understandably upset when I drove her to Luke's to pack a bag and pick up her car. That's why she was supposed to show up here and spend the night. That's what she told me."

"She didn't," Enid stated with confidence. "I know for a fact Lianne never made it here. My bedroom window faces her side of the house. I didn't sleep much last night. I would've heard her car pull up if she'd made it. And she didn't. Never saw her car here last night at all."

"I don't understand that," Gemma muttered as she slipped the key into the lock. With unease building in her belly, she stepped inside a dark house. Flipping on lights as she walked deeper inside, she called out to Lianne. But it soon became apparent there was no one at home.

Gemma walked down the hallway and back again. "Her bed hasn't been slept in. It doesn't look like she made it here at all. What's happened to her, Enid? Where could she be?"

"Let's not panic. Lianne Whittaker is as level-headed as any woman I know. But you should probably call Luke. Maybe they made up last night and slept in this morning. I'm not too old that I don't remember how good makeup sex is."

Any other time, Gemma's instinct would've been to laugh out loud, but she couldn't bring herself to feel the slightest bit amused.

With shaky hands, she dialed Luke's number at the clinic. When Ginny Sue Maples answered, Gemma asked the nurse if she'd seen Luke and Lianne.

"Luke's here. But no, I haven't seen Lianne for a couple of days." Ginny Sue lowered her voice and went on, "You know they aren't getting along, right?"

"I know. But Lianne didn't show up for work this morning. And she's not at her sister's old house. I'm getting worried, Ginny Sue. Could you ask Luke if he's heard from her this morning?"

"I sure will. Hang on a sec while I put you on hold."

Gemma waited. With each second that ticked by, the bad vibes just kept swirling in her head.

Instead of Ginny Sue picking up, it was Luke who got on the line. "What do you mean Lianne didn't show up for work?"

"What do you think I mean? I can't find her, Luke. I'm standing right here in Collette's living room, and Lianne's not here. She hasn't been here all night. When you got home last night, did it look like she'd packed a bag?"

"Yep. She packed one all right. She emptied one side of the closet and her half of the dresser drawers."

"Okay. Then why didn't she make it over here?"

"Good question. Look, give me twenty minutes to clear my schedule, and I'm on my way there. In the meantime, call Lando. I'll retrace her steps from my house to where you are. Maybe she had car trouble or something."

Gemma didn't think that was the reason, but it was past time to call Lando anyway. With a sinking feeling growing in the pit of her stomach, she hit speed dial.

Gemma waited on the front lawn with Enid Lloyd at her side until Lando pulled up in his cruiser. Not two minutes later, Luke pulled up in his Wagoneer.

"I drove the route she would've taken to get to here," Luke announced from the curb. He shook his head. "I didn't see her Honda anywhere. I also didn't see anything out of the ordinary. There's no sign of her anywhere. Where could she be?"

"Let's just take a collective deep breath and try to figure this out," Lando suggested, shifting toward Luke. "Where would she go if she needed to get away for a few days?"

Gemma let out a throaty nervous laugh and answered for Luke. "Portland. You think she headed back to Portland?"

Luke eyed his sister-in-law. "Jeez, I didn't think she was that upset to leave town like this and go back there. What's in Portland for her? Unless that's where the guy is that she's been texting."

Gemma glared at him. "Did you ever stop to ask yourself how she would cheat on you with a guy in Portland? Has she left town recently to hook up with anyone like that? No. She's been right here working her ass off to get that shop opened on time. There has to be a reasonable explanation for her weird behavior. There has to be. Could you, I don't know, just for five whole minutes, give her the benefit of the doubt?"

"Okay. Calm down. But you don't know what the last two months have been like for us," Luke insisted.

"Stop it," Lando commanded. "Both of you. I don't know why she left. But the fact is, she did. Now we just have to find her and make sure she's safe. I need phone numbers for her parents and any other persons in her life—past and present—that you know about."

Luke began to peruse through his cell phone and his contact list. "Here's the number for her parents. Why don't I call and see if they've heard from her?"

Lando nodded. "Good start. You do that while I do a background check on her."

Gemma made a face. "Really? Is that necessary?"

"It's routine when a person goes missing. And it's far better to do it now rather than later. I'll get Dale started on it. You guys keep trying to call around and see if anyone has seen her."

"I should've stayed with her last night," Gemma intoned as she walked back to her Volvo. "What was I thinking just dropping her off and driving away like I did?"

"If it's anyone's fault, it's mine," Luke admitted. "I handled this all wrong. I should never have told her the wedding was off at Leia's. I knew better. It's like I wanted to punish her for cheating."

Gemma had heard enough about that and whirled on Luke, this time getting up in his face. "I'm telling you she never cheated."

"Whatever," Luke muttered and stormed back to the Wagoneer.

Gemma angled toward Lando. "Your brother is about to get on my last nerve. So what's next? What do we do now? Should I start printing up flyers or what?"

Before Lando could answer, Luke came striding back up the driveway. "Well, that's disturbing. Lianne's parents haven't heard from her since Saturday when she made her weekly phone call to check in. And get this, her mother says one of her old boyfriends has been harassing them for information on her whereabouts. They're worried he could show up here in Coyote Wells. After what happened to Collette, they're in panic-mode."

Luke paced off a few steps and ran a hand through his hair. "Could I have gotten this entire thing that wrong? Could she have been dealing with an ex who wouldn't leave her alone, and I misinterpreted this whole thing for something else?"

Before Gemma could utter a reply, Luke stopped and pointed a finger. "You might be right. I overreacted. What the hell was I thinking? Where is she?"

Gemma took pity on him. "Blaming yourself won't bring her back. We need to focus on finding her. Pronto. Did Mrs. Whittaker have a name for the old boyfriend?"

"Yeah. A guy named Kirk Ritter."

"There's your background check," Gemma told Lando. "See what Dale says about him."

"It's a place to start," Lando said as he went back to his cruiser to relay the information to Dale.

Gemma and Luke followed—and waited for Lando to get off the phone with an update.

Standing beside each other, Luke put his head on Gemma's shoulder. "I'm sorry I've been such an ass."

She laid a hand on his jaw. "It's okay. I've been an ass before and know how much it hurts to own it."

"How could I have thought she was cheating?"

"Maybe you wanted to believe it. Maybe you didn't want to get married. Maybe you were looking for reasons to postpone the wedding because you just weren't ready."

Luke looked disheartened at the suggestion. "You're saying I used this as a reason to bail?"

"Sounds like it to me. What I can't get over, though, is how Lianne never said a word to me about this ex-boyfriend."

"Did you ever see her texting while at work?"

"Well, yeah. Sure. But I never asked who she kept texting. It was none of my business. Although now that I think about it, she did seem annoyed most of the time. I thought it was worry over the shop. Why didn't I ask her, Luke? Why didn't I ask what was going on? Don't answer that. I already know. I've been so busy with everything else I've forgotten how to be a friend to the people I care about. Why didn't I stay with her last night, see her through the first night of this? A friend would've been there for her."

"Because Leia put pressure on you to hurry back," Luke suggested.

"No, she really didn't. But I do remember Lianne mentioning she had a headache. All she wanted was to get to bed. I did feel like I should get back to Leia's and not leave Lando stranded there for too long because I knew how tired he was. I really needed to get to bed myself."

"There you go. Stop beating yourself up. I'm the one who needed to be there for her and wasn't."

"Enough blame to go around," Gemma asserted as she saw Lando take another call. "Look, maybe we have news."

Lando blew out a breath and signaled for Luke. "Dale put out a BOLO on Lianne and her car. But this Kirk Ritter guy is bad news. He went to jail a year ago for assault after a fight in a bar. He got out two months ago."

"January," Luke mumbled. "Damn. That's when she first started acting weird and texting like crazy."

"That's not all. Dale is still trying to pinpoint exactly where Ritter is. He had a job at a construction company in Portland. But we haven't heard back from his employer yet on whether or not he reported for work today. We'll keep trying to contact the company. There is one other hitch. Ritter was supposed to check in with his parole officer yesterday. He never showed."

Luke felt sick to his stomach. "Great. It's looking more like she either got kidnapped or took off on her own to avoid dealing with this jerk."

"Maybe. But I'd caution against jumping to conclusions right now."

Gemma couldn't believe what she was hearing. "You two are actually suggesting Lianne drove off into the night on her own, leaving behind her job, her business, which hasn't even opened its doors yet? No way. Lianne would not do that. The woman I know is stubborn as a mule. She's resolute about getting that business up and running."

Luke scratched his chin. "Yeah, you're right. She wouldn't walk away from Collette's Collectibles. She has big plans for that place. So this jerk kidnapped her."

"Again, it's way too early to speculate, so let's not. I've got Jimmy patrolling the highway east of here and Payce keeping an eye out on the backroads to the north. We'll find her."

"Come on, Lando," Luke began. "I know how these things work. With a twelve-hour head start, this guy could be anywhere by now."

"True. But if this Ritter guy did abduct her, we should find her car somewhere nearby. Right? He can't have driven two vehicles at the same time, one to get here and the Honda she drives. He had to use one or the other to get out of town. Right now, we don't know what vehicle Ritter is using. That's his advantage. But if he's our guy, he had to have ditched a car around here somewhere."

For the first time all morning that gave Gemma hope. "You're right. What about checking surveillance video from Luke's neighborhood?"

Luke shook his head. "My neighbors aren't that savvy. I don't even have a security camera installed. But after this, you can bet that'll change."

"I think I'll shut down the shop and start driving around town," Gemma offered. "I can't go back to work without trying. I'll start with the south end near the old drive-in movie theater."

Luke bobbed his head toward his truck. "That's a good idea. I'll take the highway north of town and circle back to the square."

"And I'll notify Zeb to keep an eye out near the Rez. That way, we've covered all the bases." Lando slapped his brother on the back. "We'll do everything to find her, Luke. You've got my word on that."

6

Gemma, like Luke, put everything on hold and cruised from south to north. She drove past the old Wolf Creek Bridge under construction, pulling over briefly to watch the crew lay the foundation to widen the road. At some point, she even passed Luke twice, heading in the opposite direction. Despite driving down every street and scouting every corner, she turned up nothing. There was no sign of Lianne or her Honda Civic anywhere.

After three hours of covering every section of town, she gave up and headed back to the shop. She found Leia waiting outside on the sidewalk, clutching her cell phone.

"No luck, huh?" Leia asked.

Downhearted, Gemma unlocked the door to the store but kept the CLOSED sign turned around. "None. It's time to print up missing person flyers. Wanna help me get the word out?"

"That's why I'm here. I left Mom at the restaurant to deal with the tail end of the lunch rush. I just got off the phone with Luke, though. He's beside himself with worry. What do you think about this ex of Lianne's, this Kirk Ritter? Could he have grabbed her last night after you dropped her off?"

"Here's what I'm thinking happened," Gemma said as she fired up the coffee machine so it would warm up. "I think Lianne went into Luke's house and got her stuff like she planned. Then, when she came out of the house to get in her car, she loaded up whatever she'd brought with her. This guy must've intercepted her somewhere along the route to Collette's house because Enid Lloyd said she never pulled into the driveway."

"We don't know that for sure, though."

"We kind of do. That house had a layer of dust. Lianne never made it to the bedroom." Gemma thought she heard a noise coming from the storage area. She tilted her head to listen, then reached out to grab Leia's arm. In a soft voice, she leaned in, "Did you hear that? There's someone back there."

Leia's face broke out in a grimace. "I didn't hear anything."

Gemma had heard a noise. She was sure of it. She picked up the only weapon accessible to prove it, a marble rolling pin.

Ready to hit whoever was back there over the head, Gemma crept down the hallway carrying the heavy object clutched in her right hand. When she got closer to the storage room door, she cocked it back like a baseball bat, ready to swing for the fences, and then yanked open the door. She hit the lights. But all she saw was the stack of boxes that held her latest delivery of chocolate supplies.

She cut the lights and backed out. But she heard the sound again. This time the scurrying noise sounded like it was coming from the other side of the wall.

"That's the storage room next door," Gemma whispered. "I'm sure of it. Come on."

Gemma took off back down the hallway and into the main dining area of the shop. Still carrying her heavy rolling pin, she stepped into Collette's Collectibles and headed straight to the rear of the building.

Marching past boxes that hadn't been unpacked yet and glass displays yet to be stocked, Gemma reached the storage room. She yanked open the door only to let out a scream when she spotted Lianne hiding behind a stack of boxes.

Lianne held up her hands and shrieked, "It's me. Don't bash me over the head."

"You scared the life out of me. Where've you been? What the hell are you doing hiding in here? I've been out looking for you all morning."

"Sorry. But this is the only place I could think of to hide out, so—," Lianne's voice trailed off. Then she took a deep breath and added, "It's a long story."

Leaning into the storage room behind Gemma, Leia noticed that Lianne wore the same clothes from the night before. "How long have you been in here?"

"I waited until Gemma closed up this morning before sneaking in the backdoor."

Gemma relaxed her hands on the rolling pin, then placed the heavy object down on one of the boxes. "Does this have anything to do with Kirk Ritter?"

Lianne grimaced. "You know about him, huh?"

"We figure that's who you've been texting," Gemma said, grabbing Lianne's arm and pulling her out into the hallway. "We know he got out of jail in January."

"Benefits of marrying a cop, I suppose," Lianne noted as she hesitated to venture farther out into the heart of the store. Instead, she hovered near the boxes of books, sticking close to the backdoor in case she had to make a quick exit.

"Let's all sit down and hash this out," Gemma suggested, pulling her by the arm and leading her back into the chocolate shop.

Lianne resisted, though, and shook her head. "I can't be seen just sitting in here having coffee. You need to lower those blinds and make sure I stay out of sight."

Gemma and Leia exchanged furtive glances. It was Gemma who headed out to the front of the store and began to lower the blinds. All of them. "If that's what it takes to get you to start talking to your best friends, then...whatever."

While Gemma fixed it so that no one could see into the shop, Leia ushered Lianne to a table and pushed her into a chair. "You've had all of us worried sick about you all day. That includes Luke. It's time to tell us what's up with all this secrecy. And I'm not talking about the past eighteen hours. I'm talking about what's been going on since January."

Gemma set a bottle of water in front of Lianne. "In case you get thirsty during this interrogation."

"Look, I get that you're upset with me," Lianne began as she twisted off the cap to the water bottle. "I don't blame you guys. I don't even blame Luke, for that matter, for thinking the worst of me. Kirk Ritter is a nutcase. He's threatened me with violence. I tried to handle it myself without bringing Luke into it. That's all I'm guilty of. Luke has his practice to consider because Kirk is a threat to that, to our way of life. Kirk was a nutcase long before he ever saw the inside of a jail cell. That's why I ended things with that reckless, stupid man in high school long before I moved to Coyote Wells. I'd even forgotten about him until he somehow got hold of my cell number when he got out of jail. That's when things started to deteriorate."

"Why didn't you just tell Luke the truth?"

"Because Kirk threatened to kill both of us if I told anyone. Not only that, he threatened to kill everyone around me if I didn't get him twenty thousand dollars by this Thursday."

"Twenty thousand dollars? Who does this guy think he is, threatening you like that and then demanding that kind of money? What made him think you had that kind of cash on hand?"

"Someone back in Portland mentioned I was opening a business. Kirk got wind of it and took that to mean I had money, big time money."

Gemma rubbed her temples. "I'm sorry, Lianne, I'm sorry you're in this boat, but you're not making a lick of sense. None of this makes any sense at all. Why didn't you speak up? Just once, couldn't you have said something to me right here at work?"

Lianne covered her face with her hands. "See? This is the reason I didn't want to tell you or Luke. Look, Kirk wanted money to leave the country, or else he'd kill Luke, then start killing my friends. That's what he said. And I believed him. I've seen him beat people up for no reason, and I got scared. He didn't start off with the first text wanting that kind of money. At first, it was just a hundred or so wired to this money outlet in Portland. But last Friday, he started upping his demands. He got greedy."

Gemma finally sat down across from Lianne. "Once you give a blackmailer anything, they always come back for more. Didn't you learn anything from Leia's ordeal with Tiffany?"

This time, Leia sat down, too. "This Kirk must know something about you that you don't want Luke to know. Am I right? Because that's how blackmail works. That's what Tiffany used on me with Zeb."

Lianne nodded. "I've been on edge for two months, carrying around this secret. Afraid. I couldn't tell anyone the reason."

"That's just not true. But we'll get to that detail later," Gemma inserted. "Right now, let's get to what happened after I dropped you off last night."

"I went into the house, gathered up my stuff, took it out to the car. That's when I spotted Kirk's truck parked down the street. I knew he was watching me. I didn't want him following me to Collette's. Or anywhere else, for that matter. That's when I got this brilliant idea to try to lose him. So I started driving around town, leading him through streets unfamiliar to him. I turned into neighborhoods trying to confuse him. But at some point, I realized I was low on gas, so I pulled into Farley's garage. Imagine my shock when I realized Farley was still there working on a car. Anyway, I explained the situation to him, and, bless his heart, he said he'd fill up the tank and that he'd keep my Civic out of sight. He even offered me a place to stay for the night."

Leia traded angry looks with Gemma. "So, let me get this straight. You could tell Farley what was going on in one stop, but you couldn't level with the man you're going to marry next month? Or us? Have I got that right?"

"I know you're angry…"

"Damn straight, I am. And I'm getting angrier by the minute. It's tough to listen to this. Maybe because you'd rather let Luke, let all of us, believe you were cheating rather than set us straight about this ex-boyfriend of yours. That's low, Lianne."

"Kirk is violent. Okay? And spending a year in jail did not help his temperament any. Eventually, I knew he'd demand more money. I knew the hundred dollars here and two hundred dollars there wouldn't be enough to keep him away from Luke. And then, one day, I realized he'd eventually show up to get more in person. I didn't want to touch Luke's money, so every time Kirk upped the ante, I took the money out of savings, *my* savings. It didn't take long for Luke to catch on to all the texts, though. He's not stupid. But by this time, it was easier to let him believe I was interested in someone else than to own up to the six thousand or so dollars I had already given Kirk."

Gemma eyed Leia. "If you think about it, it's not that different than Tiffany blackmailing you to keep a secret from Zeb. In fact, that's the same thing you did to keep Tiffany quiet about Taylor Rainford. It's the same principle. You were afraid to tell Zeb the truth, and Lianne is afraid to tell Luke she's already given Kirk a lot of money."

Leia blew out a breath and stared down at Lianne. "Okay, I get it. What's the secret you're afraid Luke will discover? What's this jailbird holding over your head?"

Lianne blew out a tense intake of breath. "We went to high school together—Kirk and me. We used to hang out. One Friday night, he picked me up in a brand-new convertible sports car. I don't know what kind it was. But I knew it wasn't his. When I asked about who it belonged to, he cracked some joke about borrowing it from a friend. I knew it wasn't true. I figured he was lying. Kirk didn't have that kind of friends. But I got in anyway. I was sixteen. About four hours into the evening, the cops pulled Kirk over for stealing the car off a dealer's showroom floor. We both got arrested, but only Kirk got charged with car theft. I think they called it grand larceny. I was charged with accessory to theft because the car was worth about twenty-five grand. I did community service. Kirk went to juvie. He's harbored resentment toward me ever since. He's been in and out of jail for minor stuff, mostly breaking and entering, burglary, that sort of thing. But last year, he got into a fight in a bar and beat someone unconscious. They sent him to prison for that."

"How well did you know this guy in high school?" Gemma asked.

"I lost my virginity to him if that's what you mean," Lianne admitted. "It wasn't my finest hour, or his, for that matter."

Leia snorted with laughter. "Tell me about it. I just don't see why you didn't tell Luke this back in January and save yourself all this heartache."

"I was embarrassed, okay?" Lianne barked. "I was three months away from marrying my dream guy, a doctor, a respected member of the community. Do you think I wanted Luke to find out about Kirk? Or my youthful stupidity? Trust me. I didn't. I wanted Kirk to go away and leave me the hell alone. I wanted him out of my life for good."

"So your idea of fixing all this was hiding like a thief in your own storage room?"

"Have you seen him around town? Kirk. Is he still out there looking for me?"

"Not that I know of," Leia answered. "What kind of truck is he driving?"

"A pickup, black, 1980 Ford. He loves vintage trucks and stuff. His uncle owns a used car lot." Lianne rattled off a license plate number from the night before.

Gemma's eyes widened. "I'm impressed. Not sure I can explain this all to Lando, but I'm impressed you got his license number."

Lianne sat up straighter. "You can't tell Lando any of this."

"Of course, I can. And I will. We need to get this jerk back in jail. How will we do that if we don't enlist Lando to nail this guy?"

"But you can't. I'll be mortified, totally humiliated. And if Lando knows, so will Luke. He can't know any of this."

"Come on, Lianne," Leia started. "We've all done stupid stuff. God knows I have. And so has Luke. You don't know the half of it. You can't be this upset over a joyride that ended with you charged as Kirk's accomplice. It's the fact that this guy is the one who popped your cherry, isn't it?"

Lianne's cheeks blushed a bright pink. "Maybe a little. It's embarrassing to admit I used to run around with a guy like that."

"Get over it," Gemma said, a sharp tone in her voice. "How do you know this guy hasn't figured out where you work?"

"Because he hasn't. I never said he was smart."

"Well, either way, you can't continue to sit in a storage room forever. I'll take you to my house, and we can both sit down with Lando and sort this mess out."

Lianne looked skeptical. "No way. Lando is all about supporting the family, no matter what."

Gemma crossed her arms and leaned across the table toward Lianne. "Duh. He's loyal to his brother. Once we explain why you did what you did, he's the only one who can help you. Tell her, Leia."

"Does it matter what I say? Really?" Leia patted Lianne on the arm. "She's right. We Bonners are family-oriented, but Lando's a fair man. Even I know that he's your only option."

"Now that we've cleared that up," Gemma began. "We have to figure how to get Lianne out of here without this Kirk jerk seeing her." She snapped her fingers. "I got it. We'll use the panel truck out front. I'll drive around back, down the alley, and you be ready by the backdoor of your shop to hop inside when I text you that the coast is clear."

"I don't know. I'd feel safer staying put."

"If he does figure things out, you'd be trapped in here," Leia pointed out.

"Here's a thought," Gemma stated in matter-of-fact, no-nonsense terms. "Kirk knows your sister's name, right? There's a big sign over your shop that says Collette's Collectibles. It's only a matter of time until he puts two and two together and waits you out."

"You're right. Besides, I have to face Luke sometime."

"Exactly. Let's get ready to move."

"You were really thinking about handing over twenty grand to this asshole?" Luke roared. "Just like that, without a single word to me about it. Never once asking for my help."

"I wouldn't have used a penny of your money," Lianne yelled back. "That was the point of attempting to handle it by myself. I didn't tell you or Gemma or Leia. That should tell you right there I was trying to handle Kirk alone."

Gemma had gotten everyone together in Lando's office for a friendly confab between all parties. Hoping for a civil discussion, she could tell by the angry shouting that it was starting to turn ugly again. She glared over at Luke. "Last night, you thought she was cheating. I would think you'd be relieved now to know the truth. Cheating versus blackmail is an entirely different problem altogether."

Leia got to her feet to defend her friend. Staring Luke down, she folded her arms across her chest. "Before you come unglued, what she was thinking and how she intended to handle the situation wasn't that different from what happened with Tiffany last fall. Need I remind everyone here that I was willing to do anything to keep Tiffany in check."

"Yeah, and look how that turned out," Zeb growled. "I feel for Luke. He's the injured party here."

Leia turned her icy stare on her husband. "The point is everyone in this room rallied behind me to get rid of Tiffany." She aimed a daunting scowl on Lando. "If I'm not mistaken, you even threatened her with charges. You had evidence, witnesses, phone calls, and threatened to use all of it against her. It's not so hard to believe that Lianne felt like she could handle this situation without dragging our brother into a blackmail scheme. Of course, now we realize our brother is as ungrateful as a rattlesnake."

With the momentum shifting to their side, Gemma stood up. "Well said. If you don't understand that Lianne was doing everything she could to keep Luke out of this sordid business and away from scandal, then you haven't been listening. She was trying to protect his reputation and overall good standing in the community."

She tossed her laser-focus at Luke. "This afternoon, that doesn't seem to be anything anyone cares about. The truth. We're laying out the truth."

"But what kind of partnership do we have if Lianne doesn't feel she can bring a problem like this up over breakfast?"

"You don't have to bother about sharing breakfast with me any longer. That's a fact," Lianne said. "We're broken up. We're not scotch-taping this weak relationship back together again for any reason. We're done. I'm not sure why we're even sitting around here. Kirk Ritter is my problem, and I'll deal with it."

Lando cleared his throat. "If we're all finished screaming at each other, I have something to say." He shifted in his chair to look at Lianne. "You're wrong about this being your problem. The minute Kirk Ritter set foot in Coyote Wells, he became mine. He's violated his parole by leaving the state of Oregon. When I find him, and I will, he'll be shipped back to Portland in handcuffs."

"There," Gemma stated. "Right there is why we're here. Lando will find this guy."

Luke pushed to his feet and looked over at Lianne with sadness in his eyes. "I'm glad you aren't missing anymore. I'm glad you're safe. I'm sorry about all of this. But you can't say I didn't try to talk to you about it."

Lianne shoved out of the chair. She took two steps toward Luke, getting nose to nose with him. "I was trying to protect you from this, to insulate you from Kirk Ritter! If you can't see that, then you're not the man I thought you were." She stomped to the door and glanced back at the man she'd intended to marry. "I'm done with this farce. I told Gemma it was a bad idea. I'm done with the faux outrage you can barely muster. Your outrage seems to be focused on the twenty-grand. I did not give him that kind of money, nor would I even if I had it, which I don't. For the past two months, I've done nothing but try to steer Kirk away from you and your practice. That's why I left last night without a fight. I'm out of here now. Do what you want. All of you just do what you want."

Having said what she wanted to say, she threw open the door and marched down the hallway to the women's restroom.

Everyone who remained traded looks all around. It was Gemma who darted out of the room and followed Lianne without a word to anyone else.

Luke threw up his hands. "I don't know what to say anymore. Nothing I say..."

Leia cut him off. "Oh, boohoo. You brought this on yourself. When I told Zeb about Tiffany, his first response wasn't about money. I think you wanted to believe Lianne cheated. You were looking for a loophole out of this wedding, and you found it. Congratulations. You're not getting married."

7

After the disastrous blowup, Gemma decided to drive Lianne over to her grandmother's house on Dolphin Way for safekeeping until Lando could lockup Kirk Ritter.

Sitting in the passenger seat of the Volvo, Lianne seemed edgy. "Are you sure this is okay with Paloma?"

"I told you she's fine with it. The plan is to sneak you in through the rear of the house using the sliding glass door."

"Just look for a black truck when you go down the alleyway. What if I see him? What if he comes to Paloma's?"

Gemma reached over and squeezed Lianne's hand to calm her down a bit. "Call me. Call Lando. Paloma has my number on speed dial. Right now, I just want to get you settled in. You're the one I'm worried about. You seem not at all like yourself."

"Why? Because things have changed, and I won't be your sister-in-law?"

"Give me some credit, okay? I'm worried you might not want to live in the same town as Luke. You might chuck it all and head back to Portland next week."

"I wouldn't do that. However, Coyote Wells has definitely lost some of its allure for me. Where did it all go so wrong, Gemma? How did I lose control of this situation to the degree that it broke up what I once thought was a solid relationship?"

"I've been there, remember? Lots of water under that bridge, a bridge I'd rather not go near again. We've all had rocky patches. You know that it's true."

Lianne let out a full-blown, depressed sigh. "Yes, but now I'm stuck with a six-hundred-dollar wedding gown and no place to wear it. Should I sell it on Facebook Marketplace or Craigslist?"

"Why don't you keep it? I know you can't return it."

"Because every time I look at it…the thing reminds me of Luke and what might've been."

If Gemma had been wondering when Lianne's waterworks would kick in, she didn't have to wait much longer. She wasn't prepared when the tears came swift and in gut-wrenching sobs.

It broke her heart to see her best friend so shattered. Gemma pulled the Volvo to the curb and unfastened her seatbelt. She scooted closer, taking Lianne in her arms. Knowing the woman needed time to pull herself together, Gemma sat there in the front seat, rocking Lianne back and forth, trying to soothe away the tears and calm her down.

But no matter how long Gemma waited for Lianne's grief to subside, her best friend's heartbreaking sobs grew louder, deeper.

Lianne couldn't stop crying. In between the rasping and weeping, she poured out her heart, everything she'd been saving up over the past twenty-four hours. "What am I going to do without him? I loved him more than any man I've ever known. We seemed to be so right for each other. And he tossed it all away. Me. He tossed me away for a fishing trip." She snapped her fingers. "Just like that, we're finished, no more Dr. Luke Bonner. And for what? Why? Because I didn't tell him about some stupid, stupid man from a dozen years ago. Is that fair? If he really loved me, why should any of that even matter now?"

Gemma kept hugging, and Lianne kept bawling.

"What will I do now, Gemma? What? Luke was the love of my life, or so I thought. I believed in him. But he didn't believe in me."

There wasn't a lot of reassurances Gemma could provide other than the truth. "Who knows why couples don't work out? Who knows why love sometimes isn't enough to keep two people together?"

"Do you think he stopped loving me, and that's why he reacted the way he did?"

"I don't know, Lianne. I wish I did. I'm no expert in matters of the heart, least of all relationships."

The two women sat there for a full half-hour on the side of the road before Lianne had cried herself out. She shifted in her seat. "I'm okay. Well, not really, but I'll be okay."

"You'll get through this," Gemma assured her. "I'll be there for you every step of the way. Are you ready to get settled for the night? Because Paloma's house is just around the corner."

"Sure."

Gemma drove down the alleyway, then stopped at the rear of Paloma's Mediterranean-style bungalow. She used the patio door at the back of the residence to usher her friend inside. Rapping on the glass got the attention of Dinkums, Paloma's West Highland terrier. Gemma reached down and scooped the little dog into her arms. But her goal at the moment was to make Lianne feel at home.

"You settle in here. When it gets dark, I'll run by Farley's later to retrieve your suitcase and bring it by. In the meantime, Paloma has everything you need to relax for a bit, drink a glass of wine, and chill before dinner. Get your mind off what happened."

"I'm happy for the company," Paloma uttered. "We've all suffered the loss of loved ones. Breakups are hard. But you'll get through this."

Lianne smiled. "Thank you for having me. I'm sorry to impose like this."

"Nonsense," Paloma spat out. The elderly woman might need a cane to get around, but she hadn't lost her quick wit. "Since when does a friend dropping in equate to an imposition. The day that happens is the day they stick me in the ground. And I'm not ready to go just yet."

"Thank goodness for that. She's definitely as much a live wire today as she was twenty years ago," Gemma concurred, running a hand through Dinkum's thick coat. "Is there anything you need right now? I could run to the supermarket and pick up groceries."

Paloma shook her head. "I ordered food yesterday, and Two Sisters' delivered it within an hour. Say what you will about Dinah and Dharma, but those two women know a thing or two about running a grocery store and getting orders out on time. I think Lianne and I will be just fine. No need to worry about us."

"Didn't you tell her about Kirk Ritter?" Lianne asked. "I should just go. I don't want to put anyone else at risk."

Paloma tapped her cane on the floor. "Of course, Gemma told me about that lowlife. He tries to come around here, though, and we'll give him what for, won't we?"

Gemma wrapped a free arm around Paloma's shoulders. "The grand dame has spoken. And just so you know, I tell this woman everything, so no holding back on any level. It seems Kirk Ritter doesn't scare her one bit."

"Maybe it should," Lianne cautioned. "Are you sure you want me here? Because I could just as easily stay at Collette's house."

"Are you prepared to fight back if this scumbag comes calling in the middle of the night?" Paloma asked. "Because I am."

That made Lianne smile again. "Sure. I'll sleep with one eye open if I have to."

"That won't be necessary," Gemma assured them. "Lando has promised he'll have Payce keep an eye on the place until this Ritter guy is in custody. They're all working double shifts."

Gemma pivoted toward her grandmother. "Which reminds me, did Ben Zurcher ever mention that he was looking into the Copeland murders?"

Paloma's mouth wrinkled in a frown. "Why would he do that? Ben retired ages ago. What's the former postmaster doing investigating murders like that? Are you saying before someone shot him Sunday night, he was carrying on his own investigation?"

"I shouldn't say any more than that," Gemma advised as she tried to change the subject. "So if you ladies are set, I'll get on the road. If you need anything, let me know." She put Dinkums down on the floor before turning to Lianne. "I'll get your suitcase here by nine-fifteen. Farley says he'll meet me at the garage at around eight-forty-five. I'll text you when I'm pulling up in the driveway out front, so you'll know it's me coming to the door. Don't let anyone else in unless, you know, it's Van or Nova."

"Van and Nova took the kids camping," Paloma snapped. "They won't be coming here unannounced. You tell Lando for me to do his job and find this guy. We'll sleep better with him off the streets."

Gemma hugged her grandmother harder. "Yes, ma'am. I'm on my way to meet Lando now."

Luke sat alone in a back booth inside Captain Jack's, nursing a beer.

The restaurant had been in his family for decades. Just like his dad had done when he was alive, his mother had worked her butt off over the years to make sure it didn't close its doors. So when Lydia Bonner slid a plate filled with fish tacos in front of him, he had to smile. "It must be Taco Tuesday."

"You know it is," Lydia said as she scooted in across from him. "Are you gonna be okay? Calling off the wedding is a big deal. I have to say I didn't see that coming. I thought you and Lianne were perfect for each other."

"It's a mess. I've screwed this entire thing up from the get-go, going all the way back to January."

"I'm sure you didn't screw it up on your own. Do you plan to take a few days off, push some of your appointments back a few weeks? You could go up to the cabin, take some time for yourself and try to figure out how it all went south."

"Thanks for the offer, but I need to get back to work tomorrow."

"Eat then. Want another beer?"

"Sure. I could probably use as much alcohol as I can get tonight."

Lydia patted his hand. "I know you don't mean that, so I won't dwell on it." She looked up to see Gemma enter through the side door designated for pick up orders. "I still think a few days up at the cabin would do you good."

Lydia went over and greeted her daughter-in-law with a hug.

But it was Gemma who bobbed her head toward Luke. "How's he doing?"

"It's like he's missing his best friend."

"I just left Lianne, and she's a basket case. Breakups are awful."

"Do you think this one will stick?"

"No idea. The thing is, I'm not even sure how we got here. One misunderstanding, one lie, one mess."

"Tell me about it. Your order should be up by now. Lemme go check."

Gemma watched as Lydia went around to the grill where Leia was hard at work. She ambled back to where Luke had finished eating his dinner. "You okay?"

"Not really. How's Lianne?"

"She's..." Gemma struggled to find the right words. "She's taking it hard."

"I hope she isn't thinking of leaving."

"She might. She misses Portland sometimes. You know, misses what the bigger city has to offer. Malls and shopping and a more robust nightlife than our little patch offers."

"See? That's another reason we're not compatible. I didn't know she missed Portland that much."

"It's where she grew up. We're all partial to coming back home. Look at me. That's why I'm here. As for Lianne, she's built something here or thought she had. She's tough. She'll stick it out for the new business. I'm sure of it. She's not a quitter."

"Is that a swipe at me? Am I the quitter? After all, I'm the one who called it quits."

"I didn't say that."

"Yeah, but you were thinking it?"

"So now you're telling me what I'm thinking. Great. You can be an ass sometimes, Luke. Look, I don't blame you for being upset with her for not telling you about Ritter. But you could've easily pressed her to find out what she was hiding. You didn't. I think you were looking to bail, beginning to get cold feet. That's on you, not Lianne. Unless you accept some responsibility, I'm not even sure the two of you could be friends."

Luke tossed down his napkin. "Gee, thanks for the vote of confidence."

Gemma swiped a hand through her hair when she saw Lydia hold up a paper sack filled with food. "My order's ready. Just remember, you and Lianne had something special once upon a time. You cared about each other. Don't let Ritter win. Don't let him change how you feel about her."

Lando had spent hours studying the photographs from the Copeland crime scene. He figured that if he could solve who killed the family, he'd also have Ben's killer as well.

The answer had to be here somewhere in all the files. He just had to see the big picture.

Just inside the doorway, Gemma held up the bag of food. "Burgers and fries. Hope you're hungry. Your mom added a ton of fries."

"I'm starving. After you left, I wasn't sure you knew I preferred a burger to tacos."

"How would I ever forget that?"

"With everything that's going on, I'd be surprised if you remembered. Did you get Lianne settled?"

Gemma began to unpack the food. "Yeah. And she broke down and cried for at least forty minutes this afternoon on the way."

"I wondered about that. She was so stoic while she was here. I thought it might not last."

"It didn't. The waterworks broke like a dam bursting. And I just saw Luke having supper at Captain Jack's. He looked miserable. Why is that?"

"I'd say it started when Luke jumped to conclusions, and Lianne didn't set him straight. Two months is a long time for trust issues to fester. I gotta sit down and eat. I'm about done in looking at these pictures." After organizing the photos, he shoved them back into the box.

"Disgusting and gruesome," Gemma acknowledged as she flipped up the Styrofoam container and picked up her burger. "I asked Paloma about Ben. She didn't seem to know he was digging into the Copeland case, either."

"I haven't talked to anyone yet who did, or anyone willing to admit it anyway. I find that odd."

"It's just so weird that he never brought it up to you. His unwillingness to talk to you about it says he didn't trust you, Lando. There's no other way to look at it."

"I know. That hurts. But knowing Ben had that box of evidence in his office all those times I looked in on him makes me angry."

"On the drive back to City Hall, I started thinking about who could've killed the family. If the sister didn't do it or hire someone to do it for her, then maybe Mr. Copeland made someone very angry at the mercantile. Maybe there's something in his background that prompted the killings.'"

"If that's the case, then why wouldn't the killer just murder Todd at the general store when Todd was there by himself? Why kill the entire family?"

"Okay, so that theory rules out employees or former employees. Opportunity there would favor a colleague. But you're right. If they wanted Todd dead, they'd probably just kill him at the store. They wouldn't need to kill everyone in the house."

"I'll look into employee records as soon as we're done preserving everything inside Ben's house. Not a small task. You should see this office. He had everything laid out like a detective."

"Take me inside there tomorrow. Let me get a feel for what Ben was thinking."

"I can do that. At this point, I could use all the help I can get."

Lando's cell phone went off just as he crammed the last French fry into his mouth. "Bonner."

Dale was on the other line. "Hey, Chief, I was headed home to get some shuteye before taking over from Jimmy at Ben's house. I drove past the old drive-in theater, south of town. I spotted a black pickup sitting in the parking lot. It looks to me like there's a guy inside who's asleep."

"Good work, Dale. I'm on my way. Don't approach him. Wait until I get there. And stay out of sight. But don't let him pull away."

Dale laughed. "No chance of that. I'm sitting at the entrance, blocking the only way in and out with the cruiser. He'd have to ram his way through."

"You stay put. I'm leaving now."

The old Cactus Flower Drive-in Theater had sat abandoned since the last owner died in the mid-2000s, and his kids didn't want any part of tossing money into a failed enterprise.

The screen was still up, and the speakers still stood, spattered throughout the parking lot. But it was the concession stand that had taken the decrepit hit. The snack bar, long boarded up, was a mess of crumbling concrete, a cracked foundation, and a ceiling about to give way. The horrible condition of the place was probably why Kirk Ritter had chosen to remain in his truck where he could catch a few hours of uninterrupted sleep.

Thanks to the pickup's proximity to the entrance, Lando and Dale managed to sneak up on the parolee and take him into custody without incident. Because they made an arrest, Gemma could pick up Lianne and drive her to Farley's garage to retrieve her car.

"You're sure it was him?" Lianne wanted to know.

"He had a driver's license that said so." But Gemma held up her cell phone just in case, where Lando had texted her the guy's mugshot. "If that's him, then he's in jail as we speak."

Lianne's shoulders relaxed. "That's Kirk all right. Thank you. I want to thank Lando, too."

"Technically, Dale was the one who spotted him. I just want to say one thing, and then I'll shut up about it. I saw Luke earlier, and he looks as miserable as you do."

"How am I supposed to feel about that? Secretly, I'm glad he's miserable. But I'm too tired right now to think straight."

"I know. I'll follow you home and make sure you get settled."

"Thanks. I should probably stop calling it Collette's house now. Kind of like you should stop calling where you live your grandmother's. Speaking of which, Paloma seemed disappointed I was leaving. I feel bad about that."

"We'll have lunch with her on Saturday to make up for it. How does that sound?"

"Normal. I'd love that."

"Then we'll make it a date."

8

When Gemma and Lando finally went to bed that night, they were both bone tired.

"What a day," she said as she pulled the covers back on the bed. With great care, she crawled between the sheets. But when she realized Lando wasn't doing the same thing on his side of the bed, her head popped up again. "Why are you not getting ready for bed? What's wrong?"

"I just got a text from Jimmy. He spotted someone hanging around Ben's place."

"And what I'm hearing is that there's no way Jimmy can handle this on his own, right?"

Lando cocked his head to study her. "As much as I'd like to crawl in beside you, I do have to go check on one of my officers. It's about backing up your own."

"Just like backing up family," Gemma repeated. After snuggling in, her shoulders slumped as she grudgingly kicked off the blanket. "As mayor, I should go with you."

"Nope. Not necessary. I'm the police chief, and as such, I'm the one who goes out in the middle of the night. If there's a problem, then I'll text you."

"Fine. But I won't sleep until you get back."

He skirted the bed to place a kiss on her forehead. "Go to sleep. I'll try not to wake you when I get back."

"I won't be asleep," Gemma muttered, pouting in a way that made him smile.

"Sure, you will. You're practically slinking down in the covers now. Look, I gotta go."

"Text me," she said, shouting after him as he rushed out of the bedroom.

The dogs took the opportunity to leap on top of the bed to burrow next to Gemma. She took the comfort but reached for the TV remote. If Lando thought she'd fall asleep, she'd show him she could wait up. After spending a few minutes flicking through the channels, Gemma settled on a rerun of Golden Girls. Bored silly with the outdated plotline and old jokes, she was asleep in a matter of minutes.

While Lando droved over to Ben's house, he knew there were times the job called for late nights and sacrifices. He'd made it a rule a long time ago that he would never ask his officers to do any kind of work or show up for any shift that he himself wouldn't do.

Tonight was one of those times.

He pulled up to Ben's address, parking his cruiser in the driveway behind Jimmy's. He spotted one of his best friends standing outside on the walkway leading to the porch waiting for him. "Whatcha got, Jimbo?"

"At ten-thirty-five—some eight minutes ago—I walked the perimeter and noticed fresh footprints at the side of the house. They weren't there yesterday. Since we just had that heavy rain, it's not difficult to see that someone was walking around here within the last hour or so. The impressions are that recent. But as I headed back inside, I caught movement. No doubt someone is out there. You told me not to leave the house unguarded no matter what, so I couldn't follow. That's when I called you."

"You did good. Stay put. Protect the integrity of Ben's office no matter what. I'll walk the neighborhood and see if I pick up on anything." Lando took out his flashlight and headed around the house toward the backyard. But when he reached the corner, he spotted a shadowy figure standing thirty feet away from the patio. Before he could take off after the hooded figure, he heard glass shatter. A whoosh of orange flames shot out from the bedroom window at the back just a few feet in front of him. A series of loud pops and bangs ensued.

Coming from the front of the house, Lando heard Jimmy shout, "The house is on fire!"

Lando's first thought was to make sure Jimmy didn't do anything stupid. But when he rushed around to the front, he reached the porch just in time to see Jimmy dash inside to try and put out the blaze himself.

Against his better judgment, Lando darted inside amid black smoke. But it wasn't as thick as he'd first thought. Charging down the hallway, he found Jimmy in the rear bedroom slapping blankets and bedding down on the floor to smother the flames.

He ran over to help stomp out the burning bedsheets. When that didn't seem to work fast enough, he gathered up a comforter, then ran to the bathroom and soaked it in water. When he came back, he tossed the entire duvet over the flames. It took both men to finally snuff out the blaze.

With soot on his face, Jimmy turned to Lando and bellowed, "That had to be a homemade molotov cocktail. You know that, right? Did you see who threw it?"

"I saw somebody who wore a hoodie toss the bottle," Lando answered, wiping the sweat from his brow. "You okay?"

"I'm fine. Scared the bejesus out of me, but I'm fine. You?"

"Yeah. At least we kept it contained to the bedroom."

"This time," Jimmy surmised. "My bet is they'll be back."

"I agree. Which is why we need to get Ben's office documented and get all of this packed up."

"I'm about halfway done taking the photos. But I'll work through the night if I have to."

"I'll use my camera phone, and we won't leave here until we've finished. That is, right after I board up this window. Seen any plywood lying around we could use?"

Jimmy took out his phone. "No, but Dale comes on duty at midnight. I'll ask him to wake up Mac Taylor at the lumberyard and pick us up enough to close this window."

After Dale showed up with the material, the men got busy getting organized.

Jimmy and Dale started to board up while Lando headed to Ben's office to begin taking photos, which he arranged under separate folders for easy reference later. He took pictures of every single piece of paper in and around Ben's desk, then began to box everything up.

By the time the trio pitched in to load all the boxes out of the office and into Lando's cruiser, it was almost five in the morning.

They'd worked all night to preserve Ben's collection of evidence. So when Lando looked up to see Gemma climbing out of her Volvo, he was surprised. "What the heck are you doing here?"

"I would've been here sooner, but I fell asleep."

Lando cocked his head to one side to stare at her. She looked like she'd just crawled out of bed. She was even still wearing her fuzzy slippers. He put his hand behind her neck, and brought her closer, kissed her hair. "You're a sight for sore eyes. But I need to secure all these boxes right now. I can't go home until I do."

"That's okay. I'll help."

"Are you sure?"

"Positive. I'm not going back home without you. You need to sleep, too." For the first time, she saw the broken window and the black soot where the house had caught on fire. Even in the darkness before sunrise, she made her way over to inspect the damage. "This is why you had to check on Jimmy last night, isn't it? Did Ben's killer do this?"

"Probably. His main goal was to destroy evidence. The good news is we were able to contain the fire and keep it to the bedroom."

"How come he started it there? Why not set fire to the office? You did say all the stuff was in that one room, right?"

"Yeah. But I don't think the killer was that picky. He wanted the house to engulf, and it didn't. We lucked out there. Come on. I'm bone tired. I'll follow you to the station, and we'll get this stuff under lock and key."

"Afterward, how about I make you some eggs before you get to bed?"

"Thanks, but not necessary. After we get everything put away, I just want to crash for at least four hours of uninterrupted shuteye."

While three-fourths of the Coyote Wells PD took advantage of some downtime, Luke started his day seeing a string of patients he'd bumped from the day before.

As busy as the doctor's office was, it didn't stop Ginny Sue from trying to gossip in between appointments. "Do you think you and Lianne will patch things up?"

Luke had been jotting down notes in a chart when he spared Ginny Sue a glance. "I doubt it since she's not speaking to me. Look, could we just not talk about it. And just so you know, our relationship shouldn't be fodder for the rumor mill, that includes my patients."

"Don't worry. The people I've seen this morning are mostly talking about Ben Zurcher's murder anyway, and how somebody tried to set his house on fire. Thanks to Jimmy and Lando's quick actions, though, the damage wasn't too bad. We've got a damn good police department, don't we?"

Luke grunted and went down the hallway to see another patient.

Ginny Sue took out her phone to text Gemma. *Luke's in a bad mood. I'd say he's missing Lianne. How are things on your end?*

Standing next to Lianne as they unboxed a crate of pottery from the Reservation, Gemma read the text message and smiled. When Lianne wasn't looking, she sent back a reply. *Same here. Lianne is miserable. I'll keep you posted.*

"Are you sure you don't want to go home and take a nap?" Lianne asked. "Hard to get through the day on four hours' sleep."

"I got more than that, more like five and a half. But poor Lando was dragging by the time we finished unloading all those cartons. And sleeping during the day is always tough. Lando deserves some quiet. That's why I dropped the dogs off at Paloma's to chill."

"Your grandmother is a pistol. She was so wonderful to me last night, making me feel better about everything."

"She's been through a lot in her life."

Lianne looked around the shop. "What do you think our chances of success are here?"

Gemma shifted her feet and elbowed her friend in the ribs. "Are you kidding? We should clean up during tourist season. You know, that was always something that carried Marissa from one season to the next. She knew the tourists were her bread and butter and that they'd faithfully show up during May through the first week of September."

"That gives me hope," Lianne confessed. "I've been a bit worried."

"I know. We'll get through this and make it a success. How did you sleep last night back in your house? Notice I didn't call it Collette's place."

"Thanks for that. I was so exhausted that when my head finally hit the pillow, I was out within a few minutes."

"Same here. I was wondering what you were up to this Saturday night."

"I suppose nothing. Why? Is Fortitude playing? If that's why you're asking, then I should probably pass. I'm sure Luke will be there."

"Tell me, honestly, is there any hope at all for you guys to reconcile?"

"Why are you asking me that? He's the one who wants to go fishing next month. I say, let him go."

Gemma heard the door ding in the chocolate shop. She left Lianne standing in the middle of the new store while she went to help a customer. But before filling the order, she texted Ginny Sue. *Lianne's not budging. You'll need to do more on your end.*

So much for trying to play mediator.

"I don't think you should meddle," Lando told her later when they met for lunch at Captain Jack's. Over chicken fried chicken sandwiches, he took a sip of iced tea. "It's up to those two to get back together or stay away from each other. Your getting involved just muddies the water."

"It's a small town," Gemma pointed out. "They both have to live here. Wouldn't it be better if they got along, worked out their differences so we could invite them to the same get-togethers? Seriously. Wouldn't that be the optimum outcome?" When he didn't say anything, she tossed down her napkin and blew out a breath. "I knew I shouldn't have mentioned it. I should've kept it to myself."

"No, I'm glad you did. But Luke has to realize that he was wrong. Lianne wasn't cheating."

"He certainly got you worked up. That didn't take long, either. You were ready to throw Lianne to the wolves Monday night."

"Hey, I thought he knew what he was talking about, okay? I did. I thought he had evidence that showed Lianne was interested in someone else. I thought he could back it up. Why else would he use an excuse like going to Leia's for dinner and then drop the bomb that it's over?"

"Evidence, huh? He thought she looked guilty."

"Yeah, but I can't arrest someone for looking guilty, whatever that even means. She didn't help matters by keeping Ritter a secret. Secrets tend to blow up in your face. That's why you should stay out of their business. Stop trying to put them back together. Maybe their relationship just wasn't meant to be."

Gemma let out a sigh knowing she and Ginny Sue had their work cut out for them. She didn't intend to share the plan with Lando, though, so she changed the subject. "Any idea who set Ben's house on fire?"

"Payce spent his morning walking around the area behind the house. He took molds of a few footprints he found, but that's about all we've got. The bottle used for the molotov cocktail was an ordinary beer bottle. But I sent it off to the lab anyway, hoping for DNA. If we're lucky, we might even get fingerprints off it. I've been thinking about what you said. If the Copelands were targeted, financial gain had to be the reason."

"That means a family member. Was there life insurance?"

"All financial information is yet to be determined. We are talking about a twenty-year-old case. Maybe you could carve out some time this afternoon to help me go through the stuff we pulled out of Ben's office."

For the first time all day, Gemma brightened. "Really? That would be great. I'd love to go through the stuff and see what you've got."

"Then let's do it. We'll box up the food and get back to the office. I feel like I'm already playing catch up. Every minute counts."

Gemma nodded and signaled for Lydia to bring them a box. "We could've met in your office. Imagine catching a killer who's already murdered five people."

Lando frowned. "We don't know that yet. You shouldn't make assumptions like that. We need to find a concrete link between Ben's murder that leads to the Copelands. The note Ben held in his hand isn't enough. Until we find something tangible, we have two separate homicide investigations."

9

That afternoon, the separate murders began to blur together as Gemma and Lando organized Ben's notes.

After slipping on a pair of latex gloves, they laid out everything from the fifth box of evidence—or everything they believed came out of the carton Ben had stolen—then stood back to study the photographs of the Copeland crime scene.

Lando pointed out the killer's point of entry. "Their backdoor had been jimmied from a previous break-in. The incident is listed in the files. As a result, the backdoor didn't lock properly. No doubt the same one you used to get in a couple of days ago."

"It was eerie walking into that kitchen. Right away, I began to see what the house looked like in 2000, see the spot where the kids helped their mom bake cookies at the counter. The same thing happened to me in the dining room. I could see the family eating dinners there, sitting around the table on special occasions like Christmas, Easter, Thanksgiving, enjoying themselves. They seemed like a happy family, inside and outside. I didn't pick up on any tension like wife-beating or serious squabbling going on or any abuse of the kids. Nothing sinister like that."

Lando knew she was doing what she could to help. Although twenty-year-old visions of a happy family seemed important, something had gone wrong, something that led a killer to murder the Copelands in their beds.

When he found Gemma staring at him, waiting for him to comment, he cleared his throat. "Just because they came off as squeaky clean doesn't mean there wasn't another angle. We have to find what brought the killer to this specific door, find the reason they were killed."

Gemma glanced at the pile of notes on his desk. "Wading through that mess of a paper trail is the only way."

"Many of the evidence bags contain pieces of paper that came from the crime scene. Other bags contain items found all around the Copeland house. The problem, as I see it, is knowing Ben had all this in his possession. Maybe for years."

"Which means he probably contaminated everything we're looking at."

"That's the issue. A defense attorney would make it a big deal. We should keep that in the back of our minds as we proceed. But if Ben was able to figure out who killed the Copelands, then so can we by using this same stuff." He picked up a baggie that contained a bloody sock. "When you see stuff like this with blood still on it, know that it needs to be re-sent to the lab for DNA testing."

"Uh, I hate to ask the obvious, but why hasn't stuff like that already been sent before now?"

Lando shook his head. "This case hasn't seen any attention since right after it happened. Ben was the only guy who thought to peek into a box to see if he could figure it out."

For five hours, the two sat across from each other, digging through an assortment of plastic bags and paper sacks, organizing the evidence into piles depending on what went to the testing lab.

Lando kept an inventory list. Whenever they examined an item, it was checked off and cataloged before setting it aside depending on its destination.

"Most of this will go back under lock and key. But these shoes…"

"Go to the lab," Gemma finished. She stared at the pair of ordinary canvas running shoes, size eleven. "Tell me again how you know these didn't belong to Todd."

"Because every other pair of shoes in Todd's closet was a size ten."

"Why would the killer leave behind a pair of cheap shoes?" Distracted, she touched the amulet around her neck. The four stones sent a charge of electricity through her. The sudden heat had her releasing the totem as if it had turned into a burning piece of coal.

She glanced down at another baggie, then reached for one containing the plastic dolls, a matching set of four. All the baby dolls wore diapers and a pink top. Each doll fit in the palm of her hand.

"I think these dolls signify the four victims," Gemma revealed. "Why would the killer bring these to the scene, though?"

Lando leaned back in his chair and scratched the stubble on his chin. "It would appear that we have a real whodunnit on our hands."

Gemma got to her feet and stretched her back. "Yeah, but what I don't get is how you can say Ben's murder isn't connected. He obviously figured out the puzzle."

"After several years," Lando charged, feeling a slice of envy. "Ben didn't do it overnight. He had years to study the clues."

"Then we'll need to do the same."

Lando grinned at the self-assured statement. "It might mean a twenty-four-seven focus."

"What's different about that than any other case we've cracked?"

Interrupted by the ringing of his cell phone, Lando sat up straighter. "It's Jeff." Without a hello, he began firing questions at Tuttle. "What do you have for me? What caliber weapon am I looking at?"

"Thirty-two caliber. Close range. I'm afraid Zurcher didn't stand a chance."

"Good to know. Keep me posted if anything else pops."

"Will do."

After ending the call, Suzanne knocked on the doorframe and stuck her head in. "Sorry to interrupt, but I have Sadie Sawyer at the front desk making such a fuss. She wants to make a formal complaint about Jimmy giving her another parking ticket down at the market."

Gemma rolled her eyes. "Note to Lando. Ben didn't have these kinds of interruptions. Life invariably intervenes, shifting the focus to other things. In this case, I wonder if Ben ever had to go head to head with Sadie Sawyer?"

"Tell her to stop parking in a loading zone, and Jimmy will stop writing her up."

"I've told her that for the past six months. But does she listen?"

Lando waited for his wife to head out the door before picking up the phone. When Zeb answered, he went into his pitch. "You wanted details about Ben's murder, right? How about making it official?

You and Leia come for dinner tonight, and we'll discuss the problems I'm facing with the investigation."

"Leia's working until close. Does the offer still hold?"

"Sure. Come hungry. I think Gemma mentioned she's making homemade pizza."

Tossing together a homemade pizza after work was news to Gemma. But once she accepted the fact there would be one more at the table for supper, she went grocery shopping. She arrived back home with everything she needed. The best pizza started with the best ingredients, pepperoni and Italian sausage. From there, she added the best jar of sauce that Two Sisters stocked. And for the pizza dough, she went with the brand that Leia used at the restaurant.

Standing at the kitchen counter, she rolled up her sleeves and got busy. After preheating the oven, she spread the dough into two round pans. With toppings enough for two pizzas, a veggie for her, a meat lover for the guys, she used two jars of sauce as a thick base, then added the main ingredients, topped with enough cheese to create a gooey pie. After sliding the pans into the oven, she fed the dogs and set the table.

When the doorbell rang, she assumed it was Zeb but was surprised to see Lianne standing on the stoop bundled up in her coat and gloves.

"I hope I'm not interrupting anything, but I need to talk to you."

"Come on in," Gemma said, ushering her into the living room. "I just put pizzas on to bake. Homemade. Stay and eat with us."

"Are you sure it's okay with Lando?"

"Lianne, stop that. You're welcome here any time. Give me your coat and get comfortable."

While Gemma hung it on the peg in the entryway, Lando appeared on the stoop wiping his feet on the mat.

Behind him stood Zeb, who shuffled his feet doing the same thing.

Lando sniffed the air as he began removing his jacket. "Hey, Lianne, how's it going?" he asked before leaning in to peck his wife on the cheek. "Are you staying for dinner?"

"Looks like," Lianne returned. "How's it going, Zeb?"

"Good. You?"

Lianne sputtered with laughter. "Oh, I don't know it could be better."

Zeb's face split with a sheepish grin. "Sorry. I should've thought before I asked."

"No, it's okay. I'm not complaining. I hope you guys won't start treating me any different than when Luke and I were together."

"Absolutely. No problem. As far as I'm concerned, you're just one of the guys like usual."

"Good," Lianne noted as she felt Gemma tug her into the kitchen.

"Okay, spill it. Please tell me you aren't here to announce that you're leaving Coyote Wells?"

"What? No. I'm here to ask if you'd let me spend the night, just until the Oregon authorities pick Kirk up and take him back to Portland. Staying by myself, I feel on edge. Every little sound scares me."

Gemma frowned. "But you said you were okay."

"I lied. Every time I close my eyes, I see Kirk's face peering into my bedroom window. I know it's irrational, but it freaks me out. I'm not used to sleeping alone."

"No, it's understandable. The guest room already has clean sheets on the bed. You're welcome to stay here as long as it takes."

"There's something else. I was thinking about moving up the grand opening to next month. I'm not getting married in April, so I might as well open early."

"But the whole plan was to get the tourists in here for a huge turnout."

"That was the plan, but things change. I thought I'd send out invitations, handwritten, and invite everyone in the County. After all, showcasing local artists is what the store is about. We should support our own."

After removing the pizzas from the oven, Gemma nodded. "Okay, it sounds like you've given this some thought. I support whatever you decide. If you want to open next month, let's do it. Let's make it happen."

During supper, the two women put their heads together, discussing what needed doing over the next six weeks. While they ate, Lando and Zeb talked murder.

"I need you to go through the evidence, make sure I'm not overlooking anything. For the first time in my career, I'm not exactly sure which murder to tackle first. But I figure if I find out who killed Ben, the Copeland murders will fall in line."

Gemma looked over at the men, turned her stare on Lando. "He certainly didn't like it when I walked through the murder house."

"I told you Jocelyn Williams called in a complaint about trespassers," Lando explained. "By law, I was duly bound to show up and run you off."

"But you haven't even bothered to talk to that woman about her sister's murder."

"I've contacted her. She promised to come into the station and sit down for an interview."

"When?"

"Jocelyn says she won't have time until Friday."

"So it's Jocelyn, huh?" Annoyed, Gemma picked up her glass of iced tea. "Well, isn't that nice and civilized. Since when does the prime suspect get to cherry-pick the time she comes in and answers questions?"

"Since she's not at the top of the list," Lando snapped.

Before Gemma could argue her point further, Lianne twisted in her chair. "You know, I didn't mention this before, but last night I started thinking about old Ben. I saw him last Thursday afternoon talking to a man. He was standing right across the street from the shop, pacing back and forth on the sidewalk, like he was waiting for someone to show up."

"Why didn't you mentioned this two days ago?" Lando barked from the other end of the table.

"Excuse me if I was a little busy getting dumped," Lianne fired back. "Besides, I didn't remember what I saw until last night. It just sort of popped into my head."

From underneath the table, Gemma kicked Lando in the shin. "Apologize for that outburst. It's been a crazy three days, and you know it."

"Yeah. Sorry," Lando muttered, his attitude changing from surliness to downright polite. "I'm gutted over this case. Okay? I haven't had much sleep. There are factors in play that I'm not comfortable talking about right now. Let's start again. Did you happen to recognize the man Ben met? Could you describe him to a sketch artist?"

"I suppose so. He was about forty-five or so, but no older than fifty. His hair wasn't graying yet. He was medium height, maybe five-ten. I do remember how he was dressed, though. He had on a dark blue running suit and wore a pair of gray trainers. And when he eventually strolled up to Ben, the two just started talking, not arguing or anything. Which might mean what I saw was completely harmless."

"Or maybe not," Zeb countered. "When a guy like Ben goes out in a rainstorm to meet his killer, it's a big deal to backtrack his final days leading up to his death."

"Thanks for that explanation," Lianne said. "Even though I'm not a complete dunce. I do watch crime shows on TV. I know what happens in a homicide investigation."

"Yeah, well, I tried to walk the old murder house crime scene and got dragged out by the cops," Gemma complained.

From the other side of the table, Zeb leaned back and studied his counterpart. "I have to agree with Gemma on this, Lando. It's been my experience that cold cases need all the help they can get. If the case isn't even on oxygen and it's been dead for twenty years, what's so wrong about letting Gemma walk the crime scene? Is there a specific reason this sister doesn't want anybody in the house?"

"Good question," Gemma piped up. "It's not like we were bothering the tenants or the owners. That house has been vacant for two decades. She doesn't even rent it out. The only people who go up there these days are trick or treaters who want a good scare on Halloween or lovers who use it for a make-out spot."

Lianne looked over at Lando. "Gemma has a point. Why does this sister hire a groundskeeper to keep people away from that old house? There's nothing inside to steal."

Lando shook his head. "The logical explanation is that trespassers could start a fire. Vandals could trash the place. No property owner wants strangers traipsing in and out of an empty house." But even he was starting to see the emptiness of those reasons. He finally threw up his hands. "Okay. I'll make a point and go see her first thing tomorrow morning."

"Want me to come along?" Zeb asked. "It might be a good idea to show strength in numbers, have two members of law enforcement show up on her doorstep and catch her off guard."

Lando picked up his beer. "Nothing's ever easy, is it?"

"Nope. Not when you're dealing with five murders. Just to cover your bases, you might include paying a visit to this caretaker. What's his name?"

Clinking his beer bottle with Zeb's in a show of teamwork and support, Lando shoved his chair back. "Bruce Barnhart."

"We should find out where he was in the early hours of Monday morning."

Gemma looked around the table. "That would be great. But you also need to find out where this guy was the night the Copelands were murdered."

Lianne got up to clear the dirty plates. "And does this Bruce Barnhart fit the description of the man I saw Ben talking to on Thursday?"

"Actually, he kind of does," Lando admitted, scratching his chin.

"See?" Gemma began. "The thing about small towns is that there's always somebody who sees something suspicious or thinks someone's out of place. There's no shortage of people willing to help you find the guy who murdered Ben."

"And that poor family," Lianne said as she disappeared into the kitchen.

Gemma bobbed her head back toward her friend. "By the way, Lianne's spending the night here until Ritter leaves for Oregon."

Lando frowned. "What does she think he'll do escape from my custody?"

"You never know. It's for certain the guy doesn't respect the rules post prison. He thumbed his nose at the authorities and took off. Look how devious he's been so far," Gemma replied, bounding into the kitchen carrying two empty pizza pans.

"She can trust me, you know," Lando pointed out. "Lianne can trust the Coyote Wells PD to do their jobs."

Zeb chuckled and shook his head. "No matter what you say, I doubt you could convince Lianne of that. This guy's been the bane of her existence now for months. She won't believe her ordeal is over until you make sure he's put some distance between them."

"I could show her the CCTV where we keep a constant watch on Ritter or any other prisoner for that matter. It just so happens he's the only guest we have at the moment."

"Doesn't matter what you say, she'll still worry."

"Women."

Zeb grinned. "Yep. Tell me about it. And now you have two in the house."

10

At breakfast the next morning, Lando wandered into the kitchen only to find a stressed-out Lianne standing at the coffee pot. "How'd you sleep?"

"Oh. Hi. Sorry. My mind was a million miles away."

"At our house, we call that waking up." After filling his coffee mug, he looked across the counter and decided to put her mind at ease. "Look, it's okay to be worried about Ritter until he's out of the area. It wouldn't be normal if you weren't concerned. But he's not going anywhere. He won't escape if that's what you're worried about. He's staying put until either the US Marshals assume custody for transport or the Portland police do it. Either way, one of the agencies right now is working on the paperwork."

"What's taking them so long?"

"It's not like Ritter is a serial killer. He's not the biggest catch from the ten most wanted list. He's a petty criminal that nobody cares about except the state of Oregon. It takes time to process his extradition. There are steps that the County prosecutor has to follow."

"How long do you think it'll take?"

"Monday. He'll be out of here by Monday."

Lianne huffed out a sigh. "I suppose that seems reasonable enough."

"Look, I'll try to speed up the process as much as I can. I'll make some calls when I get to the station and see where his paperwork stands. Not to get you out of here, but to make sure you're at peace about heading home when you do go."

"Thanks for that."

"No problem."

Gemma staggered in, already fully dressed. She had on a pair of skinny jeans paired with a black turtleneck sweater and a pair of square-toed black boots. "Oh, good. You made coffee. I could kiss you."

Lianne smiled and pushed the creamer closer to the coffee pot. "You look good. Meeting?"

"Nope. But I decided not to wait for Friday to go casual. I had a shipment of chocolate delivered yesterday that needs unpacking. And that chore tends to get messy. This time, I'm prepared to get dirty." Gemma studied her friend, who was decked out in a similar outfit—jeans and an oatmeal-colored sweater. "How'd you sleep? Was everything okay? I forgot to turn up the heater before I went to bed. I hope you didn't freeze. That guest room can be drafty this time of year."

"I felt like I had fifty blankets on me," Lianne said. "Seriously, you left like four on the bench at the foot of the bed. How could I possibly get cold?"

When the doorbell rang, Gemma fidgeted with the creamer before turning to Lando.

"I'll get it," he volunteered, pushing off the counter to head out to the hallway. Through the peephole, he spotted his brother standing on the stoop. After flinging open the door, Lando stepped outside. Lowering his voice, he whispered, "Lianne's here."

"Yeah. I know. Your wife texted me as much about twenty minutes ago. I think there's been a covert operation to get me here. Well, it worked. I need to talk to Lianne."

Lando cocked his head, acknowledging the dark circles under Luke's eyes. "Did you sleep at all?"

"I managed a few hours. Are you going to let me in or not?"

"Couldn't this wait until she gets to work?"

"Knock it off," Luke snapped, pushing past Lando. "I'm in no mood to put up with your crap this morning." Storming up to the door, he marched inside and down the hallway on a mission. "Lianne! Lianne, where are you? We need to talk."

Lianne rounded the corner. "About what?"

"I'm sick of this. I miss you. I want you to come home—our home. I'm sorry. I acted like an idiot. This is all my fault."

Lianne's breath hitched. She started to sob. "No. It's all my fault. Everything. I should've told you about Kirk. I shouldn't have let you think I could be with anyone else but you."

Luke rushed toward her, taking her in his arms. He brushed her hair back and took her chin. "I love you, Lianne. That's the truth of it. I never wanted to go fishing. I still don't. Marry me. Let's do it today, tomorrow, whenever you say."

"You mean that?"

"I do."

A breathless Lianne turned in his arms. "I don't care when. I just want you. If you want time to think…"

"No. I don't need time. I'll marry you today, right now."

Lianne sputtered with laughter. "We'll get there. I have to go to work and so do you. What about Sunday afternoon?"

Behind the couple, Gemma made a thumbs-up sign. "Right here. Right in the garden. Weather permitting. I'll check the weather." From the back pocket of her jeans, she brought out her cell phone and swiped through to the forecast. "Sunny. A little windy, though. Otherwise, the weather looks like Sunday could work."

"You're all crazy," Lando stated. "There's no way you can pull off a wedding by Sunday?"

Gemma grinned. "Watch us. We love a challenge."

Lando shook his head and walked back into the kitchen. "I'm fixing cereal before work. Anybody interested in breakfast, grab a bowl."

"He's just grumpy," Gemma said as she threw out her arms to encircle Luke and Lianne. "Seriously, if you want to get married Sunday or any time in the next month, the garden won't be in full bloom like it would be in April, but it's still a darn good place to hold the ceremony."

"I don't want to rush Luke," Lianne offered with a chuckle.

Luke kissed the top of her head. "Don't worry about me. I'll show up. What about you?"

Leaving the couple to work it out, Gemma turned on her heels and headed back to the kitchen.

Lando looked up from his cereal bowl. "You think you're pretty sneaky about getting Luke over here, don't you?"

Gemma got down a bowl from the cabinet and joined him at the table. "Nothing sneaky about it. I called and asked him straight up if he was happier without her. He said he wasn't. He took it from there."

Lando clucked his tongue. "He did look miserable when I opened the door."

Gemma swatted him on the arm. "Then don't give me a hard time about it. It was just a matter of time before both of them realized it was silly to stay apart."

"You know best," Lando supplied. "Before you hit me again, I really didn't think their spat would last this long."

"Now that my work here is done, what have you got on the agenda for today?"

"I promised Lianne I'd check on Ritter's paperwork. Then I need to head out to Jocelyn's house and have a little talk with her."

"Hmm. Is Zeb going with you?"

"No. Why?"

"Mind if I tag along after I get my chocolate delivery squared away?"

Lando cocked a brow. "You are the mayor. If you want to come along, I can hardly stop you."

"That's a warm invitation if I ever heard one. I just want to get a feel for who this woman is. Anna Kate's older sister sure didn't trust Jocelyn Williams very much. I want to see for myself why that is."

"Sure. I don't mind. In fact, maybe that's a good idea."

"Then I'll finish up and head to the store. What time is good? Will ten o'clock work for you?"

"Make it nine-thirty."

"Does this Jocelyn work?"

"No. She apparently lives off a trust established by her parents and left to her and Sandra when the women were in their early twenties."

Gemma stopped eating, her spoon held in mid-air. "Can you say motive? When did you find out that little detail?"

He held up his phone. "Dale finally dug a little deeper into the Trask family. It turns out, they were quite well off, leaving the bulk of their estate to their two daughters, Sandra and Jocelyn."

"When did the parents die?"

"1998. Automobile accident coming back from a trip to San Francisco. It seems they were on the 101 on a rainy night and veered off the roadway for some reason, ended up in a culvert upside down.

The couple was killed instantly. Dale has asked Marin County for the accident report, so we'll know more when that comes in."

"You're not willing to say it, are you?"

"Say what?"

"That Jocelyn Trask Williams just moved to the top of your suspect list."

While waiting for Gemma to get to the station, Lando did another deep-dive background check into Jocelyn Williams. As much as he wanted to believe she hadn't been involved in the family murders, he was beginning to think his predecessor had left out a huge chunk of the puzzle. He went back over Reiner's investigative notes. He reread portions of the lab reports, then studied the crime scene photos.

By the time Gemma knocked on his door, he had concluded that Jocelyn had been lying all along. "You're not gonna believe this, but Jocelyn's airtight alibi might not be so airtight."

"I thought she was out of town, away at college."

"According to Reiner Caulfield's notes, yeah, which is what I based my original belief on. But reading further into the notes from weeks after the murders, it appears Jocelyn's sorority sisters were confused about the date. It turns out, Jocelyn might have lied about being at her apartment that night. Then, several months afterward, her friends remembered that she'd gone back home for her birthday."

"When's her birthday?"

"October 14th, the day after the murders."

"What's in the file is all very vague, isn't it? It looks like you have a discrepancy, something tangible in the reports to bring up to Jocelyn. Because you obviously don't want to tip your hand that Ben's murder and the Copeland murders might be connected. At least, not yet."

"True. That could be trickier than I first thought. Won't she wonder why we're there now, especially right after Ben's death, showing up at her doorstep, asking questions?"

"We need to come up with a cover story, a reason to ask questions, but not enough to arouse her suspicion." Gemma ambled over to the bank of windows that looked out on Water Street, crossed her arms to think.

After several long minutes, she snapped her fingers. "What if we tell her we received a grant from the federal government to look at cold cases? You're there because you want to reopen the case and need to go over her story again. We make her believe that the files are a mess, make up some story about water damage from the storm Sunday night. You convince her you need her input to recreate where she was that night, to eliminate her as a suspect. It's routine. You're talking to everyone the Copelands knew. I'm there as mayor, as a bit of a skeptic. I'm not sure the case is solvable. Not sure we should throw money into the case. That sort of thing. We tell her there's not much forensic evidence available. In other words, we lie. Together, we make Jocelyn believe that I don't want you wasting time or money on a cold case that doesn't warrant the grant money."

Lando shoved to his feet. "My God, that's brilliant. You must've been a damn good lawyer."

"Not really. My heart was never in the job."

"Then, I like the way your mind works. If you're ready, let's get to it. I'm anxious to hear what the woman has to say."

By far, the largest house on Shell Bay belonged to Jocelyn Williams. In grand fashion, it sat apart from the rest of the neighborhood by taking up the entire end of the block. Built during the mid-1930s, the mission revival style house had added a touch of colonial through the years. As a throwback to another era, the original architect made sure he showed off all its unique features. From each bell tower to every gable, the estate was a picture-perfect example of the houses that spoke old money. From the separate balconies to the curved dormers, to its ornate statues out front, to its massive red barrel-tile roof, it could have starred in its own Hollywood movie.

Any other time, Gemma might have wanted to explore the grounds. But she doubted that would ever happen. For one thing, the two-story Williams house was enormous. It had an immaculate green lawn that stretched its way from front to back and around the corner to the expansive gardens, the cabana, and the pool house.

Lando drove past an iron gate to reach the circular driveway, which led to an arcaded porch. Gemma stared up at the beige stucco exterior covered in gnarled vines of English ivy.

"Wow. I remember trick or treating here as a kid. The Trask family didn't own this back then."

"Good memory. No, back when we were kids, the Trask family was still living on the ranch north of town."

"Interesting. Does Jocelyn still own that property as well as the one near Moonlight Ridge?"

"Are you kidding? She owns it all."

"And the plot thickens," Gemma muttered as she followed Lando up to the front door.

A maid, dressed in a black uniform and a white apron, answered the door.

Gemma decided the outfit was a little over the top for Coyote Wells.

"My name is Lando Bonner, chief of police, here to see Mrs. Williams," Lando began, flashing his badge.

"Is she expecting you?"

"No. But Mrs. Williams did agree to see me later in the week in my office. I decided our interview couldn't wait that long. I need to talk to her today."

"Mrs. Williams is out by the pool. I'll tell her you're here. Wait in the library. I'll show you the way."

After leading them down the hallway and into a large room off the main thoroughfare, they were left to stare at the massive floor-to-ceiling shelves filled with books.

"This looks like something out of a movie," Gemma concluded as she ran her finger along the spines. "These books don't even look like they've ever been cracked open."

Lando followed along behind, reading off notable titles. "Some of these are hard-to-find first editions."

"Really? What do you think of her taste in books? Aside from *Lady Chatterley's Lover*, that is."

Lando counted a slew of books once banned by a whole host of nations. "She seems to be particularly fond of D. H. Lawrence."

"She's certainly a big fan of emotional health and sexuality," Gemma determined after studying the woman's desk calendar. "It looks like she's recently placed an order for books in the self-help category."

They waited another ten more minutes strolling through her massive collection of titles, making small talk before the lady of the house bothered to put in an appearance.

Jocelyn Williams looked much younger than her forty-two years. Slim, with a swimmer's build, she floated into the room wearing a wraparound skirt over her swimsuit, her golden-brown hair pulled back in a ponytail.

"I thought I made it clear I wouldn't be available for an interview until Friday."

"You did. It looks like you're available now. Because as chief of police in charge of opening cold cases, I have the right to change the time and place for an informal interview anytime. You can look it up in the city's charter."

Jocelyn's jaw tightened. "I see. So this is informal? Because if it isn't, I can opt for my attorney to be present. No? Should I do that now, Chief?"

Gemma spoke up, going into her pitch about the federal grant. "I'm here because I don't believe the Coyote Wells PD has the evidence to warrant spending the money to reopen your sister's case. Sorry. That's just the way I feel. To be honest, the files are a mess. You're probably not aware of this, but some time ago, someone stole the actual evidence. If that wasn't bad enough, the storm we had Sunday night damaged most of the boxes stored away in the basement. Water damage. My husband is a great cop, but even he can't perform miracles when it comes to solving a case that goes back twenty years without actual evidence."

"Wise woman," Jocelyn stated, dropping into a leather club chair. "Very well. I'll leave calling my lawyer for another day. What is it you want to know?"

"Where were you the night Sandra and her family was murdered. It seems with the notes that are still readable; there's a discrepancy in your story."

Jocelyn narrowed her green eyes. "There's no discrepancy. I was at home in my apartment, the one I had off-campus at San Francisco State. I shared an apartment in a house with six other girls. You're welcome to check."

"Oh, I will," Lando assured her. "But the murder happened on a Friday night. How is it that a college senior is at home on a Friday night?"

"I don't remember why I was home. I just was. Then the next morning, I was still there asleep in my bedroom when one of the other girls banged on the door and told me I had a phone call. If I remember correctly, the call came in about eight-thirty. I went out to the hallway to pick up the phone, and the person on the other end was Chief Caulfield. He was the one who told me Sandra was dead, and so was the rest of her family. My sweet nieces were gone; my brother-in-law was gone. I was completely devastated."

"So there's no one who would have wanted the entire family dead?"

"I don't think so."

"Did Chief Caulfield ever theorize who might've killed them?"

"I believe he mentioned it was a vagrant or someone passing through town. Is that it? Are we done here?"

Lando lasered his eyes on Jocelyn. "Yeah. I think that clears up any questions I might have. You do realize I'll need to verify everything you've told me."

"Of course. Lots of luck tracking everyone down after such a long time," Jocelyn challenged. She got to her feet. "If we're done, I'll have Mrs. Nance show you out."

"That won't be necessary," Gemma maintained. "I think we can find our way back to the front door."

"Do you think it's worth opening such an old case?" Jocelyn asked as her guests started to leave.

"Probably not," Gemma stated before steering Lando out of the room and down the hallway.

Once outside, her hands started to shake. By the time she opened the door to the cruiser and got into the front seat, her body felt bruised and battered. She felt like she'd climbed to the top of a mountain and down again.

Lando settled behind the wheel and shifted in his seat. "I think Jocelyn bought it. I don't think she caught on to the ruse."

But after starting the engine, he looked over at his wife. "What's wrong with you? You look like you're either steaming mad or like you've seen the devil himself."

"I think maybe both. My God, Lando, I think she did it. I think Jocelyn killed the Copelands. Now we just have to figure out how and prove it."

11

Lando decided they should go over everything with Zeb and get his take. He drove over to the Reservation and met the tribal police chief inside the Windhorn Grill for lunch. Zeb had already settled in a back booth by the time they got there.

After placing their orders, Lando began going over the narrative, then leaned back and waited for Zeb to offer up words of wisdom, or maybe a new direction in the investigation, maybe even a new strategy. But he was disappointed in the first thing out of Zeb's mouth.

"So this Jocelyn was a cold fish?"

"Cold fish is a polite way of putting it," Gemma retorted. "She was more like a piranha with fangs. And arrogant."

Unsettled, Lando tightened his jaw. "That's not the point. I went in there, giving her the benefit of the doubt. I came away thinking she was guilty as hell. Jocelyn wasn't just cold; she was indifferent to the murders. Learning that I might re-open the case didn't seem to bother her one way or the other."

Gemma nodded. "It's like she's gotten away with murder for twenty years, and she's not afraid. She's arrogant enough to know there's no evidence linking her to the crime."

"And there's no way you can prove she was even near the murder house?" Zeb remarked. "What about these sorority sisters? After such a long time, their stories may have changed."

Lando blew out a breath. "I have Dale trying to track them down now. But frankly, if charging her with murder hinges on her sorority sisters, then Jocelyn might be smug for a reason. I'm not sure that would be enough to convict her in the eyes of a jury. I need something tangible, concrete, like DNA to show she was at the scene."

"What if she got a boyfriend to do it? Or hired someone off the street," Gemma proffered. "In a case like that, her alibi would be solid."

"Murder for hire is damn hard to prove," Zeb pointed out. "I should know. I had a case like that several years back, drove me nuts. It was a sordid mess to try and untangle the web of deceit and lies. Took me damn near two years to make my case and get enough on the daughter to charge her with conspiracy in the murder for hire plot."

"Daughter? So the daughter killed who? Her parents?" Lando asked.

"Yep. She hired someone to kill both of them one night when she was out playing blackjack at the casino. There was surveillance footage of her playing at the time of the murders. She obviously thought that would be enough to keep suspicion off of her."

Gemma felt disgust build in her belly. "Why'd she do it? Money?"

"Oh, yeah. She wanted the estate. Her parents were sitting on valuable ranch land estimated at five and a half million about two minutes from where we're sitting right now. She didn't want to wait until they died naturally, thought she'd move the process along to suit herself."

"Greed makes people do crazy things," Lando uttered.

There was a pause in the conversation while a waitress with the nametag that read Maggie handed out their food. Burgers for the guys, a spicy chicken sandwich for Gemma.

But as soon as Maggie left, Lando resumed his reasoning. "I find it strange that Sandra and Jocelyn's parents had a car accident two years before the murders. The Trasks are dead, buried two years when someone comes along and wipes the Copeland family clean off the map."

Before digging into his meal, Zeb shook his head. "I don't much care for coincidences like that."

Gemma turned to stare at Lando. "Maybe that's it. Maybe the parents getting killed triggered something in Jocelyn. Maybe this college kid decided she wanted the entire pie for herself. As long as Sandra and her kids were around, it diluted the pie. Jocelyn would have to share. Did she seem like a woman who enjoyed the idea of splitting an inheritance?"

"No, she didn't," Lando agreed. "Jocelyn seemed like she was swatting away an annoying fly. And the fly was me."

"I saw no fear in her eyes that you might uncover her sinister plot. Confidence is what she oozed. Which is the reason we need to come up with how she pulled it off. Who was the likely person she used?"

"Don't get tunnel vision?" Zeb warned. "Before you take off on this theory, make sure you've eliminated all other possible suspects from the picture."

"You mean like the 'vagrant passing through town' theory?" Lando proposed. "How do I do that? 'Passing through town' is a hard one to nail down. Plus, I don't buy it. Do you know how far Moonlight Ridge is from the main highway? What did the person do, wander around until he found just the right farmhouse with a tricky backdoor that wouldn't lock right?"

Zeb picked up his iced tea, sipped. "It's not unheard of. There was a case down in Texas where a nutjob drove from Missouri looking for someone to kill. He saw a huge cross off Interstate 40 near Amarillo and took it as a sign. He exited off the freeway, drove around until he came to the first farmhouse, got out, and killed an entire family."

"But in our case, it wasn't a stranger," Gemma insisted. "Little Julie recognized her killer. That means she had to have met him at least once before that night."

Zeb and Lando traded looks.

Lando thumbed a gesture over toward his wife. "That's what happened when she walked the crime scene."

"Maybe we should do that again," Zeb suggested. "The three of us. After you get a warrant, of course, maybe we should go back there. Turn the place on its end and let Gemma do her thing."

When Lando sent him a wide-eyed look, Zeb added, "Hey, what could it hurt?"

"It's an empty house," Gemma added. "There's nothing in it to hurt. However, I didn't check out the basement. Lando showed up before I could do it."

Zeb grinned. "There you go. A reason to go back and see what's in the basement."

Unconvinced, Lando munched on his fries. "And how do you suggest I get a judge to go along with that?" But he no sooner had the words out of his mouth when the answer came to him. "Wait. I'll use Ben's note to link the two cases together. Essentially as we sit here now, that note connects one to the other. That's what cracked opened the door for me to the Copelands in the first place. Until I can prove otherwise, that's the way I should approach the whole thing."

"A fine line," Zeb murmured. "But if you write the request a certain way, it might work. Judge Hartwell likes a clear, concise argument. Attach a copy of the note or what's left of it. Doing that could slingshot you to a win."

Lando wiped his mouth with a napkin and took out his cell phone. "I'll get one of the guys to start the paperwork now. Come on, Gemma. Let's head back to town and get this done."

"I'm not finished with my sandwich yet," she protested as he tugged her out of the booth. "Wait. Slow down. At least let me ask if they can wrap it up to go. I'm still hungry."

Zeb signaled the waitress. "Maggie, could you box up their order? They need to take off."

"No problem," Maggie said with a smile, hurrying back to the counter to retrieve the boxes. When she came back, she handed them off to Gemma. "Sorry, you guys have to rush out of here."

"Not half as sorry as I am," Gemma grumbled as she dug out the money for a tip. "This is one of the best sandwiches I've had in a long time. What's your secret?"

"It's in the sauce. The cook uses a dash of apple cider vinegar to tamp down the heat of all the different hot peppers he throws in there."

"Be sure to tell him how awesome it is," Gemma said, handing off the cash.

Maggie's face broke into a wider grin. "I'll be sure to."

"See ya," Gemma said to Zeb. "Once Lando gets the warrant, will you meet us there?"

"You bet. Text me when you're ready to go."

It was late that afternoon before Hartwell signed off on the warrant.

Since there was no electricity at the farmhouse, Lando knew they'd have to rely on natural light for the search. And this late in the day, whatever natural light the house provided wouldn't amount to much.

That's why he asked Gemma to round up every flashlight she had at the store and home while he scoured the building for any at City Hall. After gathering up as many LED lanterns from storage that he could carry to the squad car, he texted Gemma.

You ready?

On my way. I found five. Is that enough?

Plenty. I managed to find several lanterns that we used when we searched the woods last winter for Winnie Clover's dog. I think we're good to go.

Several minutes later, he watched as Gemma pulled her Volvo into the City Hall parking lot next to his cruiser. She got out toting a gym bag.

She held it up. "I brought the flashlights along with a few bottles of water just in case we get thirsty. And some snacks."

Lando slid his Ray-Bans on and stared at her. "Why? It's not a weenie roast."

She elbowed him in the ribs. "I feel like we're going on an adventure to a haunted house. Sue me if I'm excited about it. The feeling I have right now is similar to how I felt when I went out there on Monday. Something keeps pulling me back."

Lando patted his jacket pocket where he'd put a copy of the search warrant for safekeeping. "With this, we get to stay as long as we like. You've got hours to walk the grounds, set up camp in the basement if that's what it takes."

"Let's hope I don't have to do that." Gemma stuffed her bag in the rear cargo hold of the SUV before settling into the front seat. "Did you call Zeb?"

"Yup. He'll meet us there. How's Lianne?"

"Back to walking on air, in love, caught up in planning a wedding for the first week of April."

"What happened to Sunday?"

Gemma snorted with laughter. "Common sense and logic finally kicked in. But we could've definitely pulled it off in a pinch."

"You really believe that?"

"Sure. Why not? There's no waiting in California. They get the marriage license today; we throw together a party on Sunday with all their family and friends and call it a wedding ceremony. Done deal."

"Sounds okay to me."

"Men," she muttered with a shake of her head. "Turns out, when push comes to shove, Lianne wanted something a little more romantic than a thrown together event. She and Luke are both okay with waiting three more weeks. Besides, it'll give Lianne's parents a chance to get down here and be part of it. Mr. Whittaker wants to be there to give away his daughter. And who could blame him? Remember, Lianne is the only child they have left. And Lianne feels she owes it to them to see a real wedding, not a rushed, hack job."

"Okay, that makes sense. It's just that this morning they were all lovey-dovey and anxious to get it done."

"As I said, when the heat and smoke faded, clearer minds prevailed." Gemma twisted in her seat and caught a glimpse of another vehicle following them. "Is that Dale?"

"Yeah. He has the original search warrant and plans to hand-deliver it to Jocelyn."

"Darn. I'd like to be there to see her bony face when Dale hands it to her. What's the copy in your pocket for then?"

"The caretaker, Bruce Barnhart. That is if he gives us any trouble."

Dale veered off toward Shell Bay and the Williams' home while Lando continued northward to Moonlight Ridge. "The plan is for Dale to text if there's a problem."

"What is Jocelyn gonna do? Send her lawyers to stop us?"

"Even a lawyer recognizes there's no fight to stopping a legal search warrant."

Driving through the Oyster Landing neighborhood and around to the Ridge, Lando made a turn onto a paved road and pulled over.

"You're waiting to hear from Dale, aren't you?"

"I don't want the caretaker coming out with a shotgun and pointing it at us. Then I'd have to have a confrontation with an armed suspect."

"Suspect. I like that. You think he'd go to such extremes to keep us out of the house?"

"Who knows? But I'm not taking any chances. Barnhart was the guy who called the cops on you Monday."

"I don't like him already."

Lando's cell phone buzzed with a text message. He picked it up and announced, "It's done. Dale says Jocelyn was not happy about it."

"Too bad. She probably didn't think you'd ever reopen the case."

"Or was hoping I wouldn't."

He stepped on the gas and pulled up to the farmhouse, then spotted a man in his late fifties with graying reddish hair standing outside his pickup, blocking the entrance to the driveway as if waiting for them. "Ah. This must be Bruce Barnhart in the flesh."

"Not what I expected."

Lando rolled down the driver's side window. "We're here to execute a search warrant for the house and outbuildings. Your boss has already been made aware."

"That a fact? I'll need to see some paperwork."

Digging in his pocket for the copy, Lando slapped it into Barnhart's hands. "There. We're good to go. Now please move your truck and vacate the premises. You're not allowed on the property while we execute the warrant."

The man's face contorted with rage. Anger filled his gray eyes. "Fine. But you idiots should know there's no electricity in there. You'll be hunting for God knows what in the dark."

Lando sucked in a breath. "That's okay. We're aware and came prepared. You need to leave. Now."

This time, Barnhart didn't argue. He lumbered back up the pavement and got in his truck, backing it out of the driveway with enough attitude to last until next Christmas. The grumpy caretaker didn't go far. He made a point of turning his pickup around and heading across the street where he could watch the goings-on.

Now with a clear path to the house, Lando pulled into the driveway and got out. He skirted the cruiser to unload the lanterns he'd brought and directed Gemma to grab the flashlights.

By the time Zeb parked his cruiser behind his, Lando had already opened the front door.

Dressed in his tribal police uniform, dark green shirt, and khaki pants, Zeb walked up to the pair and bobbed his head toward the gawking onlooker. "I take it that's the nosy caretaker?"

Lando pushed his sunglasses down on his nose and glared across the street. "Barnhart. Pissed off, uncooperative, and not happy about us being here."

"But why? It's an empty house."

"That's what I'd like to know. By the way, thanks for coming. Dale's bringing some camera equipment should be here any minute. I asked him to videotape this tour as we walk around the house."

"Maybe start with taking a photo of Barnhart pouting across the street," Gemma mumbled as she walked past the men and into the house.

Dale arrived and started shooting the video, beginning with Barnhart himself, which prompted the caretaker to get back into his pickup and speed off down the road.

"Let's do this," Lando said, following Gemma into the entryway.

Gemma couldn't stand still for long, though. She led the way past the living area and straight into the kitchen. "It's best to begin here with the point of entry that night, which as we know was the backdoor."

She hesitated, her mind circling, trying to grab back what she'd felt just days earlier. But it wasn't happening. She touched her amulet, clutching the stones in her left hand as she tried to lay claim to the same strong vision from Monday. But once again, the energy eluded her.

Closing her eyes, she refused to give up. She willed the power to come back, to take her back to the past, to get a clearer picture of who had invaded the family's space that night. What should've been a safe place had turned into a death trap.

Standing there in the middle of the kitchen, a sudden spurt of light emerged in the darkness. She latched onto that and floated back in time twenty years.

She heard children's laughter, the spontaneity of innocence. It came from Hallie and Julie sitting around the supper table. The two were giggling, retelling some funny incident that had happened during the week in class. They were talking about school, their teachers, what had gone on during recess. A glimpse of happiness during supper, eating their final meal, on the last night of their lives.

The scene tugged at Gemma's heartstrings, knowing that at the moment in time, the girls had only a few hours left to live.

There was no arguing, no fighting, no dissent. There was only laughter and love as the two girls helped their mom and dad clean up the dishes. It was all so typical, so routine. Just another Friday night spent at home.

Until the darkness came.

Gemma saw it then, saw what she'd missed before—a narrow door at the end of the kitchen leading down to the basement. She went over and turned the knob. The black hole that beckoned was the basement staircase, a narrow set of steps without a railing.

From some distance away, she heard Lando call out and ask if she needed a flashlight. She felt him press the cold metal handle into her hand. She let the beam of light lead her down the steps and into a damp, musty space that reeked of earth and age.

At the bottom of the steps, she shined the light up against the four walls. Before going any further into the abyss, she illuminated the ground beneath her feet. She heard some kind of animal scurry away and hide behind the furnace.

She could make out the footsteps of Lando, Zeb, and Dale descending the stairs behind her. Knowing she wasn't alone, she crept further into the cellar. Like a chasm, it seemed to gobble her up. She walked to the middle of the room. That's when she spotted the hooded figure at the back, sitting on top of several empty crates. Waiting. The killer had stacked them in fours next to each other like a fortress to protect himself from discovery. If anyone had checked the basement that night, they would've missed him, sitting there, hidden away like a coward, waiting to strike. By the time the family went to bed, the killer had already been inside the house for hours.

Her breath hitched.

"What's wrong? Are you getting anything?" Zeb asked.

"He was here the entire time. He was already in the house, hiding down here in the basement. He might've come in by way of the backdoor, but it was earlier in the day, much earlier, when Sandra went out to run errands. The killer simply snuck inside and waited. He ate snacks out of their pantry. The killer was definitely male. Jocelyn wasn't here that night at all."

Disappointed, Lando studied his wife. "Are you sure?"

"Positive. The killer had dark hair, black. He had brown eyes and stood about six feet in height. He wore a hoodie and a pair of jeans."

"Sorry, but that description could fit half of the males in California," Zeb groaned.

"True. But I also saw the logo on the black sweatshirt he had on. It said San Francisco State in white lettering."

Lando cut his eyes to Zeb's, then to Dale. "Are you getting all this?"

Dale nodded. "Every word."

"As things go," Lando began. "It's not much by way of evidence set in stone. But as theories go, Gemma just hit it out of the park, a home run."

"Yeah," Zeb said in agreement. "Now we just need to find who Jocelyn was friends with back in 2000 that fits that description. Black hair. Brown eyes. Six feet. Do you think you could describe what you saw to a sketch artist?"

With a mouth that felt dry as dust, Gemma squeaked out, "Absolutely."

"Then we take that and start making a list of who Jocelyn ran with back then," Lando confirmed.

"Friends or lovers Jocelyn *used*," Gemma corrected. "It might have taken her months and a string of lovers before she could talk anyone into murder of this magnitude. It's a twisted kind of boyfriend who liked her enough to kill for her."

In the glow of multiple flashlights, Lando shoved a bottle of water into Gemma's hand. "Drink. You look white as a sheet."

After taking a long slug, she wiped her mouth. "I won't lie. This was hard. I saw the kids, the parents. There was no row that night, no argument, no confrontation. The killer hid out down here until the family went to bed. It was a simple plan, but a cold-hearted, calculated maneuver, Lando. The one goal was to get rid of the entire family, leave no survivors. The man who carried out Jocelyn's plot was a soulless, heartless coward."

12

In the days that followed, it went without saying that Lando's job was to track down and find the cruel coward who'd hidden like a rat before killing the Copelands in their beds.

With Gemma and Zeb's help, he took over the conference room, recreating Ben's office using the pictures they'd taken. He spent hours studying crime scene photographs, going the extra mile to lay out the evidence as he dragged each old item out of boxes.

He went from lead detective to a man obsessed who couldn't stop thinking about Jocelyn's role in the murders. After becoming fixated with the case, only then did Lando realize what had driven Ben to steal the box of evidence.

"Ben must've figured out Jocelyn was behind it," Lando conceded. "He needed something in that box of evidence to lead him to Jocelyn."

"Which means you're looking at Jocelyn as the one who murdered Ben?" Zeb offered.

"Not necessarily," Gemma stated. "Think about it. The woman doesn't look like she'd get her hands dirty. She'd send someone else out in the rain to do it for her."

"Unless she ran out of stooges," Lando offered as he shifted his feet and scratched his chin. "Barnhart is the likely person she'd ask. But we'd never get that old man to turn on her. He's too loyal."

"Agreed," Gemma said. "Plus, after looking at Dale's video of the caretaker, Lianne says she's certain that's not the man Ben talked to on the street. So maybe it was an innocent encounter."

"I don't mean to throw water on the fire here," Zeb countered. "But I just wanna make sure we're not traveling down the rabbit hole with no way out. Tunnel vision is never good for an investigation, least of all one that's this old."

Lando cleared his throat. "I hear ya. But robbery wasn't a motive. Nothing was taken from the house. I've studied the Copeland family bank statements, studied the Trask Family Trust until I'm blue in the face. The only real motive I can find is the money. If Sandra and her kids died, the trust makes it clear that the pot of gold goes to one person—that person is Jocelyn. Money has to be the motive here. Greed speaks for itself. I'm not sure why Reiner Caulfield didn't see that upfront."

"We see the same things he had on hand, and you still have no hard evidence leading back to the sister," Gemma pointed out. "Maybe that's why Caulfield didn't move on it. With Jocelyn's alibi what it is, you have nothing concrete even twenty years later. And unless something surfaces from that pool of friends she had, you're in the same boat as Caulfield."

Reluctant to accept that truth, Lando plopped down into one of the club chairs. "I've got Jimmy and Dale working the phones, trying to find people who went to San Francisco State and knew Jocelyn. So far, they've sent that sketch of the guy in the basement to every single roommate who ever lived in the same house as Jocelyn. Nothing. I've got Payce going through yearbooks, talking to her college classmates, talking to her professors from 1996 to 2000. I've personally been trying to match up Gemma's sketch of the man in the basement to anyone remotely connected to Jocelyn. It might be all I've got, but I refuse to give up."

"No one's talking about giving up," Zeb asserted. "It's just...why don't you go back and do a deep dive into Jocelyn's background?" He held up a hand in protest before Lando could argue. "I know you've done the usual. But I'm talking about something broader, something that puts her under a bigger microscope. Did she have a drug problem? Was she ever arrested as a teenager? Was she a troubled girl who envied her older sister so much that she had her killed? Stuff like that."

"I suppose it's worth a try," Lando grumbled.

"If manpower is the problem, I could put someone on Jocelyn's deep dive," Zeb advised.

Lando let out a sigh, stretched his back, then ran a hand through his hair. "That's not fair to you or your staff. It's not even nine o'clock, and I'm already exhausted. This case not only hurts the brain, but it's physically demanding."

Zeb picked up a photo showing the massacre in Julie's bedroom. "I wouldn't have offered if I didn't have the time. Right now, I'm thinking of those kids and how they died. We can't let whoever did this get away with it."

"Okay. Sure. You do what you can, and I'll keep at it on my end."

"Look, I need to get going," Gemma announced, shoving to her feet. "Hopefully, I have customers waiting for me to open up this morning. Why don't we all meet at Captain Jack's for lunch?"

Zeb stood up to leave. "Sounds like a plan. In the meantime, I'll call you if I hit the mother lode of information."

Gemma stood behind the counter this Friday morning in her element, serving up espressos, bagging chocolate, and fetching things like napkins to a crowded eating area. With spring in the air, it seemed everyone had shown up craving chocolate.

Chocolate with a side of gossip. Because many customers wanted to linger over coffee and talk about Ben Zurcher's murder, rumors began small like a tiny pebble tossed into a pond then fanned out to encompass giant waves.

Every customer seemed to toss in a pebble of their own. Everybody had a different belief about what was going on.

Gemma listened, caught bits and pieces of dialogue that only intrigued her more and drew her into their conversations. Some were downright silly. Like the ones who thought Ben got caught up in a drug deal gone bad. Others were far less crazy. Some had decided early on that the killer lured Ben there to blackmail him. Over what was never made clear.

Lianne bounded in from her yet-to-open shop to fill up her mug with coffee. "Wow. You look super busy."

"Surprised me too. How are things with Luke?"

"Isn't make up sex the best?"

"Why ask me? Lando and I have been getting along like a well-oiled machine. From your answer, I'd say things are better than fine."

Lianne grinned. "Better than fine. Want me to help out for a bit? I've finished unpacking and stocked most of the inventory I have on hand."

"Are you saying you've got time on your hands?"

"That's what I'm saying."

"Tell you what. Could you get the people coming in the door now while I bag up some candy for the orders stacking up?"

"You got it," Lianne said, her voice laced with fresh enthusiasm.

For the next few hours, they served a steady stream of locals that kept the women hopping. By noon, the crowd began to thin out, leaving a few stragglers like Ansel Conover and Ellen Emberley behind picking up their orders to-go.

Ellen, who co-owned the garden center with her brother Shaun, slapped down their most recent advertisement on the counter. "Don't forget we have our pre-spring sale starting today. If you ladies need to refresh your perennials, now's the time. We got in pallets of the prettiest orange phlox I've ever seen. Not to mention the cutest blue and white geraniums that'll make your gardens pop with color."

Gemma elbowed Lianne. "We should go look around at lunch before they sell out of everything. Lando's meeting me at the grill at twelve-thirty. Zeb will be there, too. Call Luke. See if he can break away from his patients for lunch, then we'll go peruse the garden center afterward."

"I hope Luke can make it," Lianne said, taking out her cell phone as she walked off to the rear of the store for some privacy.

"I can always count on you, Gemma, for the first big buy of the season," Ellen boasted.

"That's because I have a huge garden that needs a lot of work this time of year. Please tell me you haven't already sold out of those big purple dahlias. I have my heart set on adding them to the flower beds this year."

"We have a slew of colors to pick from, and now's the time to get them in the ground for summer blooms." Ellen angled toward Ansel. "What about you? You're a gardener. Stop by later. Bring Elnora when she closes up the library. We'll still be open. I have her favorite ranunculus in stock."

Ansel's face broadened into a smile. "Oh, she'd love that. But we probably won't be able to get there today. I'm painting the living room, and the house is upside down in a mess. I just stopped in here to get my chocolate fix. How about setting aside a full tray for pickup tomorrow, though, say around two?"

"You got it."

Gemma finished bagging up Ellen's order and went to the cash register to ring it up. "We'll see you around two o'clock today."

Ellen said her goodbyes and left. Ansel, however, wasn't as eager to go. "Any news on Ben's murder? Any idea who did it?"

Gemma patted the man's hand. "Ansel Conover, you know I can't divulge information like that even if I had a clue, which I don't. All I know for certain is that Lando is working overtime to find the person who did it. Do you have any idea who would've wanted Ben dead?"

Ansel scratched his head. "That's the thing. Ben just wasn't the kind of guy who got into trouble. All this nonsense about blackmail and drugs is downright dumb."

"I know it is. It must be difficult to hear stuff like that, knowing it isn't true. Did you ever hear Ben talk about anything he might've been working on, you know, in retirement?"

Ansel leaned across the counter and lowered his voice. "He was obsessed with the Copeland case. You remember that one, right? That family murdered some twenty years back. Maybe you were too young to remember how gruesome it was. Last time I saw Ben, he mentioned that he might've come across something significant."

"Really? And did he say what that was?"

"No. Looking back, I wished I would've asked. My friend's gone now, and I wish I'd taken more of an interest in what was obviously important to him. But I didn't."

"It's not your fault. You didn't know that would be the last time you spoke."

"True. But I'm kicking myself for not being more inquisitive."

Aren't we all? Thought Gemma as Ansel headed out the door. She skirted the counter to lock the front door, so they could head out for lunch and caught Lianne talking to her contractor, Billy Gafford.

"I'll have everything installed in the back by the end of next week, the plumbing for the bathroom, everything. So if you want to open in April instead of May, I don't see a problem."

The guy who had been so antisocial at first was now downright friendly. She could attribute Billy's turnaround to the faith Lianne had placed in him. The rehab from the ground up on Collette's Collectibles had given Billy a new lease on life. Or so it seemed.

"You take your time," Lianne assured Billy. With a sheepish smile, she added, "The wedding's back on for the first week in April. That means we both still have weeks to get the shop ready if I open the first of May."

Billy grinned, and the small gesture changed his entire face. "I knew the guy would come to his senses eventually."

"Yeah? Well, I wasn't so sure. But thanks for all the hard work you're doing."

"A great job," Gemma said with a nod. "You've made an old pizza parlor look like a million bucks."

Billy's cheeks turned red at the praise. "It wasn't a difficult job."

"It was," Gemma returned. "I know gutting the place wasn't easy, especially in the back. But hey, the hard part is behind us. The dust has settled, and it's almost ready for the grand opening. We're heading over to Captain Jack's. Want us to bring you back a burger?"

"Nah. Winnie Clover wanted me to drop by and give her an estimate on remodeling her bathroom. I thought I'd do that during my lunch hour. Of course, I won't be able to start until I finish up here. Winnie knows that."

"Not a problem," Lianne stated. "I'm glad you've lined up more customers."

"Me too. I'm awful tired of making that drive back and forth to Crescent City every day. I like having my customers here in town."

"You'll get more," Gemma assured him. "Collette's Collectibles will be your shining accomplishment. When it's finished, and we've opened the doors, you could include it in a brochure for future clients. Come May, the place is bound to be the talk of the town."

At Captain Jack's, there was already buzz about the wedding. The couple got peppered with questions as soon as they sat down. They each took turns answering questions from nosy diners about when they'd see their invitations in the mail. Some asked about the locale. Others wanted to know just how they'd patched things up so fast.

After Lydia shooed the curious away from the table, she urged the couple to put their heads together and come up with a real plan.

"We do need to sit down and finalize things," Lianne told Luke. "We should probably do it this weekend."

"Why don't you guys take some time for yourselves?" Lando suggested. "Do what Leia did before she married Zeb. Spend some time up at the cabin. Enjoy the peace and quiet now because the closer it gets to the big day, the crazier it'll get."

"That's not a bad idea," Luke replied. "We could use some quality time together. We could go up tonight and stay until Sunday afternoon."

Lianne's eyes danced with excitement. "Let's do it. Unless Gemma needs me."

"No way. Go. Lando's right. You guys need some alone time."

"It worked for me," Leia said as she dropped off a tray of appetizers—crispy spring rolls and crab puffs—they could all share until their orders were ready. "I figured you guys were probably starving. I know Zeb is." She bent down to press a kiss to her husband's lips before turning to Luke. "We're so glad you guys worked things out, and the wedding's back on."

"I'm pretty happy about it myself," Luke admitted, picking up a crab puff and popping it into his mouth.

Zeb took a sip from his glass of iced tea. "I honestly thought you guys might forego the drama. That's why everyone was so shocked when it happened."

Lianne forced a smile. "It's best we leave all that in the past and move toward the future. Our future."

"Since we're on that topic, what's the status of Ritter?" Luke asked.

Lando caught Lianne cringing at the name. "He waived extradition. He wants back in Oregon. Somebody from Portland will be here Monday to pick him up."

"Thanks, Lando," Lianne muttered. "I'm grateful."

"We're both grateful," Luke corrected.

"Happy to do what I could to speed things up."

When the food arrived, Leia plopped down next to Zeb to join them. The group finally moved on from the Ritter topic to other things.

Digging into the meal with gusto, they chatted about the wedding.

"I know she has her dress," Gemma began. "Leia and I were there when she picked it out."

Leia nodded. "Be ready to get blown away, Luke."

"Shh," Lianne cautioned. "Don't jinx me. I could end up getting a bee sting on my nose or fall and poke something in my eye. My face could literally blow up overnight."

Luke leaned over and kissed her hair. "If any of that happened, I'd still be blown away."

"He's in love again," Lando cracked.

"I was never out of love, not completely anyway," Luke corrected. "Kind of like you were with Gemma."

Lando raised his glass of tea. "Touché. Here's to second chances working out better the second time around."

Gemma elbowed him in the ribs. "We were apart for years. They were barely apart for two days. It's hardly a second time around kind of thing. More like a spat that got out of hand."

"Could we just move on from said spat," Lianne suggested. "Once Ritter leaves, I never want to think about him again. So could we not bring up the situation every time we get together?"

Leia nodded. "Sounds good to me. No sense beating a dead subject."

After lingering over a generous ninety-minute lunch, Gemma looped her arm through Lianne's and tugged her toward The Crazy Daisy next door. "Come on, let's celebrate you and Luke getting back together for real by picking out your wedding flowers."

Amused, Lianne poked a finger in Gemma's ribs. "I thought you wanted to browse through the perennials?"

The women broke apart as they entered the garden center through the double doors on the building's north side. "That too. Good thing we can do both in the same afternoon."

Lianne gravitated to the display of houseplants. "What's with you lately? You seem so much more relaxed and a lot less stressed out by the mayor's job."

"I'm glad somebody noticed. Sometimes, I take the mayor's paperwork home with me and go over it there. Sign on the dotted line here and there. It's quiet and gives me time to peruse contracts and documents better. Then I go over the store inventory. Keeping up with ordering stock is critical. I check the website for any orders that need mailing. Box those up and take them to the post office. And then, somewhere in between all that, I take the time to make chocolate. My customers have been great about it. That's when it finally sunk in that I can handle both jobs. Then there's you."

"Me?"

"Yes, you. You're the backbone, the glue that holds everything together. You're always willing to step up every single time I need you. If not for you, I'd have to give up the mayor's job. Because I could never give up the store. Not ever. Through it all, you never once complain. It occurs to me that I've never had a friend quite like you before. Never. Not even Leia. You're the best. Which is the reason I've decided to pay for whatever flowers you want for the wedding. The sky's the limit." She held up a hand. "No. Don't give me any grief about it. My mind's made up. It's my small way of saying thank you to the bestest girlfriend I've ever had."

"You mean that? I'm finally someone's BFF?"

"Yep. Totally. You are my best forever friend. We've been through a lot together."

Lianne wiped away tears from her cheeks. "Can I confide something to you?"

"Sure."

"I was never that close to Collette. I loved her dearly, but she was always doing her own thing, going her own way."

"Like moving to Coyote Wells and leaving Portland behind?"

"Exactly. Collette was a terrific person, a wonderful sister, but we were never best buds. Maybe it was the age difference. She was the older sister and got to do everything first."

Gemma slung an arm over Lianne's shoulder. "I don't want to take Collette's place, but we're closer than best buds. Think about how much time we spend together, and yet, we rarely argue about anything. We're about to venture into a new business together. Have we ever disagreed on the basic decisions attached to opening a new store?"

"No, not really. Although we did kick around different names for the shop. Maybe now would be a good time to mention that I'm having second thoughts about naming it Collette's Collectibles."

"Really? Why?"

"Because I'm not sure the name reflects our goal. Showcasing local artists means the shop would benefit from a better name, one that reflects our purpose. Sure, the name honors Collette. I mean, that was my original mindset getting this off the ground. But is that the best marketing label for what we're doing?"

"I can see that you've given this some thought. Why now?"

"I have. If I'm honest, I've been kicking it around for about a week now. And I've wondered how to tell you that I've changed my mind. I was worried you'd be upset about making the change this close to opening day. But then I asked Billy to weigh in. Just now. Turns out, it isn't too late to change the name of the shop since Billy is willing to make another sign. I could keep the original sign up in the back somewhere, maybe set up a little corner as a homage to Collette, putting the things she liked on display there. Wine. Books. Chocolate. Plus, Billy assured me he didn't mind creating a brand new sign."

"And do you? Want to change the name? For real?"

"Look around you. This garden center has a cool, excellent name. Remember last fall when we were banting around names. One of your suggestions was The Craft Factory. Do you remember that?"

"Yes, but you had your heart set on…"

"I know. But now I don't. I mean, I've done some serious thinking these past few days. I've realized that you were willing to let me turn the shop into a memorial to Collette. No matter how stupid or silly it was. I've now realized the name is all wrong for what the shop is all about. It's not about Collette anymore. It's about the town, the larger picture. It's about the local artists who trust me, us, enough to sell their paintings, their crafts, like their handmade quilts. It's about you and me running a successful business together. And closer to my heart, it's about me becoming a permanent part of the town as Mrs. Luke Bonner, not Lianne Whittaker, Collette's sister. My heart is with Luke. I know that now. Collette might've been the reason I came here, but Luke is the reason I want to stay and make my home here."

"Are you sure this is the way you want to go?"

"Yeah, I'm positive, one hundred percent sure."

There, standing in the middle of the orchid aisle, Gemma threw her arms around her best friend. Arms locked around each other, the two women did a happy dance. "Then you should probably tell Billy this afternoon we're changing the name to The Craft Factory."

"I already did," Lianne said, sputtering with laughter and holding up her phone as proof.

13

The twelve hundred square miles of Del Norte County held more than towering coastal redwoods and flowing rivers full of plentiful trout. The northernmost California County had its share of lush woods and rugged beaches. The locals enjoyed spectacular views of mountains and canyons. Hunters believed in its bountiful paradise. Wild turkeys shared the same ground with quail and grouse. Blacktail deer and elk wandered through a forest of verdant undergrowth. Campers might spot black bear and cougar with a cub or two trailing behind mom, especially in spring.

Five miles north of town, Flanner DelRay was out hunting for one of those wild turkeys. Living off the grid as he did, he'd spent most of his afternoon in search of one. As the sun started its arc toward dusk, he reached a point where he decided to settle for any small game he could snag.

As a last-ditch effort before dark, Flanner reached a patch of thick brush and walked through it to the banks of a creek bed where rabbits usually scampered in and out. But as he rounded a thicket of trees, he spotted what he thought was a pile of clothes left next to one of the towering oaks. As he got closer, he caught a whiff of something horrible. The stench stopped him in his tracks. That's when he saw the man's body. A dead body.

Hunger forgotten, Flanner got out of there quick and hightailed it back to his truck.

At City Hall, Gemma spent the rest of her afternoon in her office answering emails. At the other end of the building, Lando was about to call it a day when the 10-54 came in through the switchboard.

Suzanne dashed down the hallway to hand him the message in person. But as he read her hasty scribble, he was more than a little confused. "Where is this? Is this for real? You're telling me there's a dead body on the old Trask ranch land?"

Suzanne nodded. "That's what the caller said. It was Flanner DelRay, Lando. He said he'd wait around for you to get there and show you exactly where he'd stumbled across it."

"But you're sure that's what Flanner called it, the Trask land?"

"Oh, yes, sir. That's what he said. I wrote it down exactly."

"Okay. Just making certain. When I get there, do me a favor and call the coroner's office. Tuttle is probably gone for the day, it being Friday afternoon and all, but just tell them to send someone from the morgue in an official capacity. I'll relay the exact coordinates after I talk to Flanner."

"Will do."

"I'm sorry to ask you to stay late."

"I don't mind. I'll wait for your directions and then call the coroner's office."

"You're good at this, Suzanne. You're up for a review at the end of the month. Your hard work won't go unnoticed."

Suzanne beamed at the praise. "It's because I love working here. I love my job."

"It shows, and I appreciate it. Do you know if the mayor is still here?"

"She is. Want me to pass along a message?"

"Nope. I'll deliver that in person. Thanks, though." He'd no sooner said the words when his phone dinged with a text message.

Ready to head home?

I wish. There's a dead body on Trask land. Wanna tag along?

Sure. What else do I have to do on a Friday night? Who else but you could offer a girl a dead body? You make life a lot more interesting. Have I told you that lately? What other woman gets a chance at another whodunit?

You love it. Meet me by reception.

Shutting down my laptop now.

At thirty-five, Flanner DelRay had seen better times. His younger self had served three tours of duty in Afghanistan before returning home to watch his mother lose her three-year battle with cancer. If that wasn't bad enough, he had to accept that the bank had repossessed the house where he'd grown up. Mounting medical bills had eaten up what his mother had managed to put aside in savings. She would never be able to catch up on the back payments enough to keep her home.

It turned out, when Flanner got back stateside, he couldn't right the ship, either.

He'd spent months trying to find work. When he did land a job on the police force, he didn't last long—less than a year. Chief Lando Bonner had let him go. Flanner didn't hold a grudge. Mainly because he knew he had problems. Multiple times, Lando had sent him to see a therapist who specialized in PTSD. But six months in, the counseling hadn't helped. Flanner was well aware he had trouble controlling his temper. He had often taken out his anger on unsuspecting townsfolk during routine calls. He wasn't good at handling certain domestic situations that required finesse or dealing with people.

After losing his job, Flanner had started living off the grid. He'd built himself a place to live in the woods where he didn't need to interact with anyone unless he chose to go into town for supplies. That trip, he usually dreaded. But over the years, he'd learn to stretch out his supplies, so he didn't need to go there but every two months or so.

That suited Flanner just fine.

When Lando drove his cruiser past a discolored, corroded metal gate, the first person he saw was Flanner, standing next to a beat-up, rusted-out 1940 Chevy pickup truck—the only possession he had left that had belonged to his father.

Lando noted that Flanner looked agitated and nervous. He sent up a wave hoping to alleviate the guy's anxiety and watched as Flanner waved back.

From the passenger seat, Gemma breathed out a sigh at Flanner's skinny frame. "Now I see why we stopped at the restaurant and bought two burgers. Poor Flanner. I wish we could do more than feeding him for one night."

"He wouldn't take it. Trust me. He doesn't like help. I've sent social services out to that ramshackle hut he calls a cabin more times than I can count. He lives out there with no running water and no facilities. But he's a proud man who doesn't like accepting charity."

"Then how will you get him to accept the food?"

"Good question. Maybe he'll be hungry enough to eat. You hand it to him."

"Okay. But don't you think it's a good idea to let him show you where the body is before we try to get him to eat? I mean, he's obviously upset at what he saw."

"Flanner is always like that. It's what three tours of duty does to a man, especially when you come back stateside, and everything familiar has been taken away."

Lando got out and walked up to the former soldier, sticking out a hand in greeting. "How you doin' today, Flanner?"

"I was fine before seeing that dead guy. Reminded me too much of Kamdesh, let me tell you. Lost way too many that day to ever forget."

"Flanner was part of Cherokee Company, second platoon. They fought in the Hindu Kush against the Taliban, saw heavy fighting."

"Rugged terrain. Mountains. Steep slopes. Big granite rock that kept the helicopter from landing nearby. Had to land near the river instead," Flanner replied, almost to himself, his words rapid-fire.

To prevent him from getting too far off-topic, Lando nudged Gemma forward. "I don't think you've met my wife. This is Gemma."

Flanner looked surprised, then looked Gemma up and down. "You got married, huh? Got any kids yet?"

"Not yet," Gemma said, stretching out her hand. "We brought you some food in case you were hungry. It is near suppertime. And it'll be a while before we all get back home."

Flanner bobbed his head, eyeing the bag that held the food. He sniffed the air. "I could eat. Haven't eaten all day."

Lando looked around and studied the property. What once had been a thriving, working ranch now sat unattended. He couldn't help but wonder why the land sat unused. Jocelyn Williams could at least run cattle here. She chose not to. "Does the owner know you hunt on her land?"

"A couple of years back, I got permission. Met up with an older guy out here walking around one day. He said it was okay to hunt small game."

"Bruce Barnhart gave you the green light to hunt here?"

"Yeah. That's the guy's name." He turned to Gemma, still holding the bag from the restaurant. "Look, before I sit down to eat, I should take Lando here down to the creek bed."

"Nah. You stay put and dig into that grub before it gets too cold." Lando laid an index finger on the side of his nose. "Trust me, I'll manage to find the body."

"It stinks," Flanner added in agreement before Gemma shoved the box of food into his hands. "You shouldn't go down there, Mrs. Bonner."

"Gemma. Call me Gemma. No, I won't go. How about I stay here with you? That's Lando's job anyway. I'll stay here and talk to you while you eat. I have a soda in the car."

"A soda? Like a Coke, maybe? That'd be great. I haven't tasted one of those for ages."

Lando took advantage of the camaraderie forming between the two and set off down the hillside by himself. He wandered through the woods just as the light started to wane. But the closer he got to the creek, the more intense the odor of decomposition became.

He saw it then, the body. In life, the adult male had been approximately five-ten in height and around forty-five years old. His brown hair was now a matted mess of dried blood. Lando didn't recognize him, which meant he was probably from out of town. But it was the man's clothing that triggered a memory, a conversation he'd had with Lianne.

The dead man wore a navy-blue jogging suit and gray running shoes.

"Looks like we just found the guy who Ben met up with on Thursday before he died," Lando muttered to himself.

Holding his breath, he went through the guy's pants' pockets as best he could without disturbing the crime scene. But both pockets were empty.

He took out his cell phone and called Jimmy. "Bring that fancy camera equipment you bought out to Trask Ranch. I need decent photos of this guy's face. And get Dale out here."

"But it's almost dark."

"Since I'm standing here watching the sun go down, I can verify that. You'll need a specific kind of film for very little light. Get it and get out here. Now. By the way, how are you at running facial recognition software on a dead guy?"

"You know we don't have the budget for that," Jimmy reminded him. "I can send it through the County, though. They've already got their software up and running."

"Let's get the pictures first, then decide how best to ID this guy. What's your ETA?"

"Give me thirty minutes, and I'll be there."

"Tell Dale to get moving. I need this area secured. I'm sending the GPS coordinates now to both of you. It's not that difficult to find. Trask land, third entrance from the highway onto Moonlight Ridge, then down near the creek bed."

"Got it."

After ending the call, Lando re-sent the GPS data back to Suzanne as promised so she could forward the information to the medical examiner's office.

He spent some time near the body, checking the area for shoe prints. But he'd need better lighting equipment to do a real search if he wanted to come up with any evidence.

With that decision made, he started back toward the main gate to wait for Dale. But as soon as he reached the rise, he couldn't believe his eyes. Gemma sat on a tree stump next to the brooding Flanner. Gemma had him hooting with laughter. The guy who had PTSD and couldn't hold down a steady job because of his angry outbursts was in stitches over some joke she'd told him.

Flanner looked over at Lando and cracked up with laughter. "Your wife's pretty *and* funny."

"She is that. Did you get enough to eat?"

"I ate one burger and saved the other for later. Did you find him, the body?"

"Yep. He didn't go anywhere." Lando turned to Gemma. "Do you remember Lianne's story about Ben meeting the man in the jogging suit?"

"Sure. A week ago, Thursday, right?" The question finally sunk in. "You're kidding? That's who's out by the creek dead?"

"Seems so. The description fits almost to a T."

"Weird. Don't you think?"

"This entire week has been one weird thing after another. If it is the man who met with Ben, he's not a local. Which makes me wonder what happened to his vehicle?"

"Um, I might know something about that," Flanner acknowledged. "There's an SUV parked down the road further north. But I don't know if it's his or not."

"Registration should tell us. Look, could I get you to mind the store for me, Flanner? Don't let anyone but Dale or Jimmy or the coroner pull in through this entrance. Just those three guys get to enter."

"You got it. What you're looking for is a Ford Explorer, 2012 or thereabouts, candy red in color."

Lando grinned. "I see you still know your vehicles."

Flanner smiled back. "I still know a Ford from a Chevy."

"Gemma, are you staying or coming with me?"

"Are you kidding? To see who this guy in the creek is, I'll tag along."

Leaving Flanner to watch the entrance, Lando climbed back into his cruiser to travel the mile and half down the roadway. Sure enough, Gemma spotted the candy red Ford Explorer before he did.

"There. It's been left on the shoulder parked at an odd angle. See?"

Lando nodded and pulled up behind the vehicle. He handed off a pair of latex gloves to Gemma before pulling on the second pair over his hands. After grabbing two flashlights from the back, Lando warned his wife, "Don't touch anything even with the gloves on."

She rolled her eyes. "I'm not a rookie at this."

From the driver's side, Lando shined his flashlight into the interior. Gemma did the same on the passenger side, illuminating the front seat.

Lando noticed a set of keys dangling from the ignition. "I see a wallet on the console."

"There's a backpack on the rear seat."

The driver's door had been left unlocked. With great care, Lando eased up the handle to get inside. After retrieving the wallet, he stuck his head back out and flipped it open, squinted in the dim beam of the flashlight to read the name on the driver's license. "Wallet belongs to a Daniel Lee Albrecht from Pleasanton, California. His credit cards and two hundred bucks in cash are still here."

"Not a robbery then. Want me to check the glove box for the registration?"

"Go ahead."

She opened the passenger door and pressed the button to pop open the glove box. After rifling through some papers, she found an insurance card and the paperwork for the vehicle. "Same name here. Daniel Lee Albrecht."

"Isn't Pleasanton a suburb of San Francisco?"

"Yep. Give or take fifty miles away."

"That's what I thought."

"What now?"

"We find out what Mr. Albrecht was doing here on the side of the road."

"And why he met up with Ben. Do you think Ben killed him?"

"No idea. But the name Albrecht keeps rolling around in my head. I think it was in Ben's notes. Could Ben have maybe asked him to come up here to talk about the Copeland case?"

"That would mean Mr. Albrecht had information. Now, he's dead, too. I'm beginning to get the sense that whoever killed the Copelands has a strong desire to keep it under wraps."

"Even if it is Friday night, Tuttle needs to get a team out here to go over this car before we haul it to the impound lot."

"Knowing Jeff Tuttle the way I do, his Friday night involves a woman somewhere within fifty miles of where we are. If you're trying to track him down, start with Tina Ashcomb. That's his latest wannabe squeeze."

"Good idea." He patted his pockets, took out his cell phone to snap pictures of the SUV and the mile marker before walking back down the roadway to the cruiser. "Let's get out of here."

By the time Lando pulled onto Trask land again, Dale had secured the perimeter and took a statement from Flanner DelRay. In contrast, Jimmy had arrived at the scene with his camcorder. Starting with Flanner, he'd gotten him on tape about finding the body.

"Don't you ever get tired of living off the grid?" Jimmy asked his former colleague, who looked gaunt. The man had dropped at least thirty pounds since Jimmy had seen him last.

"You know I don't do well around people."

"Yeah, but you could eat regularly. I know you could probably get a job again. I'd see to it."

Gemma overheard that last part. She leaned in near Lando's ear and whispered, "Look, why can't we help Flanner get back on his feet? Standing here right now, I know two vacant houses. You haven't rented out your old house, and neither has Lianne rented Collette's. He could live there, maybe feel like a person again."

"You can try, but Flanner won't do it."

Gemma did try, giving him her best pitch. For thirty solid minutes, she tried to get Flanner to see the benefit of living in town. Even Dale tried. But Flanner held firm. The man refused even to consider the prospect of moving back to town.

In defeat, she watched him trudge back to his rusty pickup truck and head off down the road.

Determined to do something for a man who'd served his country with honor, she tuned out the scene down by the creek bed. Instead, she spent her time formulating a plan.

She would find a way to integrate Flanner DelRay back into the community, the town where he'd grown up, the place where he'd lived until heading off to fight a war, a war that had turned him into a hermit at such a young age.

14

Saturday morning found the Coyote Wells PD working overtime. Spread out in the conference room with crime scene photos of Daniel Albrecht, Lando caught everyone up to speed on the murders.

Standing in front of a long, rectangular whiteboard, he jotted down critical points. "Ben and Daniel Albrecht were both shot in the head with the same caliber weapon, a .32," Lando told his crew.

"Daniel Lee Albrecht was at San Francisco State at the same time as Jocelyn Williams. He's on my list of people to call back," Dale told Lando. "Now I know why he never returned my call."

Payce skimmed through the photos. "How long did Tuttle think he'd been dead? Albrecht?"

Lando took a sip of lukewarm coffee. "About a week, which puts Ben in the timeframe for it. But I don't for one minute believe ol' Ben killed him."

"Any preliminary info from Tuttle?"

"Only that the bullet wound to the back of the head was in approximately the same area as Ben's. Whoever the shooter is, he or she knows what they're doing. Plus, Tuttle thinks the bullet might've come from the same weapon. That means one killer killed both men. But we won't know that for certain until Tuttle makes it official."

Jimmy perused through his notes. "How long do we have to wait? Because we could be tracking all .32 calibers in the area."

"Probably until Monday," Lando muttered as he turned back to the whiteboard. "I texted Lianne a photo of Albrecht. She recognized the running suit and confirmed that was the guy who Ben met up with on Thursday."

Dale stood up to pour himself another shot of coffee. "Jimmy and I have gone over Ben's paperwork. The only mention of a Daniel isn't Albrecht. Ben created a list of Daniels in the Bay Area. Could he have been looking for a Daniel with the last name that started with an A? Because he lists different Daniels. I have an Abbott and an Alderman along with a series of other Daniels, all with an A for the last name."

"Maybe he was searching for the right guy, and he happened on Albrecht," Jimmy offered. "There has to be a reason Albrecht came here."

"Whatever the reason, it got him killed," Lando surmised.

"What are you guys talking about?" Dale said, raising his voice. "Didn't you hear what I just said? Daniel Albrecht went to San Francisco State with Jocelyn Trask. That nugget is huge. That must be why Ben wanted to talk to him. Maybe, just maybe, Albrecht had information on Jocelyn that Ben needed to hear."

"Keep digging through Ben's stuff and everything else you can find that came out of his desk. I'll read through his notes again. The answer is in there somewhere. One of us just has to find it."

"Are we still keeping Jocelyn at the top of our list?" Payce wanted to know. "And if so, should she be under surveillance? She could try to run if we get close."

"That's a valid point. But we're limited in manpower. The crucial thing now is gathering evidence against her. If she runs, we'll get the Marshalls involved."

"I don't think she's worried too much about our little police department reopening the case," Jimmy noted. "She's an arrogant snob."

Lando cut his eyes across the room to where Jimmy sat. "Why do you say that?"

"Ask anyone around town. Jocelyn acts like the rules don't apply to her. There's a story going around that before Ben retired at the post office, he got into it with her about a claim she filed that was by all accounts bogus."

"Might be a motive for murder," Dale added. "When did this happen?"

Jimmy rolled his eyes. "About six years back. I doubt she'd wait that long to get her revenge because Ben denied her claim."

"Probably not," Lando agreed. "But look into it anyway. Anybody else have relevant input that would advance this case? Any rumors we could follow?"

"Something we should consider is Bruce Barnhart's long and loyal work history to the Trask family. The killer could be him," Dale proffered.

"Dig into his background again? Maybe we missed something the first time. Find out where he was Sunday night. Then find out where he was when the Copelands met their demise. Let's make some progress before we have another victim."

Gemma had her Saturday all planned out. After digging into Flanner's past, she decided that she needed to give him some kind of incentive if she intended to bring him back into the community. He had to have a good enough reason to try.

She knew the librarian Elnora Kidman kept old copies of high school yearbooks going back decades. All Gemma was interested in was the year Flanner graduated. She discovered he'd taken Lucy Devereux to the senior prom. There were pictures to prove it—him in his tux, her in a lavender formal—standing with their arms locked around each other.

The snapshot brought tears to Gemma's eyes. The couple looked so happy like they were headed for a bright future together. But something had happened. Gemma wanted to know the reason, which was why she moved on to search through old phonebooks.

To Gemma's delight, Lucy Devereux still lived in town. She had never married. She'd gone to college at UC Davis to get her degree in nursing. But instead of moving off to the big city, Lucy had stayed to work locally at Dr. Margaret Kinsdale's office.

Over the years, Lucy had moved up the ladder to become a nurse practitioner, who often filled in for Margaret when the doctor traveled to conferences or volunteered in other community clinics.

Gemma discovered that Lucy also worked ten hours a week for social services, usually on weekends, visiting families all over the County that couldn't afford regular medical care. Lucy traveled through the countryside at her own expense and often paid for medicine out of her own pocket.

Without ever setting eyes on the woman, Gemma like Lucy Devereux already.

Gemma's second stop that morning was Lucy's house on Pebble Way, a little rambler painted a muted mint green color with white shutters. The flower beds burst with a glorious mix of eye-popping blue sweet peas and fragrant gardenias. Honeysuckle vines climbed around the porch.

She knocked on the door, hoping to find Lucy at home.

The woman who answered looked as pretty as she had in high school. The only difference Gemma could see was that the copper-gold hair she'd had at eighteen had darkened to a reddish-brown. Lucy had on a pair of nurse's scrubs the color of teal green.

A friendly, tail-wagging mutt that looked part collie, part mountain dog with some Asian shepherd thrown in, stood next to Lucy, bumping her leg.

"Hi. I'm Gemma Bonner. Mayor Bonner. I hope I'm not interrupting anything. Because I know you're a very busy woman. I would've called ahead, but I was afraid if I called you wouldn't see me."

Lucy frowned. "Really? What's up? I was just about to head out on one of my calls." She reached down to rub her hands over the dog's face. "This is Barley. I usually drag him around with me."

Gemma squatted down to scratch under Barley's chin. "Your making your rounds is sort of why I dropped in like this. Do you recall going to school with a man by the name of Flanner DelRay? He took you to…"

"The senior prom," Lucy finished. "Sure. I remember. How could I forget one of the best nights of my life? Yes, I know Flanner, such a sweet guy. How is he? Nothing's happened to him, I hope."

"No. Well, sort of no. Could I come in?"

"Sure. But you have to make it quick. If I get a late start, I'm out in the countryside after dark, and sometimes I get lost. I don't have a great sense of direction."

"And yet, you don't let that stop you. I wouldn't want to make you late."

Lucy showed Gemma into the living room, and the two women sat down at opposite ends of the sofa.

Gemma caught her up to speed on everything she knew about Flanner. "I'm sure he has PTSD."

"Definitely," Lucy uttered. " I remember when he got back from the military. He walked into a mess of a life, which didn't help matters any. His mother, Delnita DelRay, had been fighting breast cancer for almost three years. I took care of her. The thing is, Delnita didn't want to let on to Flanner how serious it was until she absolutely had to. I told her it was time to let him know what was going on. She finally agreed. But when she did tell him, that's when he left the service to take care of her."

"Did you two reconnect then?"

"Oh, yeah. We even went to the movies a couple of times, ate out, went on long drives through the same backroads we used to take when we were dating. But let's face it, by the time he mustered out, Delnita's cancer had metastasized. It had spread to her liver, her pancreas, and her colon. She died four short months after he got back to town. By that time, she was so sick she couldn't work. She lost the family home, the home where Flanner had grown up. He blamed himself for the situation, for not coming back sooner. And, crazy as it sounds, I think he might've put some of that blame on me because I didn't tell him what was going on with her. In letters," Lucy explained.

"I used to write to him when he was overseas. But because Delnita didn't want to burden him with worry about what was going on back here, my letters, our letters, left him completely in the dark. I tried to explain that it wasn't my place to tell him about the cancer. When a patient insists on keeping her illness private, I don't have much of a choice but to follow the patient's wishes. But I don't think he understood that. He somehow viewed my silence as another betrayal in his life."

"I'm so sorry. But I just think the guy could use a break or two right now."

"How can I help? The last time I tried to talk to Flanner was when he got kicked off the force. He was so embarrassed that he took off into the woods."

"Yeah. He's still there, living off the grid in a cabin he built by himself."

"I know. Last time I was out there, he had no running water, no bathroom facilities to speak of, no conveniences of any kind. I've been out there to check on him multiple times. Lately, he won't even answer the door."

"Darn. I didn't know that."

Lucy smiled. "How would you know it? He barely comes into town every few months. And when he does, he avoids most people."

"Including you?"

"Including me."

"Do you think medication would help Flanner's...episodes?"

"I don't know. He probably hasn't seen a doctor in four years, maybe longer. So I doubt he's been diagnosed with anything officially. I tried to get him to go to the VA hospital over in Crescent City. He wouldn't do it."

"What do you think is wrong with him?"

"After three tours of duty in Afghanistan, I'd say his post-traumatic stress disorder has layers of anxiety that go deeper than we know anything about. The longer he's isolated, the harder it will become for him to be around people. It's nice of you to worry about him like this."

"He found a dead body yesterday. The incident kicked in some major memories from the war. I thought maybe you could talk to him, get him to see there was no need to be afraid of living in town. But now that I know he won't even answer the door to you, I guess there's no ray of hope."

"There's always a ray of hope. You know about a year ago, Barley started barking in the middle of the night. I got out of bed and peeked out my bedroom window to see Flanner standing in the street looking up at the house."

"Didn't that creep you out?"

"You have to know Flanner. He's not violent. It's his anxiety that makes him blurt out inappropriate things he shouldn't. Like when he was on the force, whenever he'd pull someone over for a traffic stop, he'd keep retelling people what he'd done in the war—brought on by guilt maybe. I don't know. But it's what got him fired."

"My husband is the one who let him go."

"I know."

"I've had twenty-four hours to think about this. It might be significant. Yesterday, I got Flanner talking, making conversation. It wasn't about what he'd done in the military. Believe it or not, he talked about that old drive-in movie theater south of town."

"Really? The Cactus Flower? That old place?"

"Yes. Flanner wouldn't shut up about it. It seems he had this plan once to re-open it a long time ago."

Lucy chuckled. "This probably has nothing to do with his plans, but we made out there a couple of times back in high school and again when he got out of the Marines."

"Can I ask you a personal question? You don't have to answer."

"Sure."

"Do you still have feelings for him?"

Lucy grinned. "I'll always be fond of Flanner."

"That's what I thought. Whenever you talk about him, your whole face lights up."

"It does?"

"It does. Your eyes sparkle, too."

"What do you plan to do now?"

"I'm gonna find his cabin and try to lure him back into town."

"How on earth will you do that?"

"I'm very persuasive when the mood strikes. Do you like music?"

"Sure, who doesn't?"

"Does Flanner?"

"He used to love the Red Hot Chili Peppers."

"Have you ever been out to the Duck & Rum?"

"Once or twice. I've seen Fortitude, heard you and Lando sing together. You're both really good singers. I haven't been out on a Saturday night in a long time, though. I usually stick close to home on weekends. My schedule is usually brutal during the week. I DVR my favorite programs and watch them with a big bowl of popcorn and a few glasses of wine. You're not planning a fix-up, are you?"

"No, not that. Certainly not at a dingy, loud bar with a few hundred people. It wouldn't be fair to Flanner. I first have to get him comfortable with coming into town."

Lucy glanced at her watch. "I don't mean to push you out the door, but I do have to get going."

"Not a problem. Thanks for talking to me."

Lucy let out a sigh. "Let me know if there's any way I can help."

"Actually, there is. Give me the directions to his cabin."

"That's easy. Once you get to Moonlight Ridge, drive about a mile and a half past the cutoff and take a left. Wait. I have a little map tucked away in my medical bag." Lucy went to the entryway and dug into her leather satchel. "Here you go. I hope it helps."

After studying the map, Gemma felt better about her plan. "This is perfect. Thank you. How is it he was able to build on the land?"

"His dad bought that property years ago from the Trask family. It backs up to their land. Why they sold it to him is anyone's guess. But Flanner held onto it because it's the one thing the bank couldn't take away. Flanner owns it outright. Well, that, and the old truck he drives. Like I said before, if there's anything else I can do, just let me know. I'm more than happy to help him any way I can."

"You bet. I guarantee you'll be the first person I call."

With directions to Flanner's cabin in hand, Gemma brought Rufus and Rolo along for the ride through the countryside. The dogs would bolster her first line of attack. She had a battle plan, and she intended to stick to it no matter what kind of resistance she met. She'd take baby steps on the march to victory. Flanner didn't know it yet, but he didn't stand a chance against her determination.

Following the directions, she found the property tucked back off the main road in a small clearing surrounded by a thicket of baby redwoods.

No one appreciated craftsmanship more than Gemma, which was why her first look at Flanner's cabin took her breath away. Calling it a cabin might have been a stretch. Shack didn't do it justice. No, it was more like an artfully put-together, one-room shed, built on top of cinderblocks.

Flanner's cabin was perhaps ten feet by ten feet square, constructed using mismatched lumber in various lengths. It even had two windows with green trim on each side of the front door. The door had also been painted green and looked like it had been repurposed from some other building. He'd used sheet metal for the roof.

To her surprise, Flanner had even strung a single wire for electricity that ran from a nearby power pole with a meter box attached.

He'd also found two faded Adirondack chairs that he'd set out on his "porch," which consisted of paving stones placed along the cabin's width.

Gemma loved the look of the place. She just wasn't convinced that it was a suitable spot to live and sleep, twenty-four-seven.

She got out of the car and let the dogs out to romp in Flanner's front yard. She didn't have to knock. Flanner opened the door and looked surprised to see a visitor.

"What are you doing here?"

She held up a bag. "I brought chocolate and figs. I told you yesterday that I make chocolate in my shop. The figs—don't you dare make me take them back. Birdie Sanger gave them to me, and I didn't want to hurt her feelings by telling her that I'm not a big fan. Neither is Lando. So you have to take them off my hands."

Flanner grinned. "Sure. I'll figure out something to do with them. You wanna come in?"

"Sure. Or we could sit out here on the porch. Got any coffee?"

"Yeah. But I make it strong."

"Strong is good. Can I take a look around inside while you make the coffee?"

"Sure. You have two dogs?"

"Rufus is the Lab. Rolo is the Westie. Have you ever thought about getting one for yourself?"

"Me? Nah. I can barely feed myself, let alone a dog."

Gemma followed him into the cabin. He'd taken advantage of every square foot of space, using the back wall for storage and shelving. One side wall held his built-in bunk with a mattress. Next to the bed was an old pot-bellied wood-burning stove he used for cooking and heating.

On the opposite wall was his kitchen. For counter space, he'd recycled an old bucket sink from somewhere else and mounted it into an old dresser.

"You did all this in three years?"

He scooped up ground coffee into an old metal pot before adding water, then putting it on to boil. "Necessity means getting creative. I didn't have electricity until two months ago. Some guy from the electric company in town showed up out of the blue and said I could hook up to the nearest power pole out by the road. But I still don't have running water yet. I get that from the water spigot on Trask land. I drive my truck around to fill up my tank a couple of times a week. The water's clean, so you don't have to worry about it."

"The caretaker doesn't mind you using the water?"

"Nope. Bruce's been good about it. Not all that friendly, though, which is fine by me."

Gemma wondered if Lucy had somehow sent the power company out to hook him up to the nearest power box. But she didn't want to bring it up. "Your work is amazing. Do you think you could build something like this for me to use as an extension of my grandmother's greenhouse? You know, for extra storage."

Flanner narrowed his eyes. "You want me to build you a shed?"

"Well, yes. It doesn't have to be fancy or this large. I already have a pile of scrap wood in the garage going to waste. You could decide if it's usable or not. But what I could really use is the kind of sink you have."

She noticed how skeptical he looked and went on, "Don't you get lonely out here by yourself all the time?"

He pointed to a certain section on the shelves lined with books. "I read a lot."

"Is that how you learned to do all this?"

"You really like my cabin?"

"I do. That's why I want to hire you to build one for me."

"For real?"

"Yes."

"That would mean I'd have to come into town." He shook his head. "I don't like coming into town."

When the coffee had boiled enough, he took a rag and used it as a potholder to pick up the metal pot. He used a strainer to pour the liquid into two metal cups and handed the steaming beverage off to Gemma.

The aroma of strong, freshly brewed coffee wafted on the air. They took their cups outside and plopped down in the Adirondack chairs.

She noticed he kept watching the dogs at play as they darted in and out in a game of chase.

"If you had a dog, it might help you hunt," Gemma blurted out. She handed him her phone with a link to Inez LeMond's website for Protect the Paws. She swiped through pictures of the various shelter dogs. "You just find one you like, and we'll head out there to see if you two bond, see if you're a match."

"What if I couldn't feed it? You didn't even know I was alive until yesterday when I found that body. You have no idea the lean times I've had out here. I stretch my food for as long as I can so I don't have to go into town that often."

"Why don't you want to go into town?"

"Because I always end up saying the wrong thing, and people don't like it. They look at me funny or just get mad."

"Maybe that's their problem, not yours. Did you ever think of it that way? Yesterday you told me you once had this idea about fixing up that old drive-in theater south of town. What if you could do it?"

"That was just big talk. It's just something I kept thinking about during my deployment. When you're a million miles away from home, your mind goes back to the little things that made you happy. People don't even go to drive-ins anymore. It never really made sense."

"They don't go to drive-ins because they've all closed down. You could fix it up, get it reopened. Building this cabin proves you have a talent for renovation, for fixing old things up beyond what anyone else might imagine. I couldn't do this. Most people couldn't. You did it."

"Like I said, necessity. The first four months I was out here, I soon got tired of sleeping on the hard ground in the cold."

"See? You did something about it. Where did you find the material anyway?"

"Here and there. I didn't steal it if that's what you mean."

"It's not what I meant at all. It takes skill to envision building your own house, then actually go through with it. I inherited my grandmother's house. I'm not sure what I would've done if the bank had taken it away. But I can tell you I would've been mad as hell about it, enough to put up a fight."

"I was mad for a long time. But it didn't get me anywhere."

"So you came out here to your dad's land?"

He narrowed his eyes again. "How did you know this patch belonged to my dad?"

"Honestly, I talked to Lucy. And I came out here to save you from living off the grid. But guess what? I've changed my mind. You're living just fine. You don't need me to save you at all."

That made him smile. "I see. So that's what brought on the job offer?"

"Initially. But now that I've seen your cabin, the offer still stands. How'd you learn to do this kind of work anyway?"

"My dad taught me carpentry. Long before I joined the Marines, I used to build stuff out of the garage with him supervising."

"Like what?"

"Oh, you know, things like tables, shelves, bookcases, planter boxes, that sort of stuff. I like making things, working with my hands. And I like foraging for junk too, then turning it into something I can use."

"Well, well, well. Maybe that's your job, Flanner DelRay. That's it. You could easily recycle material and make garden sheds for people. I'd buy one. You must have access to a table saw and other tools for cutting lumber."

"Any time I need to cut lumber, Duff Northcutt lets me use his tool shed. Some of the tools are outdated, but they work just fine. And he has everything I need to get the job done."

"Then would you be willing to design and build a shed for me with a sink like the one you have?"

"If you really need one, I could do it."

"I do. Who doesn't need extra storage? And I know several more people who would want one, too."

Flanner's eyes grew big at the thought. "But I'd have to go into town."

"No. You wouldn't. That's the beauty of it. You could work from here or at Duff's place. Your choice. Moving the shed into town after it's built is the easy part. Although you might have to work on-site to add shelves to the inside."

"I suppose I could manage that."

"Sure, you could. We'll figure out the logistics later. I know someone with a truck who could deliver it. His name's Gafford. Billy Gafford. He lives near Duff. This could work."

"Why's it so important to you?"

"My grandmother loved gardening and growing things. I've tried to keep her garden alive, but sometimes it's hard. I could use a shed adjacent to the greenhouse to start my seedlings. Why don't you grow your vegetables out here, Flanner?"

"Don't have much of a green thumb. The soil's not fit for growing a carrot or lettuce."

"Hmm. What if we made a trade? All the vegetables from my garden you can eat for you building me a shed?"

Flanner grinned. "That could work."

Even in the middle of a homicide investigation, Saturday nights were made for relaxing. It was possible to spend downtime thinking about something else, even enjoying an hour or two of music, drink a few beers, let down their hair.

The cover band Fortitude regularly headlined at the Duck & Rum every Saturday night, appearing on stage around nine o'clock, give or take a few minutes. Nobody made much of a fuss if they were a little late.

The town had come to expect seeing their local police force rock out to a playlist of familiar tunes. Lando, Dale, and Jimmy had been playing together since high school. When the men met up with a music teacher named Radley Fisk on drums, it seemed their group had found its forever drummer. And when they added Bosco Reynolds, a bartender, who played bass guitar, the band's sound finally began to click. But it wasn't until Gemma came back to town when they considered adding a female lead singer into the mix that everything fell into place. With her strong contralto, Gemma's voice opened up greater possibilities. Their selection of songs expanded and brought in a bigger crowd. People came from fifty miles away to listen to soft rock, hard rock, and anything in between.

Tonight was no exception. The dive bar, located at the south end of Water Street on the cusp of town, drew an eclectic group of people. Millennials, Gen Xers, and even a few Boomers jammed in around the stage.

"Looks like we have an enthusiastic bunch tonight," Lando said as he surveyed the crowd from his spot backstage.

But tonight, Gemma's mind wasn't on lyrics. It was, in fact, still with Flanner and to some degree with Lucy. She couldn't help but think about the missed opportunities. At this very moment, Lucy sat alone at her house watching week-old TV shows while Flanner sat at his place, his nose buried in a book.

Gemma yearned to play matchmaker and somehow get the two to reconnect on a more permanent basis. She had to admit that the conversation she'd rehearsed with each of them hadn't exactly gone as planned. Both talks had yielded more than a few surprises.

She'd attempted to hijack the guy and lure him back to town using the Cactus Flower Drive-in as bait. Even though she hadn't figured out the specifics, it hadn't worked out that way at all. His carpentry handiwork had changed the tide. She had to give him chops for taking a plot of land, clearing it himself and then building a place to live that suited him just fine.

And sitting down with Lucy had revealed more than a few bombshells.

"Are you still thinking about Flanner?" Lando asked, picking up his guitar.

"You told me his place was nothing more than a ramshackle hut. It's a lot more than that. He built that place himself with his own two hands, put his heart and soul into it. Seeing it through Flanner's eyes, it was a work of art. Not only that, I think he could make a few bucks building it as a garden shed."

"And you encouraged him to do it, right? Did he agree to come into town for work like that?"

"Not exactly. We haven't ironed out the details yet. But give it time. Flanner isn't exactly without friends, you know. He uses Duff's equipment all the time. And when I told Billy Gafford about Flanner's situation, his three tours of duty, and him living off the grid, Billy offered to help him whenever he needs a hand. That's what small towns are supposed to do. Help each other. My job as mayor is to make sure everybody is taken care of, able to find work, able to make a living."

Lando shook his head. "I admire your determination. But I know Flanner a lot better than you do. I've tried to get him help. I told you that. He just doesn't like anyone meddling in his life."

"Oh, yeah? Did you know that he had a girlfriend?"

"If you're talking about Lucy Devereux, that's over with."

"Says who? Are you sure about that? You do realize that's what the whole town thought about us once or twice. And here we are back together, singing in a band. In my mind, it's never too late. Lucy still has feelings for him."

"That might be. But now, they live in two different worlds. It's never going to work."

"Why not?"

"Lucy's got a place in town and a good job. She inherited that house where she grew up. Flanner is practically a hermit."

"He is not. He has potential. I'm surprised you can't see it."

Knowing this was no time to disagree, Lando put his opinions aside. "Okay. Flanner has potential. No one ever said he didn't. But he has a phobia about being around too many people. Even in our little neck of the woods that's a relevant issue, no matter how much you want him to fit in."

When she heard Adam Greendeer, the bar owner, step to the mic and introduce the band, she knew it was time to sing. But Gemma was already planning her next move. As she stepped on stage, she was more determined than ever to get Flanner back on track. As for Lucy, it was time Lucy realized that second chances were all part of life.

15

Lando and Gemma might've disagreed on Flanner's future, but the two spent their Sunday at City Hall sitting around the conference table back at work, poring through evidence.

"You know what jumps out at me?" Gemma began. "There is an awful lot of death surrounding Jocelyn Williams. Think about it. She loses her parents in a car accident off the 101 in the Bay Area. Presumably, because they'd gone down there to visit their youngest daughter. That was when Jocelyn was a freshman in college, right?"

"In 1998, Jocelyn Trask was a sophomore." Lando shuffled through a stack of file folders until he pulled one out and flipped it open. "Marin County faxed us a copy of the accident report. It's not much help, though. According to Jocelyn's account, her parents had been visiting for the weekend to make sure she was happy at school. An odd thing to say because this was her second year there. Why would they think she wasn't happy?"

"That is odd. Why would they need to make the trip unless Jocelyn made them believe she wasn't happy."

"She got them down there, didn't she?"

Gemma skimmed the report. "Rainy night. Slick highway conditions. They veer off the roadway and end up in a ditch. Both Mr. and Mrs. Trask was dead at the scene. You're right. There's not much here. Did you ever find out where Mr. Williams went? Is Jocelyn divorced or not?"

"Widowed."

"You're kidding? One more death on her plate."

"You bet. It plays into your theory that death surrounds her. It seems she met Eric Williams at SFSU in May 2000. I compared their school transcripts. Seems they had several classes together. And get this, they were married six months after the Copeland murders. April 2001."

"Interesting. How did Eric die? If you say car accident…"

Lando opened another manila folder. "Casefile, dated December 10, 2002. Eric decides to go out hunting for elk near Six Rivers National Forest. Alone. That's Jocelyn's story anyway. He's gone for two days before four other hunters stumble on a body that's suffered a gunshot to the abdomen. Later, the coroner deems it an accidental shooting, noting that Eric had suffered a gunshot wound to his abdomen, shot with his own rifle. Without anyone around to help him, he simply bled to death."

"Does that sound right to you?"

"Nothing about these deaths sounds right. The incident report says that the police never even bothered questioning Jocelyn because the ME determined that Eric had fallen and slipped on a rock. The gun discharged, shooting himself in the stomach. In fact, that's the determination from Eric's official autopsy."

"Either Jocelyn is very unlucky with loved ones, or she's clever enough to kill without getting caught. What do you think?"

"Honestly, I'm beginning to think she's the evilest woman on the planet. How many deaths are we talking about now? Both parents die in a car accident in 1998. Four from the farmhouse in 2000. Her husband Eric in 2002. Add in Ben Zurher and Daniel Albrecht that makes nine deaths in twenty-two years that have a link back to Jocelyn."

"That's a lot of dying. But there's nothing concrete that points to her except our suspicion. Here's a thought. We need hard evidence, right? Have you ever considered sending the bedding from the girls' bedrooms to the lab for any trace DNA?"

"I did that Wednesday. Why?"

"Well, both little girls died in a tiny bedroom. The killer, whoever it was, had to get up close and personal. He or she might have left their DNA somewhere on the bedding.".

"My thoughts, too, but it will take a while to get the results back. My contact at the lab says they're backed up, and it could be next week before they even get to extracting anything off the sheets and comforters. If we get nothing from that, I'm thinking of sending the pajamas they were wearing. Even touch DNA might show up on the pajamas."

"Hey, it's worth a shot. Stranger things have been known to break open a case."

"What else are you thinking?"

"It's a leap, but here goes. Jocelyn meets this guy Eric five months before her sister's family is slaughtered in their beds. She uses him to do the job, sweet-talks him seven ways to Sunday. He's easy because he's smitten with the lovely Jocelyn Trask, and if they're successful, she'll have all that money at her disposal. After the sister is out of the picture, Eric presses her to make it official. Jocelyn's pushed into a corner. She marries the guy to keep him quiet. Now, go back to Jocelyn's parents. She could have maybe tampered with the car, done something to the brakes, or cut the brake line to make it skid off the road. I know it sounds far-fetched, but that's an awful lot of dying for one woman. I just can't get past that."

Lando studied the whiteboard. "We're talking about a daughter killing her parents. Then she's at the root of getting her sister and three innocent people killed."

"Even Zeb's case proves it happens. Jocelyn must've followed Eric to the woods and shot him with his own gun. That means she is capable of killing herself and knows how to use a rifle. She grew up on a ranch. Did she ever own a .32?"

"Not that we can find. Let's face facts. We're still flailing. She could've shot Albrecht, then gotten rid of the murder weapon anywhere along the route coming back from that creek bed on Trask land. She could probably find her way around that place in the dark."

"Maybe it's still there? We could search."

"Not without a warrant. Plus, that spread is a thousand acres or more. Poking around in the dirt, it'd be like looking for a needle in a haystack."

"I know someone who has access to the land, though. He gets his water from the nearest spigot."

"You're talking about Flanner."

"During the time I spent talking to him, I never once asked him if he saw anyone near the area where Daniel Albrecht's body was found. It didn't cross my mind. Did you ask?"

Lando looked nonplussed. "No. I didn't. I don't think Jimmy did either. You know, maybe Flanner could've heard the gunshot." He got to his feet. "Let's go visit Flanner and have a talk with him.

You'll make small talk about building those sheds, then I'll ask about the other."

"There's no need to go into a ruse to get information from him or attempt to trick him into talking. Flanner's not holding anything back."

"Are you sure about that? What's his relationship to Bruce Barnhart?"

"I'd say friendly. Barnhart provides him with a place to hunt and clean water from the tap. When you're living off the grid, those two things are a big deal."

"But how loyal is Flanner to Barnhart?"

"If you're suggesting they're in cahoots with this murder thing, forget it. Flanner has no motive to kill a stranger. And that's what Daniel Albrecht was to him."

"I need to hear it from Flanner, though."

"Suit yourself. But I'm telling you, Flanner has nothing to do with this. Except for living adjacent to the Trask land, he's not involved in any way. If we're headed there, I'd like to stop at the store first and pick him up a few things."

"Like what?"

"Canned goods for one. I noticed his cupboard was on the bare side."

On the drive through the countryside, Gemma hoped Flanner wasn't hiding anything. Her intuition said it wasn't a factor. But there was always a chance she could be wrong.

When Lando pulled up to the cabin, Flanner was out chopping wood. She raised her hand in greeting, and at that same instant, a feeling washed over her. She knew then she had nothing to worry about from Flanner. On the other side of the car, however, Lando would need convincing.

Flanner put his ax down and walked over to the police cruiser. "What are you guys doing back here?"

"Just follow up," Lando began. "During the dust-up, after you discovered the body and crime techs were all over that creek bed, I forgot to ask you some routine questions."

"Like what?"

"We found out the guy's name was Daniel Albrecht. Does that name ring a bell?"

"Nope."

"The medical examiner said he'd been dead about a week. The thing is, the man was seen in town on Thursday, two or three days before he died. We don't know where he was during those few days. Did you ever hear any gunshots during that time? Did you ever see a stranger walking around out here, say Thursday afternoon or Friday, maybe Saturday night, where he shouldn't have been walking?"

"I hear gunshots out here sometimes. Hunters come and go. Local guys mostly. I know a lot of 'em. Sometimes they nose around on Trask land, sometimes even mine. Not much to hunt though on my land except a few raccoons and squirrels. I only go after them when I'm desperate. If you want anything bigger, then you gotta hunt on Trask property. I got permission. Rabbits tend to hang around the creek bed, maybe half a mile from here. That's what I was doin' there the other day, huntin' for rabbits."

"So you never saw a stranger lurking around the Trask land last week?"

Flanner paused and scratched his chin. "Nope. Not that I remember. If that guy had been out there that long, Bruce might've seen something. You should ask him."

"Yep. That's where we're headed next."

Flanner looked at Gemma. "Are you still interested in me building you a shed?"

"Absolutely. Once you get mine finished, there's a list of others who need one."

"Hard to imagine. You want shelves in yours, right?"

"I think I'd need shelves. Yeah. And I want windows similar to what yours look like. Not the same, just whatever you can find and recycle."

"Really? Okay. When do you want me to start?"

"As soon as you want to. There's no rush. But I do have a couple of questions. Do you want me to buy the lumber, or do you have enough on hand? If we're still trading, then you need to come in and pick what vegetables you want out of my garden."

"I have a stack of construction-grade wood left at Duff's. But depending on the size you want, there might not be enough."

"I'd say seven by seven would work for me. Anything larger, I might have trouble fitting it next to the greenhouse. I want it to be a focal point of the garden. So maybe we could sit down and come up with a few ideas. I really would like you to work on it at my house. There's no one home during the day. I'm sure my neighbors wouldn't bother you." When she saw how his face fell, she quickly added, "Just think about it. Okay?"

"We'll see. I'll need to figure out the logistics anyway. I could carry the cut lumber from Duff's to your place and put it together there."

"That would be great. Let's get together tomorrow afternoon and hash out exactly what I want. I also brought you a box of canned goods. Don't look at me like that. I need to unload them on someone. I'm trying to tidy up my pantry, and they're just taking up space."

Flanner grudgingly took the box of groceries. "I'm no charity case."

"I didn't think you were."

"I do appreciate it, though. Hunting these days has been spotty at best."

Pleased that he at least accepted the canned goods, Gemma pointed to the box. "As you can see, I had an assortment of beans on hand."

"I'll put them to good use. Nothing goes to waste here."

"That's what I like about the cabin. You've used every scrap of material to its best potential."

After leaving Flanner's place, Gemma shook her head. "Why is he so stubborn?"

Lando spared his wife a glance. "Stubborn? You have him accepting food from you and agreeing to build you a shed. I'd say you have him eating out of the palm of your hand. Do you know how many trips I made out here, wondering if he had enough to eat? Never once did he ever let me leave a bag of groceries. Not one single time. He took to you like you were his long lost friend."

Gemma lifted a shoulder. "What can I say? People like me."

"What do you intend to do with this shed?"

"Put it right next to the greenhouse so I can use it for my seedlings. That greenhouse will always belong to my grandmother. But the shed, I picture it as all mine."

Lando left it at that because he had to track down Bruce Barnhart via cell phone and send a string of text messages to get Bruce's attention. The caretaker didn't make it easy. The man kept dodging him up until Lando threatened to pull him in for an official interview down at the station. That pressure worked.

After wasting an hour with the back and forth, Bruce finally agreed to meet Lando just over the property line at the same gate entrance where Flanner had stood two days before.

But this summit was very different.

Lando found an annoyed Bruce Barnhart sitting in a brand-new, shiny, silver metallic pickup. The caretaker had cleaned himself up. Clean-shaven, he now looked like a boyish fifty-two-year-old with brown hair and blue eyes. After he got out of the truck, Bruce leaned against the side of his new ride. He stood about six-feet tall with a slim build.

Still sitting in the passenger seat of the cruiser, Gemma realized this wasn't the man who had worn the San Francisco State sweatshirt the night of the murders. Disappointed, she listened to the man's voice when he spoke to Lando.

"I told you a couple of times over the phone that I don't know anything about a body," Bruce insisted. "You know as much as I do. I have no idea how the man ended up dead near the creek. None."

"So you haven't seen a stranger nosing around since last Thursday or Friday where he shouldn't be?"

"No. We get hunters out here sometimes. Maybe he was hunting illegally and encountered someone else who didn't like him on his turf. It happens. But it wasn't me."

"Where were you last Sunday night when Ben Zurcher was murdered?"

"During the storm? Like any sane man, I was at home, in bed, asleep. The power went out at my place. I went to bed around midnight and didn't wake up until morning."

"Can anyone back you up on that?"

"No. I got divorced several years back. I've lived alone ever since."

"But you're very loyal to Jocelyn Williams, right?"

"She's my employer. I was nineteen in 1987 when I went to work for her parents. The Trasks were good people. And when they were killed in that car accident, I stayed on because Sandra asked me to. And yeah, I'm a loyal kind of guy. But I draw the line at killing anybody for my employer. Oh, yeah. I know what you're getting at. It was a horrible thing what happened to Sandra and her family. It 'bout killed me when I found out how they'd been murdered. But it wasn't me that did it. I'd like to find the guy who did, though."

"Okay, if that's true, why were you so reluctant to talk to me?"

"Because I don't like thinking about or talking about those little girls beaten to death in their beds. I knew those little angels. They were sweet girls, you know?"

"Did Ben Zurcher ever want to talk to you about the murders?"

Bruce shifted his feet. "That guy must've left me a dozen messages in the past six months. I brushed him off until one day he cornered me in the parking lot at Two Sisters. I told him the same thing I'm telling you. I didn't kill Sandra and Todd and those kids. I adored Sandra. She was a good mother and a good daughter. I would never have hurt any of them. Can I go now?"

"Yeah. You can go. But next time I want to talk to you, don't give me the runaround. Got it?"

Bruce nodded and got back into his truck.

"What did you think?" Lando asked Gemma after the caretaker had taken off.

"It's not him. Bruce wasn't the guy in the Copeland house that night. I don't know about Ben, though. Bruce could've killed Ben. Bruce certainly had access to where Daniel Albrecht was found."

"It makes me wonder why Albrecht's SUV was found so far from this spot. Any ideas on that?"

"I think Daniel was meeting someone out here. I think he got lured out to Trask land, which might go a long way to explaining his connection to someone in town, likely to Jocelyn. If the link is that he knew her in college, then how significant is that link. It has to be the key to him getting murdered at this location."

"Well, it's for sure Daniel Albrecht isn't likely to tell us what he knew about Jocelyn at this point."

"Not unless his corpse decides to talk to Tuttle."

"Very funny." Lando's cell phone pinged with a text message.

"Who's that?" Gemma asked.

"It's my mom. She wants us to drop by the restaurant to talk. Says she has an announcement to make."

"Sounds mysterious. What time?"

"Suppertime."

"We'll eat there, right? Because I'm starving. And I'm not really in the mood to cook."

"Sunday special is pot roast."

"Since when?"

"Since Leia got a burr up her butt and decided it was the easiest thing to cook and serve on Sundays."

16

The month of March along the northern coast of California could be a dreary, rainy place to call home. As night approached, heavy gray clouds rolled in accompanied by a cold drizzle.

By the time Lando parked his cruiser in the side lot next to The Crazy Daisy, the sprinkles had turned to heavier rainfall.

They got out of the cruiser and darted for the side door, huddling in the entryway until they spotted Lydia.

Still trim and fit into her late fifties, Lydia Bonner flitted around the dining room bussing tables with the energy of two younger waitresses. With a trendy, choppy new bob hairdo, Lando's mom didn't look a day over fifty, let alone looking down the barrel of retirement. The only clue the woman had aged at all was a few wrinkles around her warm brown eyes and a few streaks of gray in her coal-black hair.

Gemma's eyes shot around the room, searching for Lydia's main squeeze, Paul Eddington. But she didn't see Paul anywhere.

Despite Lydia and Paul's affection for each other, Gemma knew the couple still hadn't tied the knot. A bit odd since they'd known each other for several years. But that was their business, Gemma decided. No reason to get nosy and butt in with stupid questions, especially when Lydia had been sweet enough to invite them to dinner. Gemma intended to keep her mouth shut even if she did think that one part of the equation might be dragging their feet.

Watching Lydia buzz around the dining room, Gemma began to pick up on a vibe that refused to leave, one that churned in her belly and took away her appetite.

Shaking off the "bad news" vibe, she opted to focus on the positive. It brought her full circle as her eyes landed on Luke and Lianne. That couple had already tucked themselves into a cozy corner booth, immersed in each other. They were nursing their drinks with their heads together, nuzzling each other's neck, oblivious to anything or anyone else.

Good for them, thought Gemma.

Breaking into that sentimental moment, Zeb lumbered in behind them. He took the time to wipe his feet on the mud mat for that purpose before slapping Lando on the back. "Looks like the gang is all here. How about a beer?"

Lando nodded and followed Zeb straight to the bar area. Since Zeb had chosen to play bartender, Lando slid onto one of the stools.

Zeb opened the cooler and reached in, held up three bottles of Pacifica. "Gemma?"

"None for me. Thanks. I think I'll have a glass of the Gnarly Head red instead."

"You got it."

Lydia circled back to Gemma. "What's wrong? You look like you've eaten prunes on your toast this morning. If pot roast doesn't do it for you, we still have halibut I can grill."

"What? Oh, no. Pot roast is fine. What's up with you? Why are we here?"

Lydia dodged the question to some degree and replied, "Family meeting. Getting you all together in the same room, I only have to make one announcement and get the backlash out of the way in one fell swoop. Go on, get yourself a table. Leia and I will be around to take orders in a minute."

Gemma took her wine and found a seat. But something felt off. She decided to make herself useful and dragged over another table, putting two together to make room for everyone, then pulling over eight chairs. Four couples. Eight chairs. But she still hadn't set eyes on Paul.

Leia came out from behind the grill. After giving Zeb a peck on the cheek, she headed straight for Gemma. "Do you know what this is all about?"

"I thought you did."

"Me? No. I was about to head home when Mom dropped the news that she wanted us all in here for dinner, had to be tonight, or so she said. It couldn't be any other time. She even turned away customers for this event."

"You're kidding? I've never known her to do that before for a family meeting. Funny, I don't see Paul."

"Yeah. Now that you mention it, I haven't seen him around for a couple of days. But that's not unusual. As a supplier, he does have a route to work, and sometimes that cuts into his weekends with Mom."

"Really?"

"Well, yeah. Most restaurants are a seven-day effort. I'm sure some make enough during the week that they get to close over the weekend. But you know Captain Jack's, we always stay open seven days a week."

"Grilled halibut or pot roast?" Lydia shouted from across the room.

"We need to get rid of that halibut," Leia announced. "I'll grill it up. Gemma?"

"Oh, it doesn't matter to me. Whatever you have on hand. I can eat fish as long as it hasn't gone bad."

"I better double-check to make sure," Leia said as she rounded the corner back into the kitchen. After a few minutes, she called out, "Forget the fish. I think it might be iffy at best. Monday's delivery will be fresh fish. Tonight, it's pot roast for everyone or chicken sandwiches."

"Pot roast," Zeb muttered. "Something warm on a chilly night sounds good."

"I think that's a consensus," Luke added as he tugged Lianne over to the main table. "We're fine with whatever you have, though. We're mot picky."

"Anyone know why we're here?" Lianne whispered.

Lando took a pull on his beer. "Nope. But we're about to find out."

After everyone had been served the pot roast with potatoes and baby carrots, Lydia took a seat at the head of the table. She cleared her throat. "Thanks for coming. I know it was last minute. I thought making the announcement here at the restaurant, I'd avoid any awkward questions moving forward."

Luke picked up his beer and raised the bottle, prepared for a celebratory toast. "Is this about you and Paul? Have you picked a date yet? For the wedding?"

"That's just it. Paul and I have decided to call it quits. He moved out a week ago and moved back to his farm."

"What happened?" Lando asked.

Lydia eyed her oldest triplet. "It seems Paul found someone else. It seems it had been going on for about three months or so. He found someone younger and someone who didn't have a restaurant to run, someone who could spend more time with him. At least that's what he said. It's over between us. No need to make a big deal out of it."

Gemma laid a hand over Lydia's. "Any chance of working out the problem?"

Lydia's eyes narrowed. "I'm not a big believer in forgive and forget when it comes to cheating. Paul is history. The truth is, I've asked for a new supplier."

"I'm sorry," Gemma stated, entwining her fingers with Lydia's.

Leia got up to wrap her mom in a hug. "I'm glad you aren't tiptoeing around the fact that Paul cheated on you."

"I'm not trying to tiptoe around anything—no need for that. I'm a straightforward-type person. Personally, I'm glad he's gone. It just wasn't meant to be."

"Do I need to hunt him down and…"

Lydia smiled over at Lando. "No. When I found out, we tried to work it out, and we simply could not. After three months, we gave up. Now please, no more talk about it. Let's dig in and eat this food before it gets stone-cold."

"You're taking it well," Leia said. "I've worked beside you for the past three months and didn't know you were having issues."

"That's because I dealt with it when it happened back in December. After coming to a reckoning, there's not much reason to throw dishes and have a hissy fit. I accepted the fact that Paul and I were over, and that was it."

Luke frowned. "You knew back in December you guys were done?"

"New Year's Eve, to be exact. That's when I discovered all these texts and calls on his phone. They were from a woman named Jill, who lived right across from his place in Yontocket. Jill is a young widow in her forties who moved there last summer. He admitted he was smitten with her. I told him if that's what he wanted, he should leave. And he did."

"So all the while Lianne and I were having problems, you'd already decided to end things with Paul?"

Lydia picked up the wine and poured herself a full glass. "Look, I'm a lot older and a lot less likely to put up with BS, especially from a man. And especially one who has lost interest in me. It turns out, Paul and this Jill met way before Christmas, and they were immediately taken with one another. I could tell Paul just wanted a clean break. That's what he got."

"And yet Paul just moved out a week ago?" Lando pointed out.

Sipping the red wine, Lydia smiled and nodded. "Observant like a cop. Yes, Paul packed a bag the first week of January and moved out. And yes, he came back for the rest of his belongings last week. There were little things like shirts and shoes. He never fully moved in with me. Happy now, knowing all the juicy details?"

"We just want to know you're okay," Lianne opined. "We know you're strong. There's no doubt you'll be fine. But a breakup can hurt. I know." She turned to lock hands with Luke. "I realized the hard way what was important."

"I am strong. And I am fine," Lydia assured them. "When you realize it's over, there's an adjustment, sure. But I knew something wasn't right around Thanksgiving. With our relationship. Paul and I just stopped working. We weren't getting along. It happens. And by then, he'd dropped the topic of marriage. That was the first tell."

"Well, he's an idiot," Gemma acknowledged. "The man doesn't know how lucky he was to have you."

"You're right about that," Lydia said with a laugh. "I'm better off without him."

Zeb raised his beer in the air. "To Lydia. She's stronger than ever. To hell with Paul Eddington."

"To Lydia," the group chorused with drinks raised in a toast.

Amused, Lydia picked up her fork and looked around the table. "Now this is what I needed right now. Just know that after this discussion, after this meal, I don't want anyone bringing up his name. This conversation is the end of Paul Eddington as far as I'm concerned."

"No problem," Lando muttered. "We're glad you finally told us. To be honest, I had serious concerns about Paul."

Intrigued, Lydia put her fork down. "How so?"

A sheepish look crossed Lando's face. He wasn't sure he should admit to what he'd seen. But since he'd opened his big mouth, he had no choice. "About four months ago, I took a call south of town. When I finished up, I spotted Paul's vehicle parked at the drive-in next to another sedan. He was sitting in a white Toyota with a woman."

Lydia's face fell. "And you never said a word?"

"What could I have said? That I saw Paul sitting in a white car at the old Cactus Flower Drive-in?"

Lydia sipped her wine, then let out a soulful sigh. "I take it this incident happened before Christmas?"

"It did. It was closer to Thanksgiving."

She set her jaw. "So Paul lied to me about when it started up with Jill."

"It could've been someone else other than Jill."

"No, I happen to know for certain that Jill drives a white Toyota Avalon. I saw it when she helped him pack up his stuff."

"I'm sorry. Maybe I should've said something."

"You should have. But you know what? I had to see him for what he really was for myself. It's true, I did. No one else could've convinced me otherwise, especially around Thanksgiving. You see, I hadn't accepted that Paul and I were walking on eggshells back then. Even though I'm sure we were. I hadn't accepted that he seemed more distant, more distracted whenever I tried to talk to him. In other words, I hadn't come to terms that he was such a lowlife. Tough matters like cheating need to be seen up close and personal. Am I right?"

Gemma nodded. "I suppose."

"Good," Lydia began, taking a deep breath. "I say we move on. Seriously. From this point on, we never have to speak about that man ever again. Now that it's behind us, what are you doing to catch Ben Zurcher's killer?"

Zeb grinned. "I'd like to know that myself."

Lando shifted in his chair. "As long as it doesn't leave this room, I'm willing to tell you everything I know about this case."

"Which isn't much," Gemma chimed in. "But the list of dead people keeps getting longer."

"As it stands now, Jocelyn Williams is the prime suspect for all of them," Lando revealed. "Except for the night the Copelands were murdered. Jocelyn has an airtight alibi confirmed by her roommates."

"But it doesn't mean Jocelyn didn't coax someone into killing for her," Gemma explained. "Which is our best theory yet of what happened. There was a fortune to gain. So no better motive than that."

"I remember when Marissa had a major disagreement with Jocelyn," Lydia put in. "Jocelyn has a nasty temper when she doesn't get her way."

Gemma's's eyes narrowed to slits. "What did they argue about?"

"Oyster Landing. That subdivision out by Moonlight Ridge. Jocelyn already owned the forty acres that her sister's farmhouse sat on. But Jocelyn wanted more. She got it in her head that she wanted to buy out every homeowner who lived in Oyster Landing. Marissa knew most of those people who lived there had nowhere else to go. Your grandmother fought her tooth and nail over that. She challenged Jocelyn and took it all the way to the town council. And you know what? The council turned Jocelyn down. Marissa won. I don't think the woman ever forgave Marissa for it."

Gemma traded looks with Lando. "Jocelyn's mean streak just keeps popping up, doesn't it?"

Leia pushed her plate away. "Now, wait just a minute, isn't that about the same time Jocelyn made an offer on the town newspaper?"

"I forgot about that. I think you're right. She wanted to buy the newspaper."

"What year was this?" Lando asked.

Leia looked at her mother for confirmation. "About five years back. The same timeframe where she fought with Ben over a claim she'd made. She lost that round, too. That was before Ben retired as postmaster."

Lando shifted in his chair. "I wonder if Jocelyn's interest in Oyster Landing and buying the newspaper could've been what triggered Ben's interest in who killed the Copelands?"

Gemma's eyes widened. "I bet it did. Jocelyn has this irritating habit of rubbing people the wrong way. Jocelyn's snotty attitude must've pulled Ben into the mystery."

Lando scrubbed a hand over his jaw. "Yeah, and he started looking into the Copeland murders around that same time."

"But all you have is speculation," Zeb countered. "I've already said my piece about how tough it is to prove solicitation of murder without getting a confession."

Gemma sputtered out a laugh. "Not this woman. My guess is that no one could trick her into ever confessing to anything."

"Hard as nails, is she?" Zeb remarked. "And with her hefty bank account, she can afford the best lawyers in the state. Don't forget that. Sounds like what you need is irrefutable proof. DNA or a very credible witness."

"I don't have either of those things," Lando admitted. "And I'm not likely to get those unless the lab comes up with something new from one of the girls' clothing or from any one of the newer cases, like Ben's or Daniel Albrecht's. Gemma's right, though. Jocelyn has a lot of bodies stacking up around her." He ticked off the names. "It all starts with her parents, Mr. and Mrs. Trask. Then it's Sandra's entire family. Her husband, the late Eric Williams."

"Wait," Zeb noted. "Eric Williams? That wouldn't by any chance be the hunter found in the national forest, would it? That guy was married to Jocelyn?"

"Yeah. Why?"

"Because I remember that case. I have a file on it. Well, sort of. The man was found a few feet outside tribal jurisdiction at the northeast corner of the Reservation. Keep in mind the national forest is still Federal land. It's like the person, this hunter, knew he wasn't supposed to be hunting on tribal land and crawled a few feet over the boundary to the national forest to bleed to death. Gunshot wound to the abdomen, right? I mean, let's face it, his death still occurred on Federal land."

Gemma laced her fingers together, propped her chin on top. "Would Jocelyn know the boundaries that well?"

"The girl was born and raised here, grew up here," Lydia pointed out. "The only time she went away was to college in San Francisco. She knows this entire area like the back of her hand. She's most certainly been to Six Rivers before her husband died there. Her parents used to take the girls out there to camp."

Lando cocked a brow. "You're sure of that?"

"Positive."

Gemma toyed with her napkin. "Well, if you add Ben Zurcher to that list and now this Albrecht guy, technically, you shouldn't leave out poor Laura Leigh Baccarat."

Lando frowned at her. "Anna Kate's sister? Why?"

"Well, to hear Anna Kate tell it, Laura Leigh used to babysit for Sandra and Todd. The girl was like their nanny. And Laura Leigh thought Jocelyn was part of what happened."

Lydia stood up to clear the table. "Oh, I remember Laura Leigh. Sweet girl. You know, she died in a one-car accident."

Gemma's hands flew to her necklace. Clutching the stones that hung from her amulet, she shifted in her seat to stare at Lando. "Laura Leigh's car careened out of control on that roadway leading up to Moonlight Ridge. She was driving a little gray Prius. You should look into Laura Leigh's death. I don't think it was an accident."

Lando traded skeptic looks with Zeb. "Is that based on something you just saw?"

"Oh, yeah. Because Laura Leigh's mouth was getting under Jocelyn's skin. Or more like, the rumors were starting to get back to Jocelyn and not in a good way."

"This is like telling ghost stories on a rainy night," Luke ventured, getting up to retrieve another beer. "You weren't kidding when you said there were a lot of people dying around this woman. I can't say that I've seen much of her around town. Kind of glad about it now."

"That's because she usually has a staff of underlings who do everything for her," Gemma explained. "Jocelyn wouldn't dare get her own hands dirty."

Lando leaned toward Lianne. "Speaking of dirty hands, before I forget to mention it, someone from Portland PD is picking up Kirk Ritter in the morning. Nine a.m. sharp."

Lianne sat up straighter in her chair. "Really? You should've led off with that when we got here."

Lando chuckled. "I guess I should have. But you two were too busy making out in the back booth to notice much else going on."

Luke linked his fingers with Lianne's. "Guilty. Now, what else should we expect after this guy gets back to Portland? Will Lianne have to testify in court against him?"

"I doubt it. Ritter violated parole. Period. He fled the state in possession of a firearm. That probably counts more than stalking an ex."

"Sad, but true," Gemma spat out. "Violence against women doesn't seem to be a big deal for anyone these days, which brings me back to Laura Leigh. Someone wanted her to stop the wild speculation. Listen to me when I tell you that it wasn't an accident."

Lando squeezed her fingers. "I trust your instincts. Where should we start?"

"We need to ask Anna Kate what happened to Laura Leigh's Prius."

17

When Anna Kate Baccarat opened her door to find Gemma and Lando standing there, she seemed surprised to see them, even though they had called ahead of time.

As Gemma stood in the entryway, she could hear soft music playing on the stereo somewhere else in the house. Chopin's nocturnes seemed fitting for a rainy Sunday night. Although she wouldn't in a million years have pegged her old high school alum as a classical music buff. This was the same woman who'd stood in line to get tickets to see Guns N' Roses in concert. But the sound of a piano concerto in the background went a long way to show people could change given enough time.

Anna Kate ushered them into her living room. Her kids were huddled across from each other at the dining room table, heads down, noses in their textbooks, doing last-minute homework.

Gemma dropped into one of the comfy-looking chairs. "I hope we're not interrupting anything. I know this is last-minute."

"Just me yelling at my kids. They should've finished their English essays two days ago," Anna Kate bellowed, loud enough for the kids to get the message. But in a much lower voice, she went on to add, "They promised me they finished on Friday. But you know kids. Procrastinators. They put work off till the last second if you let them. It always takes that third time you ask in a certain cranky voice if they have any assignments due Monday morning that does the trick. Why they can't just do their homework without making a scene is beyond me. Then you watch them drag out a workbook at the eleventh hour. I swear if you don't stay on top of them every second, they just won't do the work."

"We are interrupting your Sunday," Gemma offered. "I'm sorry."

"No, you're not. It's always like this around here. This is what it's like when you have teenagers who spend the weekend with their father, and he doesn't once ask them if they have homework. This is what it's like divorced with kids and you're the responsible parent."

"Did Laura Leigh have kids?"

The redheaded Anna Kate looked puzzled as she took a seat on the sofa. "Well, yes. I thought you knew she did. Sienna is eighteen now. Wow. The years just rushed past me. I remember when she came to live with me. Afterward. Her father was more interested in grabbing a construction job in Denver than staying put here and taking care of an eight-year-old. I didn't mind, though. Sienna was always a little sweetheart. But it was right about that awful time when I lost my sister that Derrick and I started having serious problems."

"So it was bringing in another child that caused the divorce?"

"Oh, not really. It wasn't Sienna's fault. I'm sure Derrick was looking to bail even way back then. He was never faithful. Never. Cheated three weeks after our honeymoon." She waved off the hurt in the same way she had in Gemma's office.

"I don't like talking about it. Besides, I know you two didn't come here to listen to me bitch about Derrick. But should I prepare Sienna for an interview in advance? Do you really need to talk to her? Because I don't think she'd be much help with anything. You see, she wasn't even in the car with her mother that night. Thank God for that. I had taken her and my kids to catch a movie at the cinema. Mine was a little on the young side to sit through the entire movie without getting antsy. But I remember the movie we saw that night. *Cloudy with a Chance of Meatballs*. Not the year's best, but the kids seemed to enjoy it."

With a polite nod of the head, Lando took a seat across from Gemma. It was nice to catch up with chitchat, but he needed to turn the conversation back to why they were here. "And how long was it after you got back from the movie that you found out about Laura Leigh?"

Anna Kate chewed the inside of her jaw, trying to remember. "We got back around nine-thirty. I'd say it was close to midnight when two sheriff's deputies showed up at the door and woke us up. They're the ones who broke the news."

"So, Sienna was already spending the night with you anyway the night of the accident, the night her mother died?"

"No, not really. But the later it got, and Laura Leigh didn't show up, I just made Sienna go to bed with my two. Even though it was summer break and there was no school the next day. I try to keep my kids on a regular schedule. That way, come fall, it isn't so hard to roust them out of bed. The thing is, I never understood what Laura Leigh was doing up near Oyster Landing. It didn't make sense because I didn't know anyone who lived up there. But I guess she must have."

"Maybe your sister was on her way to meet someone," Lando prompted.

"I suppose. But at that time of night, who? I'm not even sure where Derrick was that night."

Lando's ears perked up. "Really? Derrick wasn't at home with you and the kids?"

"No. I suspected he was seeing someone on the side even then. But I could never prove it. I'd ask, but I'd get the denials right and left. Or he wouldn't look at me, or he'd just ignore the question entirely."

"Where is Sienna now?" Gemma wanted to know.

Anna Kate flashed a proud grin. "She's a freshman at Chico State. Smart as a whip that girl, wants to be a nurse. Sienna lives there now, in Chico, off-campus, in an apartment she shares with a roommate. But she's coming home for spring break in two weeks."

"Sounds like you did a wonderful job raising her. Laura Leigh would be proud of her little sister."

"I like to think so." Anna Kate lowered her voice so the kids wouldn't hear. "I'm a little confused right now. Why are you here asking questions after all this time? I mean, it's been ten years in June. Why would you be asking about Laura Leigh's accident now?"

Lando leaned closer. In a whispered voice he explained, "I'm digging through old files. Just covering all the bases. I want you to take us back to when Laura Leigh babysat for Sandra Copeland."

"Ah. I see." The realization hit Anna Kate then. "So that's what this is all about? You're finally after the truth, ready to listen to Laura Leigh's suspicions and take it seriously."

"It's complicated," Gemma tossed out.

"That it is. I bet Ben's death prompted this, am I right?" Without waiting for a reply, Anna Kate bowled on, more than a little intrigued about the interest in her sister. "So this is on the level? Official-like?"

"Yeah. It's as official as it gets during a murder investigation," Lando proclaimed. "We want to know what Laura Leigh told you about who killed the family. In detail."

Anna Kate took a deep breath. Still keeping her voice low, she began to recall what she knew. "Even as a teenage babysitter, Laura Leigh was good with kids. I mean wonderful. She had planned to become a teacher. Instead, she went off to College of the Redwoods to become a speech therapist. Several years later, she comes back home with Sienna. Sidetracked with a toddler, yes. But she managed to get her degree and started working at a clinic off the 101. So you see, she ended up working with children anyway. Laura Leigh adored Hallie and Julie Copeland. And the girls adored her right back. For years, she spent her summers in that farmhouse acting as a nanny. Wait. There's another name for it now. What do they call those young girls who stay with the kids these days?"

"You mean an au pair?" Gemma offered.

"That's it. Laura Leigh was like their au pair. She made good money, enough to pay for college down the road. But if I'm completely honest here, I think, later on, say around sixteen, Laura Leigh had a little crush on Todd, which explained why she didn't complain about working there so much. Most teenagers would, you know. But not Laura Leigh."

Gemma lifted a brow. "How much later on? And how did that go over with Sandra?"

"I don't think Sandra knew. Look, before you go making a big deal out of a teenage crush, it wasn't like that. It didn't factor into the murders. Laura Leigh never acted on her feelings. And neither did Todd."

"As far as you know, they didn't act on it," Gemma pointed out. "Maybe they did, but Laura Leigh didn't share what happened between them with you, the little sister."

Anna Kate shook her head. "No. She was too young for that. She was barely fourteen when Sandra approached her to babysit. Besides, it was just a harmless teen crush."

"So you keep saying. Are you sure Todd didn't have a thing for Laura Leigh? Maybe he picked up on her interest and allowed something happen?"

"I'm telling you, no," Anna Kate insisted. "Laura Leigh would've said something. I wish I'd never brought it up now. It was just silly girl talk between sisters."

"Did your dad ever find out that his daughter had a thing for a grown man?" Gemma asked. "Because if he did, he might've overreacted and—"

"Committed murder by killing the man and then his wife, along with their two little kids? Don't be ridiculous. No way. It never happened."

Beginning to lose her temper at the implication, Anna Kate huffed out a breath. "You knew my dad. James Baccarat was a decent guy. You're just taking my words and twisting them to make it look like Laura Leigh, or my dad was somehow involved. She wasn't. My dad wasn't, either. You're wasting your time."

Gemma held up a hand. "Okay. We're sorry. We never meant to accuse anyone in your family. We're just thinking outside the box here, trying to get a clear picture of the situation back in October 2000. That's all. We understand that Laura Leigh loved babysitting for the Copelands. Was that always the way she felt even in the beginning?"

"It was. She had that job for four years. In all that time Laura Leigh never had a problem with either Todd or Sandra. In fact, she looked up to Sandra, wanted to be like her one day. You would have to know Laura Leigh to understand that she sort of worshipped Sandra. Laura Leigh would never have hurt her in any way. She couldn't. She got along well with everyone. Why would she do anything to jeopardize the cushy job she had with the family? Like I said that day in your office, the person Sandra had a problem with was her own sister. Sandra had arguments with Jocelyn. Screaming matches. At least one a week. It was Jocelyn who gave Sandra a hard time the most."

"And what did they argue about?" Lando asked.

"I only know what Laura Leigh told me. Jocelyn wanted access to her trust fund, kept pestering Sandra about it, but Sandra wasn't having it. There were several heated arguments about the money."

"Now we're getting somewhere," Lando muttered. "Because Sandra controlled the trust?"

"She did. And she had very specific ideas about what she wanted Jocelyn to do before giving her access even after Jocelyn turned twenty-one."

Lando scrubbed a hand over his chin. "Like what? What were Sandra's requirements?"

"Like graduate from college and then get a job," Anna Kate laid out. "Sandra wanted to see her sister show some responsibility."

"So you might say that Sandra put several obstacles in Jocelyn's way?" Lando prodded.

"Yeah. That seemed to be at the heart of those two not getting along. According to Laura Leigh, the trust was huge. Millions were at stake. You see why Laura Leigh thought Jocelyn was behind the murders, right?"

"I do now. Tell me something. Do you have any idea what happened to the car Laura Leigh was driving that night? The little Prius?"

Anna Kate's forehead tightened in thought. "Wow. Good question. It probably ended up towed to the junkyard out on the highway. You realize the Prius was totaled?"

Lando traded looks with Gemma. "It's a longshot, but it might still be there in some form for a forensic team to examine."

"I'm getting a sneaky suspicion you think someone ran Laura Leigh off the road on purpose?"

"It's just a theory," Lando said as he got to his feet. "I won't know unless I dig a little deeper."

"Will you tell me what you find?"

"If…I find anything, I'll definitely let you know."

After a long day, Lando and Gemma finally made it home. Pulling the cruiser into the garage next to the Volvo, Lando shut off the engine. "It's nice to be able to park in here. Thanks for clearing everything out."

"Clearing everything out" meant finally moving Marissa's cherished Buick out of the covered parking and into a storage unit for safekeeping. Over the winter, Gemma had made the decision. But she couldn't bear to sell her Gram's car or to see it carted off by strangers. Not yet, anyway.

"No problem. It was past time we made room in here for both our vehicles."

"I know it was a big step," Lando said, picking up her hand and squeezing her fingers. "I'm grateful you took it."

"As long as you appreciate my sacrifice," Gemma cracked, trying not to overthink her decision. After gathering up her belongings, she headed for the door that led to the mudroom.

Entering the house through the side door, she walked in first and got almost knocked down by two anxious dogs.

Worked up, Rufus and Rolo met her with more than enthusiasm. Their behavior bordered on fear. Sensing that something had spooked them, Gemma dropped her bag on the bench and turned to Lando. She put her fingers up to her lips for quiet. "I think someone might be in the house."

That one caution put Lando on full alert. He reached for his service revolver and rushed past Gemma into the kitchen. The first thing he noticed was that the backdoor had been left open. The rain had splattered the kitchen floor with droplets but not enough to indicate the door had been left ajar for very long.

He darted out into the backyard to look around but was met with darkness. Left behind, Gemma grabbed flashlights out of the laundry room and slipped out into the misty rain after him. She caught up with him in the garden.

"Footprints left in the mud," Lando grunted. "See? There? I'd say size nines."

Gemma squatted down to study the boot print. "That could belong to a woman. What I want to know is what was our intruder doing in our house?"

"Good question. I'm almost too tired to think of the possibilities. But I need to take an impression of this and write up a report."

"Now? Right this minute?" But looking at the stubborn clench of his jaw, she realized he had a job to do. "Should I put on coffee? Who's on duty to take the impression?"

"I don't need anyone to take the cast but me. I'm just not sure I have plaster on hand to get it done." He took out his phone and punched a button. The call went directly to Dale.

"What's up?" Dale asked, not waiting for the usual small talk.

"Bring plaster casting to my house. There's plenty in the storeroom. I need enough for at least four impressions."

"I'm on it. See you in twenty."

"I'll put on coffee," Gemma repeated, watching where she stepped to retreat out of the garden so she wouldn't mess up the tracks.

"Might as well put out cookies, too," she said as she passed the rose bushes. But the beam of her flashlight caught a glimpse of something gold lying on the ground. She bent down to get a better look. "Lando, you'd better take a look at this."

"What?" He followed the narrow stream of light to a bulky but shiny gold chain woven in double knots lying in the damp dirt. He dug out a ballpoint pen from his shirt pocket and used it to pick up a length of the metal rope. "The clasp broke. See?"

"Yeah. That's not mine, too bulky, too heavy, too gaudy. Plus, it looks like twenty-karat gold to me. That was not here the other day. I know that for a fact. And it's right here lying two feet from those footprints like it snapped off or something while they were running out of the house."

"I'll need to bag it. Might be able to get DNA off it."

"No problem. I'll run in the house and get a baggie. It occurs to me that we must've interrupted the person when we pulled into the garage."

"That rope chain doesn't belong to a guy," Lando pointed out. "What woman do you know in town who might be able to afford an eighteen-inch, twenty-karat, gold chain like that?"

"You already know the answer. But why would Jocelyn risk coming here? What did she hope to gain?"

"Better still, what was she searching for?"

"Information about the case, maybe? I need to check the house to see if anything is missing."

Later, after getting the dogs calmed down for the night, Gemma poured coffee and put out snickerdoodles to munch on while Dale finished waiting on the plaster casts to set.

As they all three sat around the kitchen table, they tried to make sense of the scene in the garden.

"Well, I've gone through the downstairs. As far as I can tell, there doesn't seem to be anything missing. Although whoever broke in, made a mess of things in the study and the solarium."

"They went through every drawer in the desk," Lando pointed out to Dale. "And knocked things off shelves in the sunroom. Beats the heck out of me what they were looking for."

"Are you sure they didn't find what they were looking for?" Dale asked, dunking his snickerdoodle into his coffee.

Gemma wrinkled her nose at the sight. "How can you eat cookies like that? We have milk. Snickerdoodles are meant to be dunked down in milk, not coffee.'

"Says who? I like mine with coffee. Sue me."

Lando was too tired to be amused by the banter. "The way they ran out of here when they heard us pull in, I don't think they found anything."

"Which could mean they'll come back," Dale prompted.

Gemma narrowed her eyes. "First thing tomorrow, I'm getting new locks. And maybe we should think about installing one of those security cameras on the front and back doors."

"Yeah. I'll take care of that. I'm still upset that someone came into this house. My house. Our house. I'm the chief of police, for God's sake. Someone decided to waltz in here while we were gone. If they think they can do that without repercussions, I'm here to tell them otherwise."

Gemma drummed her fingers on the table while staring down at the baggie containing the rope chain. "That necklace is probably worth fifteen grand at a minimum. Why would you wear such an expensive piece of jewelry to a burglary?"

"Arrogance?" Dale suggested. "Is that gold chain really worth that much? If so, someone will definitely be missing their expensive bauble sooner rather than later. In fact, what do you wanna bet me that we get a call first thing tomorrow morning reporting that it was stolen?"

"Wouldn't surprise me one bit," Lando stated. "This could be the break we've been looking for. Even if Jocelyn makes the claim for insurance purposes, we should be able to poke a hole in the lie."

"What did you think about Laura Leigh's theory on who committed the murders?" Gemma asked Lando.

"It's not that valuable as evidence because she's not around anymore. She can't testify against anyone. It's hearsay. The only value it provides is a window into how Jocelyn felt about her sister back in 2000. That's the pot of gold, especially if you put yourself in Jocelyn's shoes at the time. Because you have a college student who wants to get her grubby hands on the money mommy and daddy left her, she's too greedy to wait until she turns twenty-one."

Eating her fill of cookies and coffee, Gemma pushed her plate away. "So we're back to Jocelyn talking a friend, a lover, a roommate, twisting somebody's arm, into killing her sister and her family to get at the trust."

"Not sure we ever left that theory. It's still viable and the best motive we have right now."

"Okay, then maybe she dangles some kind of incentive. Sex. A chunk of money. A portion of the trust. Something large enough, important enough, that a killer at heart finds irresistible, enthralled with the idea, and unable to walk away."

"Yeah, but we have to figure out how to prove it."

"Look, it's obvious ot me that Eric Williams played a part in it," Dale said. "Then she marries the guy to keep him from ratting her out down the road. Spouses can't testify against each other. Reasonable. Seems simple enough to me."

Gemma nodded. "Then she decides to kill him off in the woods, making it look like a hunting accident, no one the wiser. I mean, here we are, twenty years later, and nobody questioned the coroner's report on Eric Williams. Jocelyn strikes again, she scores, she wins again."

"Try getting a jury to believe any of that when the defendant has hired the best top gun lawyer in the state, the best money can buy," Lando pointed out. He held up both hands. "Just projecting what will happen if we get sloppy. No, before that happens, we need solid, concrete, indisputable evidence we can take to a grand jury."

Dale huffed out a breath. "Good luck with that. We're no closer to solving this than we were the night Ben died."

Gemma laid a hand over Lando's. "You know who else we should talk to about that night, the night the Copelands died?"

"Who?"

"Derrick Ross."

Lando's brow furrowed. "Why Derrick?"

"Because Derrick knew Laura Leigh. He even knew Jocelyn. Might've been years earlier, but it warrants a face to face talk."

"I'm not sure I see the connection there, other than the obvious high school classmate's reunion down-by-the-river thing. But now that you mentioned him, I can certainly buy into interviewing Derrick for one simple reason."

"What's that?"

"Derrick wasn't at home the night Laura Leigh died in that car crash."

"So?"

"It's an unanswered loose end. I don't like leaving loose ends."

18

Monday morning dawned with springlike blue skies and warm temperatures. First thing Lando did was send off the plaster casts and the baggie with the necklace to the crime lab for testing. If they could get DNA off the gold chain and match up the shoe prints, it would go a long way to solving who came into their house last night.

As if Dale could predict the future, he came strolling into Lando's office with a big smile on his face. He slapped down a piece of paper on the boss's desk. "Told you Jocelyn would report the gold chain stolen. Payce took her incident report at eight o'clock sharp this morning. She claims it must've been stolen sometime over the winter. Claims that the last time she checked was several months back when the gold chain was safely put away in a jewelry box on her dresser. She's already suggesting that the hired help must've stolen it. This Jocelyn thinks she's a very clever woman."

Lando bounded out of his chair and walked to the windows. "She thinks she has all this figured out, that she's a step ahead of us. I guess she has been for twenty years. But we'll see who's still standing at the end of this thing. I did a deep-dive background check on Derrick Ross, then studied every line for anything that looked suspicious."

"And?"

"He once had a $20,000 credit line at the casino. Around Memorial Day in 2010, he was in deep debt to them. It seems he squandered away almost forty thousand dollars. Then two days after Laura Leigh died, the balance was paid off. Derrick somehow managed to settle up and still have ten grand left over."

"You're not suggesting that Derrick had something to do with that accident, are you?"

"Not yet. But it's early. I want you to go out to the junkyard on the highway and see if they still have Laura Leigh's Prius." He yanked a sheet of paper out of the fax machine and handed it off. "Here's the registration information with the VIN."

"Are you sure that's the best use of my time? What good is it looking for a rusted out hunk of metal? That's probably all that's left."

"Look, I know it's a longshot, but Laura Leigh dying like she did just might hold the key to this entire puzzle."

"Okay. But it'll probably take me most of the day."

"I'm aware of that. Send Jimmy in. I have a special assignment for him, too."

"Oh, goodie. I hope it's as thrilling as mine."

Jimmy's task was to go back over Ben's research and see if the postmaster ever talked to Derrick Ross.

"I know it's tedious work, but it needs doing," Lando assured Jimmy.

"I'm not complaining. It's better than climbing over and around a bunch of junked up metal all day long."

"You've been comparing assignments to Dale's, I see."

"Well, he did grumble a lot before he headed out the door. Let's just say he wasn't in the best of moods for a Monday."

Lando spent the rest of his morning at home installing new locks and cameras on all the outside doors. Gemma arrived at noon to bring him lunch and get off her feet.

"I've been wearing my chocolatier hat this morning," Gemma announced, carrying in a food bag from Captain Jack's. "I brought samples for dessert."

Eyeing the sack, Lando closed up his toolbox. "I hope you didn't bring anything with fish."

"Would I do that to a hungry guy like you?" She patted his cheek before waving a carton in front of his nose. "A burger cooked just the way you like it and hot fries."

He leaned in and gave her a peck on the cheek. "That's my girl."

While they scarfed down the food, Lando caught her up on the latest about Derrick Ross. "I see now why Anna Kate divorced his ass."

"So in addition to his being this big ladies' man, cheating every chance he got, he also is a serious gambler with a problem. Who knew Derrick was such a high roller? When you go interview him, I want to tag along."

"Fine by me. Maybe you'll pick up on what he's hiding."

"What makes you think he's hiding anything?"

"Because the background check also revealed there's a wide six-month gap in Derrick's employment record beginning a few days after Laura Leigh's death. He went from a decent job at the County in the planning department to disappearing off the radar. When he does reappear, he has a cushy job at a company called River Run Limited."

"Never heard of it."

"It's a real estate holding company out of San Francisco owned by one Jocelyn Trask Williams."

Gemma's jaw dropped. "She owns companies, too? I'd be impressed if she wasn't such a coldhearted bitch."

"Let's just say she has a healthy portfolio. Several. Some of her money is in offshore accounts, spread around in various shell companies. It's what the rich do, which is why it took a warrant and another deep dive into her wealth to uncover it. Now we have an interesting link to follow all the way to Derrick's door."

"I'm not missing out on *this* conversation."

"Wouldn't expect you to. What kind of chocolate did you bring home?"

Gemma's lips curved as she reached in the bag and brought out a box. "I made your favorite this morning from scratch."

Lifting the lid on the box, she showed off her latest truffle creation. "I know how much you love Amaretto. So I mixed it with my best dark chocolate and added a hefty dose of buttercream to make it richer in flavor, then I rolled the outside in Amaretti cookie crumbs."

Lando bit into the concoction and let out a slow groan. "Oh, that's delicious. It's so much better than the hazelnut stuff you usually make on Mondays."

"I know. I'm replacing it beginning today. I think it's a flavor that better ushers in spring."

Lando took another piece out of the box and popped it in his mouth. "I predict these will sell like hotcakes. I hope you made plenty."

"I left Lianne with four trays. She loved them, too. She's thinking of serving them at the wedding reception and at the grand opening of The Craft Factory."

"You changed the name? When did that happen?"

"Lianne did. And I'm thinking of using these to persuade Flanner to build my shed right here in the backyard."

"Lots of luck with that. You haven't seen stubborn until you try to pry Flanner out of that cabin and into town."

"We'll see." Gemma shifted in her chair. "Tell me again why you're not asking Derrick to come down to the station instead of having to track him down like the dog he is."

Lando licked the chocolate off his fingers. "Not a bad idea. I could get Payce to pick him up. First, ask Derrick to come down as a courtesy. Informally, of course."

"Of course. Take the high roller by surprise because he has no idea what you suspect him of doing. Catch him totally off guard."

"I'll text Payce now. But if Derrick refuses to cooperate, which he has every right to do, we'll have to go out to his house."

"Fine by me. But he's not getting my chocolate unless he tells us something juicy."

They ended up having to make the trip out to Derrick's house. The man refused to willingly go down to the station just to talk, even informally. But it wasn't from lack of trying on Payce's part.

Payce met them on Ross's street in front of his house. "I spent twenty minutes trying to appeal to his sense of fair play, reminding him that Laura Leigh was once his sister-in-law. But he didn't care," Payce explained to Lando. "He didn't seem interested in helping explain anything. I'm sorry, Chief. I tried."

"It's okay. I didn't expect him to cooperate that easily. It plays to our advantage that he wouldn't budge an inch to help."

"Want me to hang around here?"

"No. See if you can get in touch with Dale, though. I want an update on how it's going at the wrecking yard. Preferably before I leave Derrick Ross's house."

"You got it."

Lando angled toward Gemma. "You ready to do this?"

"I'm just here to watch and learn."

He grinned. "That'll be the day. Let's go see if Mr. Ross wants to get anything off his chest."

Derrick Ross answered the door dressed in shorts and shirt. But he greeted them with annoyance written on his face. "I already told the other cop that I have nothing to say about Laura Leigh's car accident. I know we go way back, Lando, but I got nothing to say to you either."

"Yeah. I get that. But here's the thing. I just need a few minutes of your time. Because we go way back, I want to give you the opportunity to straighten me out about a few things. Because I have several questions about Laura Leigh's so-called accident, if that's not enough to get you to talk to me, I'm also working on a murder case. Ben Zurcher. You heard about that, right? So you can either talk to me here or downtown."

"Don't threaten me like that."

"Look, if you don't talk to me now, I'll come back tonight with a warrant. Judge Hartwell likes me. Fair warning, the judge usually grants me warrants for the slimmest of reasons. It's called generous leeway."

"Hey, I've got friends and a lawyer I keep on retainer."

"Good for you. But like I said, I can get Judge Hartwell to write up a warrant in the next hour based on all the questions I have and take you down to the station for an interview. It's really your choice. I could even call you a material witness and use that to get you to the station. You're welcome to bring your lawyer with you. But if I take anything to the grand jury later, you're toast."

"I don't know anything about a murder case. Ben Zurcher's or anyone else's. And I don't know why you'd question me about a car accident that happened ten years back?"

"I'd love to explain it to you, but I'd need to come in first."

Derrick sneered and spat out, "Fine."

As they moved inside, Gemma noted that Derrick was much shorter than she remembered. He stood maybe five-eight with his sandals on. He had more facial hair than he did on his head. The slight beard forming on his chin and jawline gave him a shabby look. He had lost his hair, though, either shaved it off on purpose, or it had thinned on its own. Either way, the face reminded her of the actor Tom Hardy in his bad guy role.

With somewhat of an attitude, Derrick showed them into his living room, then crossed his arms over his chest in a defensive poster. "Okay. Let's hear your questions."

Gemma cleared her throat before Lando could speak. "How long had you and Laura Leigh been having an affair before she died on that road up to Moonlight Ridge?"

In response, Lando's jaw fell open while Derrick simply slumped into the nearest chair.

When he was able to get over the shock of the question, Derrick choked out a question of his own. "How did you find out?"

Before she answered that, Gemma traded looks with her husband. "You said it before when you mentioned that Derrick wasn't home the night Laura Leigh died. It got me to thinking. Anna Kate already suspected he was cheating. She just didn't know with whom. Right? Plus, she couldn't figure out why Laura Leigh would go out to Moonlight Ridge. Remember? I just put two and two together and took a chance that I was right. It seems like I was."

She stared over at Derrick. "If you had to cheat on your wife, why did it have to be with her sister?"

"I'm not proud of it. Look, I never wanted Anna Kate to know about our affair. There's no need to tell her at this late date, either. It's true. We were sneaking around behind Anna Kate's back. But I hadn't been happy in my marriage for a long time. Deep down, Anna Kate knows that. As for the affair, one day, it just happened. It was just sex."

Lando did his best to recover from the news enough to put the fear of God in Derrick. "The night she died, you were with Laura Leigh for how long? And where?"

"Earlier in the evening, yeah."

"No, I mean, how long did you spend together that night specifically?"

Derrick licked his lips and slunk down further into the chair. "We had this habit of getting a room out on the highway at the Starlight Motel. But that night, we headed up to the little cabin I kept at Moonlight Ridge for some privacy."

"I see. You mean like a love shack sort of thing?" Lando prodded.

"I bought the place with my own money. You can call it what you want."

"Then I take it your wife knew nothing about your little love nest?"

"No. She did not."

Not surprised by his answer, Gemma had a follow-up question. "Just curious, but where was Laura Leigh's husband or boyfriend during all these bootie calls?"

"What? No. Laura Leigh never got married, not even to Sienna's father. She was a free spirit. That's what I liked about her."

Gemma traded confused looks with Lando. "That's weird. What happened to her wanting to be like Sandra Copeland, the lady of the manor, mom of the year, that sort of thing?"

Derrick lifted a shoulder. "I don't know what you're talking about. Her wild side was one of the things that appealed to me. She was unattached, available, and willing to go crazy now and again. We were having fun. We weren't hurting anyone. Neither of us was that serious about the other. I liked that. They might've been sisters, but Laura Leigh was the total opposite of Anna Kate." He rolled his eyes. "Anna Kate, the one who always had to control everything I did, who always wanted me to account for every minute of my day. No, Laura Leigh was a breath of fresh air compared to the wife."

Lando decided to take a seat across from Derrick so he could look him in the eye. "So tell us what happened the night she died, start to finish."

Derrick itched a spot on his beard. "Jeez, I'm not sure I remember exactly. I probably made up some excuse to get out of the house. I do know I met Laura Leigh at the cabin because Sienna was at our house. We had time on our hands. I seem to recall Anna Kate planned to take the kids to the mall or something. Once I arrived at the cabin, we probably made love. Afterward, I remember she got this phone call and said she had to meet someone. She got dressed, went out to the car, and that's the last time I ever saw her alive. Fifteen minutes later, she drove off the road and was killed."

Since he hadn't heard from Dale about the Prius, Lando felt like he needed to stall. But he wasn't ready to tip his hand about Derrick's gambling debts. At least not yet. "Do you know a Jocelyn Williams?"

Derrick seemed surprised at the question. "I know of her. Sure. Everybody does."

Lando managed not to look over at Gemma, who knew better. "And where is your place of employment these days, Derrick?"

"Uh, I'm a real estate agent, commercial, down in the Bay Area. I specialize in leasing retail office space."

"That's a great job. What's the name of the company you work for?"

"River Run Limited. Why is that important to this conversation?"

"Just routine questions, Derrick. Tell me this, a few days after Laura Leigh died, it seems you came into some money. Fifty grand, to be exact. It was enough to clear all your outstanding debt that you'd run up at the casino in the neighborhood of forty thousand dollars."

"What the hell are you doing checking up on stuff like that? I probably hit the lottery or something."

"You don't remember where fifty thousand dollars came from? Is that your official answer?"

Derrick began to fidget. Beads of sweat popped out on his forehead. "Look, I was devastated about what happened to Laura Leigh. After she died, that was about the time I decided to take some time off, and I left the country for a while."

"Six months," Lando provided.

"That sounds about right. I remember now. I got this job offer from River Run, and they gave me a bonus for coming to work for them."

Lando wanted to be clear about Derrick's explanation so there was no confusion. "Let me get this straight. They allowed you to take six months off before beginning the job leasing commercial real estate? Is that what you're saying?"

"Yeah. I told my boss I needed some time to heal, to get over the pain of losing Laura Leigh."

Gemma knew they had him cornered. "You needed to heal because you were that shaken up over the death of a woman you were just having fun with, right? Your words, not mine. You guys weren't serious, just fooling around, remember? So you were so upset over the accident that you needed to leave California and go where? Where did you spend those six months out of the country?"

"I went to Monte Carlo."

"Alone?"

Derrick's hands began to tremble. "I went to the beaches, soaked up the sun. A friend might have joined me there later. I don't remember exactly. Look, I've answered your questions. I think it's time I spoke to my lawyer."

Lando looked down at his phone as it dinged with a text message from Dale. "Here's good news, Derrick. I just learned we found Laura Leigh's old Prius. Early indications look like her brake line was tampered with." He held up his phone. "We have all sorts of photos to send to the crime lab now. The good news is that there's no statute of limitations on murder. You wouldn't know anything about brake lines, would you?"

Derrick wiped his sweaty palms on his shorts. "No, I wouldn't."

"Here's what I think happened. For whatever reason, you were either hired by Jocelyn Williams to get rid of your lover. Or maybe you did it on your own. But it seems strange that your sabbatical lasted six months before you went to work for River Run Limited, which is owned by none other than Jocelyn Williams."

Gemma watched fear come into Derrick's eyes.

"I'd like you to leave now," Derrick announced.

"Okay. But where were you the night Ben Zurcher died?"

"I was at home."

"Can anyone verify that?"

"No."

"Did you know a man named Daniel Albrecht?"

"No."

"Funny thing about Albrecht. He's also dead, found on Trask land. What do you think I'd find if I checked Jocelyn's passport and her travel out of the country back in 2010? Do you think I'd discover that she's the woman who joined you in Monte Carlo?"

"I think I need to speak to my attorney now. I'd like you both to leave."

"That went so much better than I ever thought possible," Lando said once he got behind the wheel. "How in the world did you figure out Derrick was screwing Laura Leigh?"

"To be honest, it was kind of a bluff. I did have a feeling about it, but I thought I'd put it out there and get Derrick's reaction. Turns out, he looked gobsmacked. What does gobsmacked mean exactly? And who uses that word?"

Lando found that funny. "It means completely shocked. And I was watching his eyes. Derrick was blown away by your question. The perfect start to the best interview I've given in years. I knew you'd landed a punch as soon as he collapsed off his feet and had to sit down. The bravado went out of him. You saw that, right? His arrogance just faded right before our eyes. I loved it. Remind me not to play poker with you."

"What happens next? Did Dale really find the car?"

"Oh, yeah. That was no bluff. And the timing couldn't have been better. Showing Derrick those pictures had him calling out for his lawyer."

"Which was the point, correct? To scare him?"

"Well, not really. But a guy with no alibi for the night Ben Zurcher died climbs to the top of the list because of his connection to Jocelyn. He could be her current stooge."

"Why do you think Derrick was so reluctant to admit that he works for her?"

"Good question. And another reason to dig deeper. Those two are linked by what exactly? How did Derrick come to be on Jocelyn's radar? The important takeaway for me was that Derrick formally denied that he ever knew Daniel Albrecht. I have him on record now."

"Yeah, but he also claimed he barely knew Jocelyn. How do you barely know the owner of the company you work for when there are no other employees? That sets it up that he's a lying sack of you know what."

"Exactly. But now he's on record changing his story about his debt, about his employment, about Laura Leigh. We just need to find out why Daniel Albrecht met up with Ben. What triggered Ben and Daniel getting killed? Was Ben getting too close to the truth about what happened to the Copelands? Then, days later, Daniel Albrecht suffers the same fate. Why? Someone must've found out that Daniel was talking to Ben. How? How did they know that? There are still big gaps to close. No doubt we still have more digging to do, a lot more, but at least now we have a firm place to dig."

"That means Jocelyn, right?"

"Oh, yeah. We zero in on Jocelyn."

To focus on Jocelyn, Lando needed to start connecting a few dots to back up his suspicions. He hadn't heard from Jimmy yet. Which was why once he arrived at the station, he headed straight to

Jimmy's desk down the hallway while Gemma took off in the opposite direction to check her emails.

The squad room was a bullpen-style open area with four metal desks arranged in each corner of the room. The placement provided little privacy. When the officers took phone calls, anybody could listen in. But since they were a tight bunch, no one ever complained.

After going through Ben's papers for the third time, Jimmy sat at his workspace, feeling frustrated. He looked up to see Lando walking into the room.

"Look, I know you wanted to see some results, but after spending hours going through this stuff, I feel more perturbed than when I started. The man's notes are barely legible, not that organized, and sometimes ol' Ben tended to ramble. Most of the names are scattered throughout a host of documents, sprinkled here and there among theories and suspects."

"If that's a long drawn out excuse for closing up shop for the day, I'd like to encourage you to stick with it."

Jimmy huffed out a breath. "Okay. But it's not like I can make something materialize out of thin air. How'd it go with Derrick?"

Lando caught him up to speed. He also shared Dale's photos of Laura Leigh's car.

Jimmy studied the pictures, swiping through the series of images. "It doesn't take a mechanic to figure out the brake line has been cut. If Derrick's story is that he had sex at this cabin with Laura Leigh right before she died, maybe while they were in bed, somebody tampered with the Prius. Then when Laura Leigh got the phone call and left, it was a perfectly timed setup. She took off down the hill and wasn't able to stop. This was no accident. The question is why."

Dale came strolling in with a grin on his face. "I might be able to help answer that."

After hanging up his jacket on the peg, Dale took a seat on the corner of Jimmy's desk. "That Prius had a previous owner. You'll never believe who bought it and drove it off the lot first."

"Jocelyn Williams," Lando provided.

Dale cocked a brow. "Okay, how did you know that?"

"I pulled the registration before heading to Derrick's."

"You might've clued me in because it seems strange to me that the babysitter for the Copelands receives a generous gift from the very person she suspected as being a killer. Ask yourself this, was the car a payoff for stopping the rumors?"

Gemma joined the men, carrying a tray with four cups of coffee on it. "That would mean Laura Leigh was blackmailing Jocelyn. Which is a great reason for Jocelyn to want her dead."

Lando took one of the mugs, lifted a hip to sit on one of the desks. "Now see, that's one of the reasons we make a good team. Because at first, I thought Laura Leigh might've legitimately bought the car from Jocelyn. Pickings are slim around here when it comes to finding a quality used car. But now, it seems obvious. The Prius was less than a year old when Laura Leigh had her accident. If it was a payoff, then we need to prove it."

"I bet Derrick would know," Gemma suggested.

"Probably. But the next time we see Derrick, he'll have an attorney sitting next to him."

Gemma shook her head. "Not necessarily. If you were to offer him a deal, down the road of course, he might just save himself and put the blame all on Jocelyn. Even if he does work for her, he could cut ten years off his prison sentence if he testifies against her."

"If it comes to that, we'd have to get creative. And right now, we still need proof that Ben got in touch with Daniel Albrecht because Daniel had key information about Jocelyn."

Jimmy let out a sigh as he glanced through several pages of Ben's notes. The information was starting to run together. "Maybe someone else could give it a try. A second set of eyes might help. I swear all this stuff is blurring together." He was about to snap the book closed when one line leaped off the same page he'd been staring at for hours.

"Wait. Look at this. Here. Wasn't Daniel Albrecht from Pleasanton? This is why I couldn't find the name. It's not here. All Ben has listed was the phone number with a 9-1-5 area code. Isn't that the area code for Pleasanton?"

Lando bobbed his head as he punched in the number listed in Ben's notes and listened as the call went unanswered. But when it went to voicemail, for the first time, Lando heard Albrecht's voice. His lips curved at the message. He hit the speaker button, so everyone else could hear it, too. "I'll be damned. Ben Zurcher, you old dog. Postmaster or not, you should've been an investigative reporter."

Gemma folded her arms over her chest. "Now, we need to figure out what Albrecht had on Jocelyn. It had to be something big.

Otherwise, why would the guy drive four hundred miles up here just to meet with Ben?"

Lando turned to Jimmy. "How many sets of fingerprints did we get out of Ben's house?"

"Maybe half a dozen. Most belonged to Ben."

"But not all. Call the lab. See if Daniel's prints were found at Ben's house."

"You think Daniel stayed with Ben while he was here?"

"Yeah, I do. Not only that, I think the two men were lured out to meet their killers—Ben at the mercantile on Sunday night during the storm, then Daniel later on when Ben failed to return home. Somebody got him to drive out to Trask land."

"Why would he do that, though?" Gemma wondered. "Why would he fall for that kind of story when he knew—or at least suspected—he might be in danger? Especially if Ben didn't return to the house?"

"Before we assume anything, we need to know if any of those prints belonged to Daniel."

"I'll get on it," Jimmy said, getting to his feet. "I'll even ask the lab about Daniel's cell phone and see if we can get a clearer triangulation on his phone, see who he talked to during his final hours."

"Ordinarily, I'd say leave it till morning," Lando began. "But we don't know who Jocelyn is targeting next. At this point, she could go after anyone."

19

That night after supper, Lando helped with the dishes while Gemma filled out her insurance claim forms for the water damage from the night of the storm. To complete the paperwork, the adjuster had suggested she attach photos of the damage. She sat at the kitchen table going through the library of pictures she'd taken that Sunday night during the heaviest rainfall.

"I'm glad I thought to take photos that show just how high the water got."

"He's not trying to deny the claim, is he?"

"She. A woman by the name of Karen Pettigrew. The name on that business card Marissa kept in the desk drawer was someone else. Unfortunately, when I asked for that person, they told me he'd died years earlier. This Pettigrew woman is a piece of work. She started by telling me that my deductible was five thousand dollars. I told her that couldn't be right. That I was looking at the policy I renewed in January. The damage didn't amount to that much. It turns out, this Pettigrew woman was looking at someone else's policy instead of mine."

"That doesn't sound very professional."

"Or efficient. It's her job to play hardball with customers. I get that. She is in the business of denying claims rather than paying legitimate ones. Anyway, I had to remind her that I'd taken pictures of the water damage in the corner of the dining area. Do you know what she had the nerve to say to me?"

"What?"

"That photographs could be doctored. This Pettigrew woman asked if I had anyone from the insurance company come out and officially verify the damage or write it up as soon as it happened. That's when I invited her to the shop to look at the beginnings of mold growing in the corner. I'll probably need to replace the flooring because it never dried out. But if the insurance company won't pay a small claim like mine, I should probably think about switching companies."

"Even with the pictures of the damage, this woman is still giving you a hard time?"

"That's what I've been saying. Yes. She told me to go ahead and send in a claim but that she'd need to come out and inspect the damage herself. What I can't figure out is why she assumed that I would doctor photos just to get new linoleum installed in one corner of the shop."

"You'd be surprised how much money some people try to hustle out of an insurance compamy."

Gemma scoffed at the notion. "I would never do that."

Sulking, she continued to pick and choose from the photographs on her phone and attach them to the online claim form. But when she came to the pictures taken outside the store, one got her attention. She stared at several shots of a hooded figure walking into the frame. She had photos of the person appearing in the foreground walking toward the mercantile. "Uh, Lando. You better take a look at this."

"What?" He dried his hands on a dishtowel so he could take the phone. After swiping through several shots, he looked down at Gemma. "Holy crap. That's not Derrick, is it?"

"No. That's a woman's build. Even with the hoodie and the all-black clothing on, you can tell. Look at the size of the feet. Having just seen the size of Derrick's sandals today, the feet in those pictures belong to someone with narrow feet. That's a female."

"Could we get these blown up to tell us more?"

"You could try. Doesn't the County have a lab that does that with crime scene photos?"

"Yeah. I'm just not sure how grainy images work from a cell phone. But hard copies might help to ID her."

"You really need those blown up to tell who it is? Who are we kidding? It looks like Jocelyn to me."

"Me too. But I need—"

"Proof. I get it. What will you do if you discover that a super wealthy woman is the person who killed Ben?"

"What do you mean? I'll arrest her. What else would I do?"

"Lando, you don't need me to point this out. But that woman will fight you tooth and nail. Whatever evidence you come up with will need to be ironclad. No mistakes. No errors."

"I know that. Why do you think I'm so concerned? Finding *the* critical piece that connects this all together is key."

"What if you dug deeper into the death of Eric Williams? Maybe he's the key. He was married to Jocelyn. If she did kill him, maybe there's evidence no one bothered to find. Why not look at his autopsy again? Get Tuttle to dig out the man's files."

"Better still, maybe we could dig up Eric Williams."

"Is there a way to do that?"

"There is if we find a good enough reason for exhumation."

As long as Lando had known Jeff Tuttle, he knew the County medical examiner was, at times, like a prickly pear that didn't like people butting into his business. The morgue was Tuttle's domain, and nobody told him what to do there. Nobody. He kept his own schedule. He did things in his own timeframe. On his own terms.

Tuttle also didn't like answering calls from pushy investigators. Those who often tried getting him to rush his autopsy results were in for a fight. For the duration of his tenure, Tuttle had resisted hanging around law enforcement types in his off hours for the very reason they might use a friendship to try and influence his professional decisions. If a case leaned suicide, Tuttle didn't want a cop pushing him to call it a homicide or vice versa.

Lando knew the guy could be a hardass about certain things. But he also knew that Tuttle wasn't perfect. After all, the medical examiner had gotten Marissa's cause of death wrong. If not for Gemma showing up when she did to put it right, Marissa's killer might have gone unpunished.

That less-than-perfect backstory from the coroner himself came into play when Jimmy met with resistance. Getting Daniel Albrecht's fingerprints out of Tuttle was turning out to be a major production.

Until Lando showed up.

"Come on, Jeff. You're not doing us any favors by stalling. You already finished Albrecht's autopsy. All I want to know is if his fingerprints match any that we found at Ben's house. I'm asking you to make one phone call to the crime lab and confirm. You can send the prints via fax. If you do it, we could have an answer before morning, maybe even make an arrest."

Tuttle slammed the file drawer closed. "Stop needling me about how to do my job. I've gotten along just fine for fifteen years without you showing up asking for these kinds of favors."

"It's not a favor. Besides, what's the big deal? It's part of your job to ID a killer."

"So you think Albrecht killed Ben and then got killed by someone else? That's the dumbest thing I've ever heard."

"No. I have a theory that Ben offered Albrecht a place to stay. When Ben got lured out of the house that Sunday night in the middle of the storm, it left Albrecht vulnerable. Someone lured both of them out in the open for one reason. And that was to murder them. I think it's because Ben was getting close to the truth, and Albrecht already knew a secret about our killer that he shared with Ben."

"Fine. I'll make the call. But I want you to do something for me."

"What? Name it."

"I want you to plan a party or something and invite Tina Ashcomb to it."

Lando narrowed his eyes. "You want me to play matchmaker for you? Jeez, Jeff, how desperate are you?"

"I like her. But she's always busy with work. If I could get her in a social setting, I think we'd hit it off."

"Wait a minute. Have you already asked Tina out once before? Has she turned you down using work as an excuse?"

"Sort of. Look, you guys are always planning get-togethers, barbecues, that sort of thing. I don't care what kind of event it is. Just include me on the guest list."

"If I do this, will you be more receptive in the future if I need access to an autopsy report? Or maybe want a body exhumed?"

"You get me a solid evening to spend around Tina, and I'll grant you an all-access pass to everything in my domain."

After brokering the deal with Tuttle, within a few hours, Lando had his answer. Ben had indeed offered Albrecht a place to stay. That's why the prints found in a guest room matched back to Daniel Albrecht. While at the coroner's office, he also got to make copies of the autopsy paperwork on Eric Williams, including all the photographs.

Lando jammed everyone into the conference room where he'd set up laptops and a projector to use so they could all see the autopsy documents in larger than life snapshots. He kept uploading the slides until he reached the one that he wanted to showcase.

"In Eric's case, take a hard look at the autopsy, line seventy-two. As you can see, Jeff Tuttle listed the cause of death as undetermined. Tuttle went on to say that he just couldn't in good conscience label the death an accident when the angle of the shot ended up coming from a straight line in front instead of how Eric would've been carrying his rifle. But the widow did her part in spreading plenty of rumors that flat out encouraged everybody in town to believe Eric had accidentally shot himself while hunting, that he tripped over a log and the gun went off."

Gemma picked up a photo from the crime scene to study. "But there's no log anywhere near the body."

"Exactly. No one had access to these photographs. They just took Jocelyn's explanation for fact. That's why no one questioned Eric's death."

"Not even his family?"

"According to the files, he had an aunt who lived in Richmond. No other relatives around to question Jocelyn's account of what happened, though. For the record, Jocelyn buried him back in Richmond, in a family plot there, within three days of Eric dying."

"So basically, what you're saying is that exhumation is out of the picture," Jimmy surmised. "Digging up a body in another county is difficult."

"No, we could do it. But it would take time," Lando said.

Gemma studied the photogrraghs of Eric's crime scene. "I don't see the problem relying on Tuttle's autopsy or these pictures."

She squinted at one photograph that depicted Eric's body lying on the ground with half his face contorted in pain. "Imagine for a moment that the way he looks right here is the last thing he saw before he died. And if we're right, his wife is the one who shot him and watched him bleed out. Is there any way you could enlarge this photo so I could get a better look at Eric's face?"

"Sure." Lando handed off the shot to Dale. "Scan this into that software app you recently bought and see if you can get a closeup of his facial features."

"Why don't I just bring up his driver's license photo from eighteen years ago? That would give you a better idea of what he looked like than half his face hidden in profile," Dale suggested.

Gemma's lips bowed into a smile. "Even better. I need to see what Eric looked like around 2000."

Dale went to his computer, typed the name into the DMV database. When the search brought up a result, he turned around the monitor so she could see what Eric Williams had looked like in life.

She moved closer to the screen to study the photograph, all the while clutching the power stones around her neck. Swallowing hard, she muttered, "That's him. That's the guy I saw at the Copeland's house wearing the hoodie. That's the man who murdered Sandra, Todd, Hallie, and Julie."

Dale looked at Lando, held up both hands. "Don't shoot the messenger, but it makes sense. Think about it. Jocelyn must've talked him into committing the murders, giving her an airtight alibi, then married him to control his mouth if he ever got chatty. She waited for the right opportunity, then killed him when he'd served her purpose, and she didn't need him anymore."

Gemma took a seat at the conference table. "My seeing Williams there at the farmhouse isn't enough. I know that. But there must be some way to verify that he was in that house and killed those four people that night. What about DNA off the bedding? Did the lab find anything?"

"Not yet. The technicians tell me it's a prolonged process to vacuum every single spot on material the size of bedding.."

"But not impossible?"

"No, it just takes time."

"I want to go back up there to the farmhouse," Gemma announced. "We'll need that caretaker's permission. That is if you've crossed him off the suspect list."

"No, I don't think Barnhart's our suspect."

"Good. Because this time I won't be run off until I'm convinced that I have something significant to contribute. And I don't want Barnhart to interfere. I need to go back to see where this all started."

"Technically, it all began with the deaths of Sandra and Jocelyn's parents. Technically," Jimmy repeated. "Just saying."

Gemma nodded. "You're right. Maybe we should start on Trask land, the place where Albrecht was shot."

"I have a better idea," Lando piped up. "While we're at the farmhouse, why don't we send Jimmy and Dale where Albrecht died. But this time, spread out and scour the area for the murder weapon."

"But we already did that," Jimmy reminded him, looking over at Dale for confirmation.

"And that day, we had crime scene techs who helped us," Dale pointed out. "Although…"

"What?" Lando asked.

Dale scrubbed his chin. "Well, we didn't drag the pond. Maybe the killer tossed the gun into the stock pond, the one used for the cattle."

"Then start there," Lando directed. "Get divers from the County. Come on, guys, we need something, anything, at this point, that leads us to Jocelyn."

"Or Derrick," Gemma added. "Let's not rule out the possibility that Jocelyn might've used another stooge to get the job done."

"Either way, we move on this fast. Whatever we find, we work through the night and act on it."

"What if we don't find anything?" Dale muttered.

"Let's not dwell on the negative," Lando proposed. "We do our jobs to the best of our ability and hope for the best."

20

Gemma heeded Lando's words as she gathered her supplies around her. This time she'd come prepared. She'd brought a bag full of items she hoped would help her get a clearer perspective of what happened that night. She already knew Eric Williams had waited in the basement for his opportunity to attack the family. But she needed more.

Bruce Barnhart had given them access to the farmhouse. But it came with a caution. "Whatever you have planned, do it quietly. Mrs. Williams made it clear she didn't want you guys out here, not for any reason, not at any time of the day or night."

"She won't hear it from me. She'll never find out if you don't tell her," Lando fired back. "You're welcome to stick around outside and keep watch."

"I think I'll do that," Bruce decided, worry in his voice. "I'll stand out by the entrance. That way, if I spot her car, I'll give you a heads up with a text message. How does that sound?"

"Works for us."

While Lando dealt with the caretaker, Gemma hauled her bag into the kitchen and set up shop there. Using the counter as her workspace, she unpacked her items. First, she burned white sage to clear her head. She used sweetgrass to build up her energy, then set out incense along the path to the basement door. When everything was ready, she began fanning the sweet smell of Myrrh into the interior of the house in hopes that it would cleanse the air and let her see the past in vivid color.

Like a reset from her previous experience, she needed to wipe the slate clean. She held her power stones up and called out to the lost souls for help, to the Copelands, to Todd and Sandra, to Hallie and to Julie.

To the spirits, she pleaded for their direction. "To the one and only Great Spirit, who guides us all, I call on sacred Mother Earth, the creator of the four winds to show me the truth. To Father Sky and Mother Moon, show me the way. Show me what happened here in all its evil. Show me the truth in cold detail. Fill me with the power of your wisdom. Here. Today. Now. Protect us from the evil that occurred here. Come to me, Great Spirit. Show me the way. Keep me on the path to the truth. Don't let me fail. Don't let me stray. There is power in the Great Spirit. Show me the light."

The ceiling began to glow overhead, like a dome illuminating its radiance, ready to give up its secrets. The floor beneath her feet began to shake.

Gemma heard Lando's intake of breath.

Somewhere between his skepticism, he'd come to realize his wife had a talent for seeing the past. He glanced up at the ceiling in time to catch a wisp of hazy mist floating from the incense. Carried on the air was the shape of a man. The face of Eric Williams stared back at him, big as life.

When the light increased, Gemma closed her eyes and centered her mind, focused. Knowing they were no longer alone, she held her power stones tighter and willed the vault to open. Locked in twenty years of mystery, at that moment, the old farmhouse gave up its darkest secret.

Through Gemma, the images jumped from the vault into that dank cellar, then the first floor. Next came the upstairs, and every room on the second floor opened. It launched a sea of knowledge, allowing her to witness firsthand what had gone down that night.

Whirring images rushed her brain, details she hadn't seen before. The sea parted and gave up more. She saw the initial attack, the blood that came with it, the determination, the rage. The second assault became more manageable and by the time the perpetrator got to the kids, he was motivated to finish what he'd started.

With the vault laid bare, the download complete, she dropped to her knees on the tile floor. Spent and exhausted, she ended up on all fours.

Lando went to her side, brushed back her hair from her face. "Are you okay?"

She nodded. "Yeah. The connection. Eric Williams drove Jocelyn's car here that night. Look for a 1996 Acura Integra. Desert Rose Metallic. Back then, there weren't that many on the road in that color. The Acura was registered to Jocelyn Trask. Eric borrowed her car. That's the mistake. That's the link back to Jocelyn."

Lando had carried Gemma out of the Copeland farmhouse and to his cruiser. He'd driven like a madman back to the house because she looked like she'd seen the dead.

Leia and Lianne were waiting on the stoop along with Rufus and Rolo.

"What took so long?" Leia hollered as she bolted off the porch to help get Gemma out of the car and into the house. "We've been waiting for almost thirty minutes at least."

"I had to make sure she had a pulse first," Lando snapped. "I've never seen her have that kind of reaction before. Scared the life out of me."

Lianne ushered them inside. "Put her in the living room on the sofa. We'll take it from here."

Sweat had broken out on Lando's forehead as he carried Gemma and rushed past them. "Are you sure? Maybe I should take her to the emergency room."

"No need. I've already called Luke," Lianne assured him, fluffing pillows under Gemma's head as soon as Lando placed her on the sofa. "We'll make her comfortable, get some tea into her, bring back her color."

The dogs huddled near Gemma's head until finally Rufus rested his snout on her chest. Shorter and unable to reach anything but her hand, Rolo licked her fingers.

"Okay, guys," Leia said to the dogs. "We've got this."

Lianne ruffled Rolo's fur. "You might as well let them stay put. They won't leave her no matter what."

Leia's lips curved. "You're right." She looked down at Gemma. "Was it worth it?" Leia wanted to know. "To see all that violence firsthand. To see the children suffer?"

"To nail the person responsible, the reason it happened. I think so," Gemma answered, her voice weak and soft. She was still trying to get her balance back, get her head to work right.

"For several long minutes...afterward...she found it tough to breathe like someone had punched her in the gut," Lando acknowledged. "Too long. The whole thing lasted probably less than fifteen minutes but whatever she saw knocked her to the floor, literally. And she stayed that way until I had to help her to her feet."

Concerned, Lianne laid a hand on Gemma's forehead. "How long did it take for her to recover? I mean, how long did it take for her to get up. Because to me, she still looks drained. See how pale her face is."

"About half an hour," Gemma explained. "Lando was great. He didn't even doubt what I'd seen."

Lianne smiled at that, winking in Lando's direction as she removed Gemma's shoes. "You two have come a long way from the days when Lando questioned everything. You've both evolved. Accepting Gemma's gift couldn't have been an easy thing for a hard-boiled cynic like yourself."

"I've learned the hard way," Lando admitted, running a hand through his hair. He bent down next to Gemma to tuck several strands of wayward hair behind her ear. "You okay? For real?"

She took his hand. "I'm okay. I told you so in the car. But you were too worried about me to listen. I just need a minute to recover."

"More like an hour." He placed a kiss on her forehead. "Maybe we should think twice about putting you through that again."

"No, it did the trick. I was able to see so much more than I had earlier. I didn't realize it at the time, but Jocelyn picked the right man for the job. Don't feel too sorry for Eric Williams. Even if the black widow killed him. He wasn't exactly a nice guy. The fact is, he'd killed before—a homeless man in Oakland—beat him to death like he did the Copelands. No. Mr. Williams was hardly a saint. And he had soulless eyes."

"You'd have to be that kind of man to murder children," Leia muttered. When she realized Gemma's eyes had locked on hers, she added, "Well, wouldn't you? Heartless. Soulless. Those two deserved each other—Jocelyn and Eric—didn't they?"

"Leia has a point," Gemma concluded, swinging her legs to the floor and pivoting to a sitting position.

Her head was still spinning when Luke came hurrying into the room. "I got here as soon as I could. Where's the patient?"

Gemma waved him away. "I'm fine. They shouldn't have called you. I hope you didn't leave your real patients to come running over here to me."

"You don't look fine," Luke said as he plopped down next to her. He took her chin, studied the glazed look in her eyes. "What happened exactly?"

Lando cleared his throat. "She went out to the murder house. Had one of her more intense visions that sent her into a nosedive. She saw the murders as they happened. It seems the killer had been waiting in the basement until the family went to bed."

Gemma swallowed hard and nodded. "Eric Williams got into the house through an unlocked window in the basement. While Sandra fixed dinner, she had music playing—a playlist of her favorite songs she'd put together on her own—U2, Coldplay, Green Day, Bon Jovi. You get the idea. Anyway, the music must've covered up any noise Eric made when he got into the house. But the most significant thing I saw was that he got to Moonlight Ridge driving Jocelyn's Integra."

"That reminds me. I need to get Payce to check that Acura's ownership records."

"It'll come back true," Gemma promised. "Trust me. Eric parked the car out of sight at the bottom of the hill. That way, when Todd came home, he just pulled into the garage like always and went into the house through the mudroom. The family ate dinner, cleaned up the kitchen, watched some television, and then went to bed. It was a perfectly ordinary night until the house grew quiet and Eric pounced. He tiptoed up the basement steps to the first floor. He then headed out to the garage looking for something heavy enough to use as the murder weapon. But he spotted the hammer lying on top of the washing machine and grabbed it instead. Eric always intended to kill the kids. It was just a fluke that Julie woke up and saw him standing on the landing. Julie recognized him and she called out, 'hey, Eric, what are you doing here?' That was the moment he took Julie by the hand and led her back to her bedroom."

Lando shoved out of his stance and got to his feet. "So, you don't think there's any way Eric would've let the kids live? Even if Julie hadn't seen him?"

"There's no revisionist history at play here," Gemma clarified. "The minute Eric saw Julie standing on that landing, planned or not, he killed everyone there. That was what he did. There's no going back from that."

"And all this happened because spoiled Jocelyn wanted her inheritance," Leia huffed out. "Do you have enough to arrest her? Because if you don't and this gets out—your theory—she'll probably sell everything she has and move out of the country."

Lando narrowed his eyes on his sister. "You can't tell anyone what we're working on. How far we've gotten. The way it stands now, I don't have enough hard evidence and I'm sure Gemma knows that."

"I'm well aware," Gemma replied. "Yeah. But Lando's sent divers out to the Trask pond today to look for the gun that killed Ben and Daniel. Hopefully, Dale will get lucky. Maybe he'll report back that they found it."

"Hope? What kind of real action is that?" Leia protested. She sent a scowl toward Zeb. "Do something."

"What do you want me to do exactly? It's not my case."

Luke glowered at his brother. "And what if the divers don't find the gun? What happens then? Will Jocelyn continue to evade law enforcement?"

"If I can tie her to those two murders, Ben's and Daniel's," Lando began to explain. "It won't matter much if I'm unable to link her to the killings of her sister's family."

"It will matter," Lianne stated. "It has to matter. Those four people can't have died in vain just because Eric Williams is already dead. Just because she's wealthy doesn't mean she should get away with her part in this."

"Damn straight. Because it's not right," Leia pointed out. "Even if you can't take what Gemma saw to a judge, which you can't, we should figure out a way to bring this woman down. And fast."

Zeb heard that last part. "Uh-oh. As a member of law enforcement, I didn't hear that."

"Sure you did," Leia responded. "Jocelyn Williams should be brought to justice for her part in the murders. Murder for hire, right? Solicitation?"

Lando shifted his feet and traded looks with his counterpart Zeb. "I can't prove money changed hands. You know as well as I do, that's the key to murder for hire. And before you ask, that's because Eric Williams never actually had a bank account. Or one that we could find. Because we checked. And checked. And checked some more. Jocelyn damn sure wasn't stupid enough to add him on her bank account. Not ever."

"You're looking at this all wrong," Gemma said. "Eric and Jocelyn were made for each other. They were users, manipulators. It was just a matter of time before either one of them killed the other. Don't you see? Don't you get it? They used each other to the greater end. Jocelyn deliberately picked a guy like Eric, a loser, a man who'd already murdered because it worked to her advantage."

"It must've been risky, though," Zeb added. "Choosing a man like that who had so many faults going against him."

Gemma tried to stand up. "Maybe she saw his faults as pluses. After all, she needed a bad boy, someone who had already proved himself to her. My guess is she tried recruiting Daniel Albrecht first, but he didn't take the bait. Probably several others, too."

"Which is the information Albrecht had for Ben," Lando provided. "He's the guy who explained to Ben how it worked, knowing Jocelyn. Then, Ben took it from there. What's the likelihood that she talked Derrick Ross into doing the crimes?"

Gemma wobbled to the kitchen, taking her time getting there. "If she did, you'd better beat her to Derrick's door. Otherwise, she'll figure out a way to eliminate Derrick just like she did everyone else."

"You're right." Lando reeled on Zeb. "You up for a joint jurisdiction task force?"

Zeb's face broke into a grin. "My favorite words strung together. Just tell me what you need me to do."

21

Dale stood back and watched the divers work the muddy pond using a grid pattern. Because the body of water curved and twisted through the gnarly underbrush of ranchland for almost half a mile, the task had lasted longer than intended. The recovery had turned into a massive effort. It might even mean returning tomorrow to do it all over again.

But Dale didn't mind. He was on a mission.

Set back a quarter mile from the ranch's main entrance was the stock pond, a murky body of water used for cattle. The spot was perhaps another quarter mile from the creek bed where Flanner had discovered Daniel's body. If they did manage to locate the gun, the logistics meant that whoever killed Daniel knew the lay of the land and knew it well enough to seek out the neglected, stagnant water as a disposal site.

Deep in thought and going over their suspect list, Dale didn't see Jimmy pull his patrol car into the bumpy field behind him. Not until Jimmy honked the horn did Dale raise his head to look up. A smile broke across his face. No one was happier to see a friendly face than Dale. He waved Jimmy over like he'd been rescued off a sinking ship.

"What's the word?" Jimmy asked, after joining his coworker on the rocky shoreline.

"As you'd expect, visibility is almost nil. The dive team tried sonar first, then decided to use ground-penetrating radar in the soft silt along this bank, believing that the weapon likely was tossed from here and then sunk into the sediment."

"It hasn't been that long since Daniel's murder. Would the gun travel that far? This pond doesn't seem to flow that much."

"That's what I thought. But the divers seem convinced the arc of throwing the weapon away would end up right where they're searching. And they're the experts. A tight-knit bunch. Haven't said two words to me since they started."

"Lonely out here, huh? Heard from Gemma and Lando?"

"I did. Just a single text message about an hour ago. As usual, the chief wasn't entirely chatty. But he did say he wants to meet up later no matter what time it is."

"Do these divers ever take a break?"

"Not so you'd notice. They're divided into two teams that tag each other when they trade-off. They go down for a certain amount of time and then come back up for the other team to take over. I've already been told they don't quit at dark either. Nightfall doesn't seem to impact the search one way or the other as long as they're under the water."

"Interesting."

"Yeah. How'd it go with Flanner DelRay?"

"Good call there." Jimmy took a piece of paper out of his pocket, handed it off to Dale. "Here's the list of cars Flanner could remember seeing out here in the past two weeks. How did you know he had a habit of writing down license plate numbers?"

"Because he told me. That day he found the body. He has this thing for keeping track of makes and models of cars. It's our good fortune that he also writes down their license plate numbers." Dale went over the list. "Looks like he's recorded every car that came within a mile of his place. A flatbed Ford truck with an Arizona plate, a Nevada semi, a big rig with California plates, and a station wagon loaded down with Utah campers. The guy's thorough, if not anal-retentive. Wait a second. Look at this. Here's a champagne gold Lexus."

Dale's head popped up. "Jimbo, I want you to check out this plate number for me."

"Right this minute?"

"Yep. Run that registration like you've just chased down a speeder going ninety in a fifty-five-mile zone."

"No problem. Be right back."

Dale watched Jimmy walk back to his squad car and sent up a prayer for luck. They needed a break.

Zeb had the same thing on his mind as he pulled down the street from Jocelyn's estate. Luke had come along to keep him company. Their part in the investigation was to keep an eye on the woman in question and make sure she didn't do a runner.

Seventy yards from her front door, the two men sat there and stared at the massive house at the end of the block. At that moment, a dozen possibilities ran through Zeb's law enforcement brain.

"Do you think she realizes that Lando is onto her? And if so, what is she planning to do about it?"

In it for the thrill of catching a bad guy, or in this case a woman, Luke shifted in the passenger seat and brought out a thermos of coffee. "Good questions. But what would happen right now if we, well you, appeared on her doorstep this very night and put the cuffs on her? Would she go quietly? Or would she fight to the bitter end?"

"I wouldn't be...putting the cuffs on her. That's Lando's job. I'm just here to provide manpower in a crunch. But to your point, I don't much think the woman would go quietly into the night. She's not the type. But that's just my cynicism working overtime," Zeb admitted.

"Yeah, but you can't discount the bodies piling up around her. They might go back years but using that, you and Lando should consider Jocelyn Williams a flight risk."

"Well, yeah. Not just that, but she's an unknown danger. She's not your run-of-the-mill serial killer. Think about it. She likes to cut brake lines, cause accidents or shoots her hubby in the middle of the woods. Most serial killers don't vary their methods. She's different that way. Between you and me, I almost wished she'd make a move so we could find out what she's up to."

Luke didn't like the sound of that. "Hey, I'm just along to keep you company. It was either that or stay behind with the women. I'm not here looking for trouble. Although I am curious as to what Jocelyn will do if cornered."

When Zeb's radio crackled to life, it broke up the speculation. Luke listened in as Lando provided the latest update.

"Dale just discovered that a gold Lexus registered to Jocelyn was spotted hauling ass past Flanner DelRay's property the day we think Daniel Albrecht died. So make damn sure she's in that house. Make certain you're watching her and not some underling who works for her."

Zeb swapped looks with Luke. "Well, she's either going to bed in an hour, or she'll try to pack up and hit the road. Either way, we're here for the night."

"No, you're not listening," Lando fired back. "I mean, make sure she's even in there. Make sure she hasn't already hightailed it out of town."

"You want me to go peek in her window? Like a peeping tom?"

"Up to you how you verify she's inside. But I need eyes on her at all times. And the later it gets, the more convinced I am she'll try to run. I want to make sure she hasn't already taken off."

Zeb let out a loud sigh. "Fine. I'll verify. Or maybe I'll send Luke out into the night. But if the neighbors bring out their shotguns, I'm blaming you for making Leia a widow at such a young age."

Lando chuckled. "That's playing dirty. Okay, I'll head over there myself and knock on the door."

"Sure you will," Zeb taunted. "Did you find the gun?"

"Not yet. Divers are still looking, which brings me back around to Jocelyn. If she got wind that there are divers out there on Trask land, her childhood home, she could bolt. See what I mean?"

"Fine. I'll make sure she's there. You keep digging for evidence that will nail her. Besides, getting out of the car is better than twiddling my thumbs."

"I'll keep you posted. If there's trouble, you know what to do."

After Lando ended the transmission, Zeb turned to Luke. "Any ideas?"

"That house probably has any number of security features like surveillance cameras. We can't just go up there and hover around the windows. Whatever it is you come up with, you should keep it simple, though."

"Like what?"

"Well, what if you placed a call inside and asked to speak to Jocelyn. Tell her there's some problem with her, I don't know, her credit card or something."

"That's not a bad idea." Zeb picked up his cell phone, the one he carried for official tribal business, which had a police-issued phone number that would show up on her digital readout.

He dialed Jocelyn's landline.

The ruse was easy enough. When the maid answered, Zeb asked to speak to Jocelyn and only her. Yes, it was urgent, he told the housekeeper. Someone at the casino had her ID and had tried to use her credit card at the cashier's office to purchase chips for the blackjack tables. Someone was there pretending to be Jocelyn Williams.

As soon as Jocelyn picked up, Zeb politely asked if she had recently had her ID stolen. Had she given anyone permission to use her credit card?

When her answers came back with worry and concern in her voice, and she answered a resounding "no" to each question, Zeb knew he was talking to their main suspect. This was not a subordinate.

After reassuring Jocelyn that the casino staff had caught the illegal credit card use in time and that there was no need to panic, Zeb hung up.

He cut his eyes across the front seat to Luke. "That was fairly brilliant. You're not bad for a doctor. Now I should probably text your brother and tell him the suspect is tucked in for the night."

"But do we know that she'll stay put?"

"If she goes anywhere, she'll have to drive right past us."

Gemma had regained her energy enough to persuade Lianne and Leia to stay for supper. She dangled juicy bits of gossip about Laura Leigh's affair with Derrick Ross over a bottle of merlot served with warm bruschetta. It was Leia's idea for an impromptu meal.

"No wonder Anna Kate dumped his ass. What a sleaze," Leia scoffed as she removed the second batch of bread covered in fresh garlic, basil, and tomatoes from the oven. "Was he like that in high school? I barely remember the guy."

"You mean full of himself?" Gemma prodded as she helped herself to a piece of toasted bread. "He's the guy who rode a motorbike up and down the halls on Senior Day, ran into Mrs. Wilson coming out of the science lab, and knocked her off her feet."

Leia shook her head. "Ah, yes. That sounds like Derrick. He was kind of a doofus even then. Hard to believe he could help Jocelyn murder the woman he was sleeping with."

"Maybe he had no idea what Jocelyn was planning to do," Lianne offered. "It's possible. Right?"

"I guess. But I was there when the doofus admitted he left the country four days after Laura Leigh died. He didn't even bother showing up for her funeral. Toss in Jocelyn's mysterious job offer coming on the heels of the accident and the money he got to settle his gambling debts, and it sounds to me like Derrick was a co-conspirator. All he had to do was lure Laura Leigh to the cabin."

"Which he did," Lianne stated. "If it's true, and Jocelyn took care of cutting the brake line, then I say throw the book at him."

"Who knows? Maybe Jocelyn killed her parents in the same way," Gemma offered before adding, "Another car accident to her credit."

With Lianne, the implication sunk in, causing her eyes to widen. "That would make her a serial killer."

"If she's responsible for murdering her sister's entire family, I think she is one." Gemma paused mid-bite and put down her bread. "Oh, my God. I just realized if Eric Williams killed before, I think I might know how to prove it."

"How?"

"He lived here, right? Back in 2001 and almost a full year in 2002."

Leia shrugged. "So? That was eighteen years ago."

"Jocelyn owns that ramshackle storage company across from the drive-in theater. I know because, like everybody else, she paid her property taxes at the end of December."

Leia lifted a brow. "And your point is?"

"Back in November, Joe Don Bowden, one of her oldest customers, received a notice from her that the rent was going up. I know because as mayor, I had to listen to Joe Don bitch about it. He wanted me to fine her or something. He also checked around and discovered that everyone who stored stuff there was put on notice. He wanted me to intervene."

"So what if she decided to charge more? We've already established that she's greedy."

"I'm getting there. The fees were going up beginning on January 1st. I forget the exact amount she asked for, but it was astronomical. No one in their right mind could afford to continue renting their storage space from her. Anyway, Joe Don mentioned he needed to find a new place to store his equipment. As a hot dog vendor, doing mostly street business, he needed a handy place to keep his extra cart and cooking equipment."

"And?"

"According to Joe Don, it's like Jocelyn decided to kick everyone to the curb at the same time to have the place all to herself. As a result, her customers started bailing way back in December. They eventually cleared out their stuff. I heard the same thing from several other people. From what I heard, they went over to that new place out on the highway called The Lockup. At the time, I didn't give it much thought. But now, maybe she wanted everyone gone for a reason."

The realization came into Leia's eyes. "And you think she wanted everyone out of there because she had more stuff to move in? Stuff that came out of her house, maybe?"

"I don't know the answer to that unless we go there and check it out. We just have to find out which storage units are hers. Tonight." Gemma glanced over at her dog. "Hey, Rufus, how do you feel about a snooping session? You'd get a treat out of it."

At the word "treat," the Lab stood up on all fours, ready to rock and roll.

"What are you planning to do?" Lianne questioned. "I recognize that gleam in your eye."

"Hey, do I know my dog or what? Rufus is proof that a Lab will do anything for a treat. Anything. He'd recite the Gettysburg Address if he thought he'd get a treat out of it."

"What about us?" Lianne asked.

"You guys want a treat, too? You're welcome to tag along. Let's see, we'll need flashlights, bolt cutters, gloves, binoculars, and our wellies."

Leia rolled her eyes. "Wellies? Really? My rain boots are at home."

"Mine too," Lianne said.

"Then I'm the one who'll go around and check the units with Rufus. Wait here. I'll just go grab my boots, the ones I use in the garden."

After Gemma disappeared into the solarium, Lianne elbowed Leia in the ribs. "Is this another ill-advised, wine-fueled mission?"

"Let's face it, her wild escapades put the thrill back in our otherwise ordinary lives. Come on, let's do this. Gemma needs us to take down a serial killer. How often is that gonna happen?"

"At the rate we're going, lots," Lianne muttered, grabbing her jacket. "But who am I to turn down the hunt for a serial killer?"

Using her grandfather's old panel truck, Gemma loaded up the dogs along with her friends and headed south of town to a small group of self-storage units called Stash and Store.

The property consisted of five concrete buildings, crumbling from four decades of harsh weather whiplash and old-fashioned neglect. Rotting foundations were a run of the mill occurrence. Not surprising since the place had been around since 1978. Each storage building had aluminum doors that ranged in sizes from the smaller five by five units to the larger garage size ten by tens.

The office was in the main building with the smaller units. A chain-link fence surrounded the land set back off the roadway in a field of overgrown weeds and rutted pastureland.

Behind the wheel, Gemma pulled up and parked the van at the entrance. She pointed to the rooftops. "See. No cameras. Weird, huh? The good news is that since there are only twenty-five units, we should be out of here in an hour, maybe less."

"Famous last words," Leia mumbled, crammed between Gemma and Lianne on the bench seat. "How did this place get so rundown? I feel like we're out in the boonies."

"Just the edge of town. But look at it. This place is hardly worth Jocelyn's trouble, yet she's held onto it through the years, then clears everyone out like there's a fortune stored here. Makes you wonder."

In the passenger seat, Lianne took her binoculars and aimed them at the various buildings. "You're right about the cameras. I don't see any. If there's something important or valuable here, why wouldn't she install surveillance?"

"Maybe she doesn't want to draw attention to it," Leia offered. "Security cameras would certainly do that, especially a dump like this."

Lianne twisted in her seat. "So what's the plan? How do you intend to get inside? Crawl over the fence?"

"I won't have to. I have the key code."

Leia's head snapped around to stare at Gemma. "How did you manage that?"

"Remember when Lando and I first went to see Jocelyn. The housekeeper stuck us in the library. Jocelyn kept us waiting there on purpose. I made use of my time. I snooped around her little secretary's desk she'd wedged between the shelves. Oh, I didn't open any drawers or peek inside the hidey-holes. She'd written down the code in plain sight on her desk calendar."

"You are resourceful. I'll say that for you," Leia uttered. "Was it your instincts that made you believe Jocelyn was bad news from that first time you set eyes on her?"

"Yep. From the moment I stepped inside her house. Look, this isn't the time or the place to talk about this. We need to get in and out fast as we can. Now, I'm taking Rufus with me to sniff each door."

Leia wrinkled her nose. "That's your big plan?"

"What's wrong with that? I told you back at the house. Besides, dogs, especially Labs, can sniff stuff that no humans ever could. Rufus has a nose for a lot of things."

"Yeah, trouble being one of them," Lianne muttered.

"I heard that," Gemma said as she grabbed one of the flashlights and hopped out. "Just for that, you can carry the bolt cutters."

Liane bounded out of the truck. "Oh, joy. I'm already feeling special."

Gemma went around to the back and opened the rear door for Rufus. She snapped the leash to the dog's collar. When Rolo tried to squeeze out of the opening to join his bigger buddy, Gemma snatched up the Westie before he could make a break for it. She handed the dog off to Leia. "You carry Rolo."

"You're sure bossy when you're like this," Leia noted. "I'm not even sure what you're hoping to find. Lianne's right. If Jocelyne ran off all the customers, most of those units are probably empty."

"I'm counting on that. But if she is hiding anything here, Rufus will sniff out what it is. I'm looking for the units with locks, hence the bolt cutters." Gemma held up a crowbar just in case. "Look, the surrounding field is muddy from the rain. I'll do the initial walk-around, and then we'll assess the situation. You might be right. Maybe there's nothing here."

Tail wagging and eager to start, Rufus pulled on the leash. Gemma punched in the code on the keyboard and followed the dog through the gate.

Lianne and Leia trailed after Gemma and the Lab, gingerly stepping down the middle of a gravel pathway to the first building.

Sniffing the ground as he went, Rufus went up to each unit, but he didn't stay for long. Instead, the dog moved on to the second building. Here, they lost the gravel pavement, and the ground turned into a muddy mess.

Leia artfully dodged puddles and pointed out bigger ones for Lianne to avoid.

Rufus made fast work of the second building and the larger units, unable to pick up any strange odors or anything out of the ordinary.

Gemma shined the flashlight on the latches and saw there were no locks on any of these doors. After clearing the second row, Rufus rounded the corner to the third building and found a concrete pad in front of it. For some reason, this building seemed better maintained than the other two. And there were double locks that looked relatively new on the middle aluminum door.

Rufus sniffed around the edges.

Gemma noticed his tail wagging faster, and his body started to shake, showing his excitement.

"What is that smell?" Lianne asked, holding her nose.

Gemma covered her nose with her hand. "That's decomposition."

"Want the bolt cutters?"

"No. I think it's time to call Lando," she replied, reaching into her coat pocket for her cell phone. She punched a number and waited. By the time he answered, she was shivering more from the discovery than the chilly night air. "I don't know where you are exactly right this minute, but I think you better get over here to Jocelyn's storage units. And you'd better bring a warrant. I think we just found another body."

By ten o'clock that evening, the old Stash and Store had become a crime scene.

Thanks to Rufus, when Lando had opened Unit Number Fifteen, the middle unit on the third row, he'd discovered a long, plastic, blue container. Inside the box had been the body of an adult male.

"I don't recognize him," Lando said. "Do you?"

Standing more than six feet away and with a scarf over her nose, Gemma shook her head. "No. He's not from around town. How old do you think he is?"

"Fifty-five, maybe. Hard to tell for certain."

"I have a reasonable explanation for being here," Gemma began. She'd practiced her speech while waiting for him to show up. "Wanna hear it?"

Lando held up a hand. "Nope. Don't care. Doesn't matter now. You may have just cracked this case wide open. For that, I'm grateful. Now I have cause to bring Jocelyn into the station."

"I suppose. But don't you need an ID or something on the dead guy first? Or an autopsy that tells how he died?"

"I already know how he died. He has a bullet wound to his head, just like Ben Zurcher and Daniel Albrecht."

"I don't get it. Why would Jocelyn put this one in here, hiding him away like this? You know, I'd look to see if anyone went missing back in November before Thanksgiving. That's around the time she sent out notices to everyone about finding another place to store their stuff. The body has to be the reason."

"I'd say hiding a body in here is a damn good reason to send everyone else packing."

"Do you need me to hang around? Leia and Lianne are getting as restless as the dogs. I think I should take them all back home and feed them."

"Sure. Get out of here. Just don't leave town. I'll need you guys as material witnesses."

"Very funny. In fact, for the top cop, you're hilarious."

"Gotta have a sense of humor through stuff like this. Otherwise, I'd lose it for sure."

Gemma leaned in to give him a peck on the cheek. "See you at the house."

"Not any time soon, I'm afraid."

"Then I'll drop everybody off and come back with coffee and sandwiches. How does that sound?"

"Sounds great. Make enough for Tuttle. I can already hear him grumbling."

22

Lando was going on zero sleep. Most of the people in his office the next morning were in the same sad shape. Luke. Zeb. Dale. Gemma. They were crammed into the room with people all talking at once.

Jimmy and Payce were the only two who had gotten a full eight hours of rest, but they seemed overwhelmed with the turn of events.

Everyone else seemed short-tempered, including Jeff Tuttle, who tossed down a file folder on top of Lando's desk. "Laura Leigh's autopsy report. Just like I said, no surprises. She died as a result of the car accident, suffered trauma to the head when she went through the windshield. Not wearing a seatbelt. She was dead on impact."

Lando ran a hand through his mop of wild hair. "But we think someone cut the brake line to her Prius. If that's true, then it would make it murder and not an accident."

"Yeah, I got the photos. After studying the Prius pictures and making sure the VIN matches, I don't have a problem changing the cause of death from accident to homicide. Happy now?"

"Not really. What about the dead guy in the storage unit?"

"Preliminary results show he's likely been there four months."

"November then?"

"Could be. The body was there through the winter. The cold kept it from decomposing too rapidly. But it did decompose on the same scale as approximately four months out."

"That's what I was trying to tell you earlier," Jimmy said. "Before all these people showed up. I checked for missing persons. There was a private detective out of Crescent City who went missing the week before Thanksgiving after telling his wife that he was working on a big case. He left his house one morning and didn't come home that night. That's the last she heard from him. Name's Samuel J. Dinsmore."

Lando's jaw tightened in thought. "That has to be the guy left in Unit Fifteen." He turned to Tuttle. "Start your ID process with that name. If it's him, it'll save you some time. What was a private detective doing—"

"The name Sam Dinsmore was in Ben Zurcher's contact list," Jimmy provided. "Apparently, Ben contacted him back in October. They exchanged emails. Dinsmore decided to take the case. And he must've turned up something important that led them to a suspect because they both end up dead as a result. Daniel Albrecht must've been part of whatever they discovered."

Dale squeezed in next to Gemma. "After the divers found the gun, a semi-automatic Walther PPK pistol, I dropped it off for testing at the crime lab. The tech reminded me that type of gun is known far and wide for very low recoil. It's deadly accurate. It might be a James Bond classic, but it's a perfect weapon for a woman. That's when I realized we should've found a casing in the basement at the mercantile that morning."

"Why didn't we? The killer picked it up."

Payce scooted in next to Dale. He held up a baggie. "Spent casings. Three. Found inside the storage locker with the dead body."

"One for Ben, one for Albrecht, one for the dead guy in the storage unit. Why do I get the feeling that no one messes with Jocelyn Williams and lives to tell about it?"

"Because she leaves a string of bodies in her wake," Gemma provided. "I started my morning searching for that unsolved murder of a homeless man in Oakland, the one I'm sure Eric Williams killed. Sure enough, two months before the Copeland murders went down, on August 13th, 2000, Robert Makepeace was found dead in an alleyway. He was bludgeoned to death with what authorities decided was a baseball bat. Oakland PD even has grainy video of the attack captured on CCTV from a convenience store across the street. But the quality is so poor they could never identify Makepeace's attacker."

Lando leaned back in his chair. "It's a shame they didn't try harder. If they could've caught Williams way back when, how many lives could've been spared?"

"By my count, at least nine," Gemma tallied. "Sandra. Todd. Hallie. Julie. Eric Williams. Laura Leigh Baccarat. Sam Dinsmore. Ben Zurcher. Daniel Albrecht. And that's not even counting her parents. No way to prove she tampered with their car before they headed back up the Coast Highway to Coyote Wells."

From the back of the room, Zeb cleared his throat. "I left one of my men watching Jocelyn's house. Jake Culross. Cody Chato will take over this afternoon."

"That won't be necessary," Lando stated. "I've got Hartwell working on a warrant for her arrest. Finding Dinsmore at her storage business jumpstarted a complicated case that until now had no links to Jocelyn. Now we have a dead body, shell casings we hope to match the murder weapon and a lot of conjecture. We need to put it all together. And we will." He looked at Jimmy. "You and Payce go out to Derrick's house and pick him up as well. We're going to take this step by step and let the trail of evidence speak for itself."

When Zeb's phone dinged with a text message, he held up the device. "Jake says Jocelyn Williams is on the move. She's loading up luggage into her champagne gold Lexus."

"Word must've gotten out that the crime scene techs are all over her storage unit. Let's go. Zeb and Dale, you're with me. Tell Culross to stop her no matter what he has to do. Don't let her flee."

Tired to the bone, Gemma brushed her hair back from her face and grabbed Lando's arm. "Be careful out there. Don't underestimate this one. I'm convinced that woman is a certified psychopath."

Wearing his tribal police uniform, Jacob Culross had stationed his unmarked police car at the end of Shell Bay to block in the psychopath's fancy Lexus from getting out of the neighborhood. But waiting on backup to arrive meant that if she pulled out of the driveway, it was up to him to stop her from going anywhere.

Jake knew he had no jurisdiction off the Reservation, but orders were orders. Intent on doing his job, he watched as the woman finished tossing stuff into the trunk of her car, then slammed the lid shut. She settled behind the wheel and cranked up the engine.

A bad feeling came over Jake when the suspect stepped on the gas and roared out of her driveway. Revving the engine, even more, she swung the car around to face him.

He heard squealing tires. He saw smoke from burning rubber. The next thing he knew she was barreling straight for him at full speed. He could see the murderous intent in her eyes as she gripped the steering wheel with white knuckles and prepared to ram his cruiser.

At the last second before impact, Jake opened the driver's door and dived for the pavement. Rolling into a patch of hedges, he watched as the Lexus careened up onto the sidewalk and took out a row of prized pink rosebushes just beginning to bud.

Clipping the hedges didn't seem to stop her momentum. She floored the vehicle as it roared off down the road.

He managed to get to his feet to radio in. "Suspect is on the move heading east on Valiant Way in a gold Lexus. She tried to ram my car. Consider her armed and dangerous."

Hopping back into his cruiser, Jake yanked the gearshift and turned the car around, then shifted again before stepping on the gas to give chase.

Hightailing it down Valiant Way, he caught sight of the Lexus rounding the corner onto the old section of the 101.

"Suspect is now heading north on the old junction road." He no sooner got the warning out of his mouth when he edged up on the Lexus. At speeds inching toward seventy, Jake caught sight of an SUV with the Coyote Wells PD insignia. The SUV cut him off and fell in behind the speeding sedan.

Pushing eighty miles an hour, the SUV soon overtook the Lexus. It wheeled in front, forcing the Lexus off the road and into a ditch.

Jake pulled up to the side of the gully, blocking the sedan so it couldn't go anywhere. He jumped out of his car. "I'm sorry. I tried to keep her contained."

"No problem. We've got her now. That's what's important," Lando stated as he marched over and yanked open the driver's side door. He saw Jocelyn bleeding from her lip and forehead where the airbag had deployed. She had a glazed look in her eyes. "Planning on taking a trip, Jocelyn?"

"My lawyer will sue your ass off for this."

"Quick recovery. I don't think so. You'll need a criminal attorney for what we have in mind. I'm arresting you for the murders of Samuel J. Dinsmore, Benjamin Zurcher, and Daniel Albrecht."

"Those charges are just for starters," Dale added. "We've got arson and breaking and entering."

"You can't prove a thing," Jocelyn yelled as Lando pulled her out of the front seat. He snapped a pair of cuffs on her wrists. When he began walking her to his SUV and reciting the Miranda warning, she tried to kick him in the legs. "Dale, do me a favor. Take this piece of trash and lock her up for me. Will you?"

"You bet."

"And finish reading her her rights. By the book, remember? I'm sick of looking at her already."

"You got it."

Zeb let the scene play out as Dale put Jocelyn in the back of his squad car and took off. He stood there in the middle of the street and stared at his youngest officer. Zeb decided the kid deserved some praise. "You did good."

"You think so? I thought for sure she'd barrel right into my car, take me out with her. She tried to run me down."

"Is that a fact?" Lando said with a grin. "You just made my day even better. She's certainly one of the most devious females I've ever encountered. Now, we'll add a charge of attempted murder of a police officer to the other stuff. How's that sound?"

Zeb slapped Jake on the back. "You'll be famous. You just helped take down a serial killer. This arrest might easily be the highlight of your career."

Still a little shaky from the ordeal, young Jake stood up taller. "I looked into the eyes of a serial killer? For real? That woman is a serial killer?"

It was Lando's turn to dish out a compliment. "Yep. It wouldn't surprise me one bit if you got a commendation out of this."

A startled Jake went bug-eyed. "No way."

Lando exchanged an amused look with Zeb. "You didn't mention to him that he was keeping an eye on one of the County's worst criminals ever?"

"Nah, I figured if he knew, he'd hit me up for a raise."

Beginning to suspect a joke in the making, Jacob Culross thought he'd figured things out. "You guys are pulling my leg, right?"

Lando shook his head. "Nope. Jocelyn Trask Williams might've killed at least a dozen people."

"That we know of," Zeb added for effect. "Could be there are more victims out there we don't know about."

Jake was starting to believe they were on the level. "Maybe I should get a raise."

"Don't push it, kid. You did let her get by you."

"She used her car as a weapon," Jake pointed out.

"Which is why he should stay put and see it towed in as evidence," Lando suggested. "Follow through to the finish."

Zeb grinned. "There. See. You get to book all that luggage into evidence and write up a report. Just keep thinking about that commendation the entire time you're doing the paperwork. It'll look good on your performance review."

"Then I get a raise, right?"

"Sure," Zeb assured the kid as he watched him make the call into the tow truck company. Zeb watched him walk back to his cruiser with a certain bounce in his step. "That should keep him energized for another month or two."

"Kids. Were we ever that young and naïve?" Lando asked.

"Not me, but you sure were."

"Oh, I don't know. I remember that time you were out on patrol by yourself and thought you saw bigfoot. If memory serves, you even called it in. Sighting turned out to be a big ol' fierce brown bear scratching his butt on a tree."

"You promised me you'd never bring that up again."

Lando tapped the side of his head. "Yeah, well, it helps to carry around blackmail material if I ever need a favor."

"A favor? You always need my help, and you know it."

Lando slapped his brother-in-law on the back. "Haven't you heard? That's what family's good for."

23

The highlight of Lando's week saw Jocelyn locked in a jail cell. But when Gemma wanted to celebrate, he had to remind her it was too early for that. What he needed was to get Jocelyn to talk before he interviewed Derrick Ross.

He had Dale bring Jocelyn into an interview room where she spent half an hour screeching about how they had the wrong person.

After giving her plenty of time to throw a tantrum and then sulk, Lando invited Gemma to join him. Maybe having Gemma there would buffer his accusations. At least he hoped it would.

It was Lando who started with a direct statement, hitting her with the truth. "Look, it's over, Jocelyn. You're not going anywhere. That stunt with the car gets you the attempted murder of a police officer. You're looking at fifteen years to life. I guarantee you won't get bail from Judge Hartwell. You know it's true. Fancy lawyer or not, we've finally figured out your sordid past. All of it. Bail is usually frowned upon when it concerns a serial killer."

"You're dreaming," Jocelyn huffed out. "Or maybe just delusional. Both of you don't know the first thing about me."

"Now that's just not true," Gemma noted. "Everything you've been hiding for the past twenty years is out in the open now. It's all over town how you did it. Lando and I decided this was always about the Trask family fortune. Nothing else but greed and money."

"You don't know what you're talking about."

Lando's mouth bowed in a smile. "Okay. Then correct us when we get something wrong. Fair enough?"

Jocelyn crossed her arms over her chest and sat there in defiant petulance, refusing to cooperate.

"I'll take your silence as a yes," Lando said and went on, "You tried to set Ben's place on fire when you realized his death prompted a new look at your sister's murder. This is what killers like you fail to realize. They make mistakes. Your mistake was killing Ben. But before we get to that, we know it all started with you somehow managing to screw with the brakes on the car your parents were driving when they visited you that day at college. You see, we obtained a copy of the accident report from Marin County. That was back in 1998. Accident investigators went over the car with a microscope, but all they could find was that the car had no brake fluid left in the system. They chalked it up to poor maintenance, a fluke. But now we know better. You wanted your inheritance and didn't want to wait until your parents died of old age."

"That's ridiculous."

"Sandra might've thought so back then, that the idea of you causing the accident was ridiculous. But Sandra soon learned just how determined you were to get that money. There was a hitch. You didn't count on one little detail. Your dead parents threw a monkey wrench into your plans. They left Sandra in charge of the trust. Since she was the oldest, she was the executor. And the one who got to make up the rules. She insisted you finish college before you got a penny. That pissed you off. Enough that you did a lot of grumbling out loud to your roommates. My team talked to them, too, individually, one by one. You spent two years trying to find someone that would kill Sandra. That way, the money would come to you, and you wouldn't have to share with anyone. You'd be in charge. That was your next project. And it began almost immediately after you buried your mom and dad. At some point in your desperation, you reached out to Daniel Albrecht, a classmate of yours at the time. You tried to persuade him to kill for you. But Albrecht was sickened by your offer. He walked away cold and never looked back. That's what Daniel told Ben. You were the link to the Copeland murders."

"Daniel Albrecht was an idiot," Jocelyn spat out. "He turned out to be a pathetic little worm with no spine."

"But then you met Eric Williams. People tell us that Eric was a different sort of guy, malleable, but dangerous. It wasn't enough that he agreed to do it. No, you needed to test his loyalty to you first. So one night, you sent him out to prove himself. You asked him to kill someone for you. And being the simplistic fool he was, Eric went out, found a homeless guy named Robert Makepeace, sleeping in an alleyway in Oakland and beat him to death with a baseball bat."

Jocelyn's lips curled into a snarl. "Eric was another idiot. I'm always hooking up with idiots. But it's not a crime to have bad taste in men."

"That's true. But Oakland PD has video of the attack," Gemma said, waiting a slow beat for that to sink in. "The thing is, after Robert Makepeace, you talked Eric into murdering Sandra and Todd along with the kids because you wanted all the inheritance for yourself. If they were all dead, you wouldn't have to share a penny of it with anyone. Including Eric."

"This is unbelievable."

"No, it's not. Eric probably never mentioned it to you. But the night he killed everyone, he left his size eleven running shoes behind. Know why? His trainers were a mess, soaked in a mix of the victims' blood. The lab found a perfect DNA sample inside the shoe, enough for a male profile that matches back to Eric."

"You don't have Eric's DNA. The man's dead," Jocelyn retorted.

"That's how we have it, from his autopsy," Lando offered. "Our coroner is a surly guy but very good at his job. He kept tissue samples because he wasn't convinced Eric's death was accidental. Another mistake, Jocelyn."

Jocelyn glared at Lando. "You think you're so very clever, don't you?"

"Sometimes, I do. You sent Eric hunting that day," Lando continued. "You followed him to the woods. You managed to kill him with his own hunting rifle. You tried your hardest to make it look like an accident. But you failed."

"Here's a newsflash for you," Jocelyn snapped. "Accidents happen all the time. I can get seven experts to claim it was an accident. My parents included. That night it was rainy. The highway was slick. The accident investigators told me that Dad lost control. They shouldn't have been traveling that night—end of story. As for Eric, he fell and tripped, and the gun went off. I'm sticking to that version."

"You do that. But it doesn't happen with that kind of rifle," Lando explained. "Our side has experts, too. I will agree that we'll probably never be able to prove it."

"Of course you won't because I didn't kill him."

Gemma linked her fingers together. "Just another accident then? Just another unfortunate person who dies because they're in Jocelyn's orbit?"

Lando pretended to rummage through a thick file folder until he pulled out another document. "Like Laura Leigh Baccarat. Laura Leigh just wouldn't shut up about how you murdered the Copelands. She made sure plenty of people around town heard her theory on why you killed your sister."

"Again, no idea what you're talking about."

"You tampered with Laura Leigh's brakes. One night you got fed up. You were tired of her running her mouth. You got Derrick Ross to lure her to his cabin. While they were inside making love, you cut her brake line. We found the Prius at a junkyard, Jocelyn. The brake line was cut."

"So? That has nothing to do with me. I wasn't even there. You should talk to Derrick about that, though. He's the one who wanted her dead. He was tired of her, tried to break it off like seven times. But the stupid woman wouldn't go away quietly."

"Derrick's down the hall in another room," Gemma informed her. "We're planning on talking to him…when we're finished with you."

Lando shuffled more papers. "Then there's the private detective Ben hired named Sam Dinsmore. Ben brought him here to work on the case, in hopes that Sam could solve it. But Sam made a fatal mistake almost from the get-go. That first day in town, he showed up on your doorstep, started asking you serious questions about the Copelands. You didn't like that. You told him to leave. But then, at some point, you changed your mind and decided he had to go. You lured him out to your storage facility with the promise to clear up some of his questions. When he showed up, you put a bullet in his head with a Walther PPK pistol. We found the gun, Jocelyn. The one you tossed into the pond on Trask land. It turns out that it's the same pistol you used to kill Ben Zurcher that night at the mercantile and Daniel Albrecht."

"You really are quite delusional."

"Not really. You see, we have a photo of you getting out of your gold Lexus that night during the heaviest rain. We have you going into the mercantile that Sunday night. The photograph was taken at the height of the storm and time-stamped a few minutes before you shot Ben." Lando slapped down the blown-up image on the table.

"Please. That could be anyone. You can't even make out who that is."

"But the gold Lexus in the background belongs to you," Gemma pointed out and had the satisfaction of watching Jocelyn's arrogance fade into pure panic. For the first time, Jocelyn looked terrified, like her past had just caught up with her.

"That brings us back to Daniel," Lando prompted. "Daniel's sister told my team that he came up here to talk to Ben about you. You see, I think Ben wanted Daniel's relationship with you on record. He wanted to hear Daniel admit that you'd asked him to kill your sister. It's called precedent. Daniel verified in his own words that during the summer months in 2000, you kept after him to kill Sandra. We found Ben's tape recorder where Daniel had spelled it all out for Ben."

"It's hearsay."

"Maybe. But that's for a judge to decide. Then we have your Lexus showing up on the road to Moonlight Ridge the night Daniel died."

"Last time I checked, it's not a crime to go for a drive in the country," Jocelyn sneered. "Especially when I grew up out there. I get sentimental sometimes and go out there to calm myself down. So what if I go out to the Trask Ranch ever so often. Sue me."

"You know Daniel was found on Trask land because you lured him there. You took out your gun of choice, the Walther PPK pistol, and shot him in the head with his back turned."

"You've been quite the busy girl," Gemma taunted. "There is something I don't understand. How long had you and Derrick been having an affair when you decided to kill Laura Leigh?"

Jocelyn chewed her lip, a nervous habit she had when she didn't want to talk. But now, sensing defeat, she leaned back in her chair and took a deep breath. "Derrick and I have been together for ten years. Ten freaking years. After spending time with Eric, I never wanted to marry again. Not ever. I'm not giving up my power for some dip wad. But I told Derrick at the start that if he wanted to be with me, he had to get rid of Laura Leigh."

Gemma nodded. "And by 'get rid of' you meant…?"

"I meant dump her ass. I didn't tell the idiot to kill her. That was his idea."

Lando shifted in his chair. "You expect us to believe that you didn't want Laura Leigh dead, although she was the one spreading rumors about you killing your sister?"

"Okay, Maybe her dying was mutually beneficial for both of us. But Laura Leigh's death is on Derrick, not me."

Gemma couldn't believe Jocelyn's cold eyes, the lack of empathy, the lack of compassion. "But you both knew Laura Leigh had a child. If she died, that child would be left alone forever."

"Oh, please. Spare me the concern. The child went to live with Anna Kate. Sienna was infinitely better off with her than her mother."

"Says you," Gemma charged.

"You obviously didn't know Laura Leigh very well. She slept with anything in pants. No one even knew who Sienna's father was. Plus, she had an affair with her sister's husband. Don't go thinking Laura Leigh was some saint just because she's dead."

"So your version of Laura Leigh's death is that it was Derrick who cut the brake line and not you?"

"I didn't kill anyone."

"Right." Lando began to gather up his files just as Gemma pushed back from the table and stood up. He looked over at Jocelyn. "I think we're done here. I'll send Dale in to take you back to your cell."

"What happens now?"

"We charge you with three counts of first-degree murder and a host of other lesser charges. We figure something has to stick. But congratulations are in order, Jocelyn. From this point forward, you'll be known, far and wide, as one of California's deadliest female serial killers."

They moved down the hallway to where Derrick Ross sat at another smaller table. But before going into the room, Gemma turned to Lando. "That might be the most heartless woman I've ever talked to, and that includes my mother."

"At least Genevieve Wentworth never murdered a dozen people to get what she wanted."

"How strong is your case? Is it solid enough to put Jocelyn away for life?"

"We have the murder weapon. We have the shell casings. We have Dinsmore's body found in her storage unit. And we'll add to all that when Derrick flips on her. I think he's one man who knows all of her secrets. No matter what he says to dispute it, no matter how much he thinks he's in love with her. When it comes to saving himself and throwing Jocelyn under the bus, I think he'll do it in a heartbeat."

"I guess we'll see. Are you ready? Got your story together?"

"Let's do this. Roll tape."

Working as a team, they used the same technique they'd used on Jocelyn with Derrick.

"This is what we know for certain," Lando started. "You killed Laura Leigh Baccarat, cut her brake line, and then left the country. Your wife, Anna Kate, filed for divorce. You didn't contest it from Monte Carlo. Where you and Jocelyn were living together for six months, having a grand old time. You didn't even stick around to attend Laura Leigh's funeral. You left your wife to raise your kids, and the little girl, Sienna, and never gave any of them a backward glance. Jocelyn set you up in this great job, this commercial real estate game because she wanted you to kill Laura Leigh."

Derrick became agitated. "Now, wait just a minute. I never killed anyone."

Gemma linked her hands together and shook her head. "That's not what Jocelyn says. She claims killing Laura Leigh was all your idea. It's what you wanted. You cut the brake line on the Prius."

"No. That's wrong. I only knew Jocelyn because of Laura Leigh. She's the one who thought Jocelyn had murdered Sandra. Laura Leigh kept going on and on about how Jocelyn got someone to do it for her. And let me tell you, Laura Leigh wouldn't shut up about it for months. Of course, Jocelyn eventually got wind of the accusations. Anyone with ears had heard the rumors. After Laura Leigh died, I confronted Jocelyn about it. Jocelyn told me to forget everything Laura Leigh had said. She offered me six months abroad and a better paying job selling commercial real estate at five times what I was making working for the County. I jumped on it. Jocelyn saw to it I got my licensing requirements in record time, and I forgot about Laura Leigh. But I didn't kill her."

"I could show you Jocelyn's taped interview," Lando prompted. "Hear it out of her mouth in her own words. Do you know all of Jocelyn's secrets, Derrick? Or just part of the story?"

"What do you mean?"

"Do you know how many times she's murdered to get what she wants?"

Panic mixed with realization crossed over Derrick's face. "What are you prepared to offer me?"

"I don't make deals. That's the County prosecutor's job. But you testify against Jocelyn, tell us the truth about everything you know, and I'll put in a good word with the DA. But I'll tell you the same thing I told Jocelyn. You're not leaving here today without a murder charge. Bond is up to Judge Hartwell. And when I lay this out for him, you won't be going home anytime soon. It might've taken us ten years to get here, but the past just caught up with you and Jocelyn Williams in a big way. So, are you ready to tell me the truth? Who cut Laura Leigh's brake line and left her kid to be raised by someone else?"

Derrick bowed his head and covered his face with his hands. He slumped further down in the chair. "Okay. I did it. Jocelyn suggested it, planned it all, and I did it. At the time, I wanted that vacation to Monte Carlo. I was bored with my life, everything about it—Anna Kate, the kids, my job. I wanted a better-paying salary, a high-flying career in real estate. I wanted it all."

"And you lured Laura Leigh to the cabin that night. The whole time you planned to tamper with the car, right? She never received a mysterious phone call to meet up with anyone, did she?"

"No. While Laura Leigh took a shower, I went out to the Prius and cut the brakes."

"And afterward, when she left your little love nest, Laura Leigh was headed to pick up Sienna from her sister's house, right?" Gemma clarified. "She was on her way down that hill to get her kid and go home. She never made it."

His voice barely above a whisper, Derrick muttered, "Yeah. What happens next?"

"We charge you with murder. You'll get a bail hearing. As I said earlier, don't count on going home anytime soon."

Out in the hallway, Lando swung Gemma around in the corridor. "Now, we can celebrate."

"Let's get everyone together tonight. Our place."

"Sounds like a plan."

Gemma patted his chest. "I just thought of something, though. Someone has to tell Anna Kate what happened to her sister."

"You're right. I'll do it."

She took his face in her hands. "It might be better coming from me. I'll get Lianne and Leia to come with me. It's a girl thing." She took out her cell phone and sent them texts. "I'll go by the shop and pick up a bag of truffles. Chocolate always helps when you're delivering bad news."

"I'm not sure that'll work with Anna Kate."

"I'm not suggesting chocolate is the answer, but it might cushion the blow. And Anna Kate does have kids. The kids will love the treats, which should go a long way in making Anna Kate a little less sad."

She gave him a quick kiss. "I'll see you at home."

"I have paperwork to do."

Gemma patted his face. "Of course, you do. We're celebrating afterward. Instead of our place, let's all meet at Captain Jack's and check on your mom. Come to think of it, I haven't prodded Flanner in a few days. I need to ask him about my shed."

"You go pester Flanner. I'll see you later at the restaurant. Let me know how it goes with Anna Kate."

24

They waited for Captain Jack's to clear out before setting up several tables for their celebration feast. At this late hour, there was no one left in town who hadn't heard the news. People were streaming through the doors, greeted by either Lydia, Lando, or Gemma.

When Jeff Tuttle arrived, Lando pointed to the end of the bar. "Tina's already here. Now's your best opportunity to make your play."

Tuttle nodded and smiled. "I owe you big time. But we won't be naming our first kid after you. It'll have to be something other than Lando."

"Glad to hear it. Because personally, I don't think you stand a chance with her. But prove me wrong. She's ordered a gin and tonic, her drink of choice. Up to you to buy the next round."

"Thanks for the heads up."

Before Jeff could head that way, Lando reminded him, "Remember the agreement. I get access to the files in the morgue if I need them."

"Yeah. Yeah. I'll remember. I'm not the kind of guy to back out on a deal."

Lando watched the medical examiner saunter off, watched as Tina aimed her charm on Jeff. "Some people have no taste whatsoever."

"What's that?" Gemma asked, following the track of his eyes. "Oh, yeah. Jeff's never going to capture Tina's attention for very long. She has plans. She wants to be the star reporter in a much larger market."

"I can live with that," Lando quipped with a grin. When he spotted Flanner standing just inside the doorway, he nudged Gemma in the side. "Would you look at that? How did you get him here?"

"I told him we wanted to thank him for his part in nailing Jocelyn," Gemma said, sending Flanner a wave. "I dangled a meal as part of the incentive. Besides, we need to sit down and come up with plans for the shed."

Lando moved in to plant a kiss on her forehead. "Nice. Move him to a quiet table in the back. I'll see to it."

"Thanks." Gemma walked over to Flanner, prepared to keep him calm in the crowd of people. But he didn't seem that agitated. "If not for you writing down the license plate and the description of the Lexus, Lando wouldn't have had enough to arrest Jocelyn. That bit of information sealed her fate."

"It had to be more than that," Flanner protested. "I didn't do that much."

"But you did. Your habit of keeping track of the traffic out that way was the missing piece we needed," Dale upheld. "It was the key that broke open everything."

"I just like to keep track of cars and such," Flanner muttered. But his jaw dropped the moment he saw Lucy Devereux step into the restaurant. He glanced over at Gemma. "You invited Lucy? Here? Why?"

"Because she's a friend of ours," Gemma said with a straight face. "We wanted all of our friends around us tonight. I've learned one thing since coming back to town. It pays to have a tight-knit community around you when your back's up against the wall. We should take care of each other more. Don't you think?"

"But…"

"No buts, Flanner. We all need help getting through this thing we call life. If you don't believe me, I just had to tell a neighbor the most heartbreaking story so she'd hear it from me instead of the rumor mill. I had to tell her an awful, ugly truth about her ex-husband and her sister. It was like an arrow to her heart. But she'll be fine because we'll see to it that she's okay. That's what we do for each other."

Gemma pivoted toward Lucy. "I'll get you two a drink. What are you two having?"

Lucy's lips curved up as she stepped closer to Gemma, then closer to Flanner. "I'm not much of a drinker, other than my weekly wine. But I told myself tonight I'd try a white Russian. Remember that time we talked about premiering the movie, *The Big Lebowski*, after we remodeled The Cactus Flower Drive-in?"

The question sparked a memory in Flanner and caused him to flash a rare smile. "Yeah. I do."

Gemma noted the spark between them. If only she could take that little ember and fan it into a larger flame. "How about I show you to a table in the back so you guys can talk, somewhere not so noisy. Then I'll get your drinks. Follow me."

Gemma prodded Flanner to move ahead and then leaned in to whisper, "Maybe ask her what kind of day she had. Maybe ask her if she'd like to go see a movie or have dinner sometime."

Flanner chuckled. "I got this. I do remember how to talk to Lucy."

Gemma patted Flanner's shoulder. Keeping her voice low, she murmured, "Music to my ears. Because Lucy cares about you, and you care about her. Now try to relax and enjoy yourself. Ignore everybody else here. Tune out the noise. And don't blow it."

"What about going over plans for your shed?"

"That doesn't have to be tonight," Gemma mused. She got them seated, then took off for the bar. "I need two white Russians," she relayed to Leia.

"Good to know we're so cosmopolitan tonight," Leia tossed out.

"Aren't we just?"

"Hard to believe you just seated Flanner DelRay and Lucy Devereux. Together. How on earth did you get him into town?" Leia glanced over at the back booth. "And look at that, he's talking to a woman."

"Not just any woman. Lucy was his high school sweetheart before he joined the military."

"I'd forgotten that. You're trying to flex your matchmaker skills, aren't you?" Leia teased, bumping Gemma's shoulder in a playful gesture. When Gemma just smiled, Leia added, "Who knew you were such a romantic? Does Lando know?"

"He does. And he rubber-stamped it. Any ideas what to do for Lianne's bridal shower?"

Across the restaurant, Leia eyed her brother Luke, arm draped around her soon-to-be sister-in-law. "Not a clue. Those two sure made up fast. Any bets on whether or not they'll make it to the big day?"

"Stop talking like that. You were no prize before your wedding to Zeb. As I recall, you were downright difficult and rude."

"Don't remind me. Ooh, here they come, the lovebirds are all over each other."

Lianne and Luke joined the two women. Lianne sipped her wine and looked over at Gemma. "I'm glad that ordeal is over with Anna Kate. I was trying to explain to Luke just how bad it was."

Luke took a sip from his beer. "That couldn't have been easy for any of you. Not sure I would've had the courage to tell Anna Kate the truth."

"You should have seen her face when Gemma told her," Lianne conveyed to Luke. "I've never felt so sorry for anyone. And after we left, Anna Kate still had to find the right time to tell the kids why their dad won't be picking them up this weekend."

Leia took a drink order from Sadie Sawyer and continued talking. "I felt sorry for Gemma. It's brutal having to tell someone that their husband murdered their sister. I thought for a minute there that Anna Kate might shoot the messenger."

Gemma picked up the white Russians. "I wasn't sure what she took harder, the murder itself, or the fact that Laura Leigh betrayed her by shagging her hubby. Now she knows the affair went on for years behind her back. That's a lot of lies built up over time to digest in one afternoon. Look, I'll be right back. I have two thirsty people who need their drinks."

She marched across the room and dropped off the beverages. "The Dude would approve. Trust me. Leia makes the best use of vodka. There's plenty to eat. Dips, chips, spring rolls. Help yourselves to the food."

Lucy held up her glass. "This is nice. Thanks for doing this, Gemma."

Flanner grinned and glanced up. "This is the best night I've had in a long time. Thanks."

"My pleasure. Now eat something. Or I'll come back and bore you silly with shed ideas."

Back at the bar, Lando and Zeb helped themselves to a beer. The two men held up the bottles for a toast, clinking the glass together. "Here's to joining forces every time we go after a serial killer."

Gemma looped her arm through Lando's. "Not to put a damper on your joining forces, but let's go find your mom and see if she needs a hand in the kitchen. We don't want to overwhelm her."

"Good idea. You're not gonna believe this, but I saw Paul Eddington sitting in his car outside in the parking lot," Lando announced. "He looked like he'd lost his best friend."

"Uh-oh. Is Paul here tonight? Does your mother know he's hanging around?"

"I don't think so. Should I go out there and tell him to get lost?"

"Let's see what she says." Gemma went through to the kitchen where Lydia stood, arranging warm chicken flautas on a tray. "Need some help?"

"No, I'm okay. Although you could make sure we aren't running low on guacamole."

"You got it."

Lando leaned in and kissed the top of Lydia's hair. "Thanks for doing this, Mom."

"Any time my boy brings down the bad guys or in this case the twisted bitch behind the Copeland murders, it's a reason to party. Did you see Flanner and Lucy together? I almost did a double-take and dropped the glasses." She sent Gemma a conspiratorial wink. "Wonder how that happened?"

"I know how it happened," Lando volunteered. "Gemma set this up. I'm not complaining. It's time Flanner caught a break. Don't you think?"

"I suppose there's no way he could get his job back," Gemma proffered.

"Sorry. No. That ship sailed. But he could fix up that old drive-in. Oh, I've heard the rumors. Maybe you could find some money in that redevelopment fund you got from the feds to help him get started." Needing a change of topic, Lando looked at his mom. "Did you know Paul's outside sitting in his car?"

"I know. He called me earlier, said he wants to get back together. Says it didn't work out with Jill."

"And?" Gemma prompted.

"I told him no. I can't trust him after the whole Jill thing. I'm okay with it. I like having my house to myself again."

"Want me to get rid of him for you?" Lando offered, turning toward the back door. "I don't mind having a heart to heart with him so that he knows to leave you alone."

"Maybe you should. I don't want Paul showing up any time he feels like it, not here at work, not at home either."

Lando did a mock salute and headed outside. But he discovered that Paul had already taken off. Making a mental note to follow up with the guy later in the week, Lando was about to head back inside when Jimmy came busting out of the side door.

"We've got a body that just washed up in the harbor."

"Male or female?"

"Lucien Thorne says male. He's the one who called it in."

"Whereabouts?"

"Straight down the street underneath the pier."

"Round up the team. Looks like the celebration for us will have to wait." Lando's face broke into a wide grin.

"What's so funny?" Jimmy asked.

"I just realized I get to tell Tuttle that his big evening with Tina is cut short."

"Let me," Jimmy offered.

"No way. I want to see his face when he has to negotiate for another opportunity."

Cast of Characters

Gemma Channing – Granddaughter of Marissa and Jean-Luc Sarrazin, now the owner of Coyote Chocolate Company, also the daughter of Genevieve Wentworth

Lando Bonner – Coyote Wells police chief, ex-husband of Gemma

Leia Bonner – Daughter of Lydia, sister to Lando and Luke, chef at the family-owned restaurant, Captain Jack's Grill

Dr. Luke Bonner – Doctor who works at the reservation's clinic, brother to Lando and Leia

Marissa Sarrazin – Gemma's grandmother, Gram, who owned Coyote Chocolate Company for forty years.

Jean-Luc Sarrazin – Gemma's grandfather, she calls Poppy

Lydia Bonner – Owner of Captain Jack's Grill and mother to triplets Lando, Luke, and Leia

Paul Eddington – Lydia Bonner's boyfriend

Zebediah Longhorn – Tribal Police Chief on the reservation

Vince Ballard – Owner of Wind River Vineyard and a real ladies' man

Collette Whittaker – Longtime administrative assistant to Vince Ballard

Lianne Whittaker – Sister of Collette, down from Portland to look for her sister

Marnie Hightower – Eighth-grade schoolteacher at Harbor View Middle School

Daryl Simmons – Former boyfriend of Marnie Hightower, basketball coach at Harbor View Middle School

Paloma Coyote – Her great-grandfather founded the town. Former mayor.

Van Coyote – Paloma's grandson, son of Michael

Nova Coyote – Van's wife

Michael Coyote – Deceased son of Paloma and Gemma's father

Coyote Wells Police Department:
Louise Rawlins – Desk sergeant, mother to Mallory
Payce Davis – Coyote Wells PD

Jimmy Fox – Coyote Wells PD and guitar player for the band Fortitude

Dale Hooper – Coyote Wells PD and keyboard player for the band Fortitude

Mallory Rawlins – Adopted daughter of Louise
Holly Dowell – Sister to Louise, birth mother to Mallory
Elnora Kidman – The town librarian
Adam Greendeer – Owner of Duck & Rum, a bar at the edge of town
Fleet Barkley – Former mayor
Reiner Caulfield – Former chief of police
Marshall Montalvo – Real estate developer, the wealthiest man in the county
Buddy Swinton – Son of Roland Swinton who owned a pizza parlor in town, now closed. Husband to Suzanne
Suzanne Swinton – Buddy's widow, who now works as dispatcher for the Coyote Wells PD
Roland Swinton – Owned the pizza parlor next door to the Chocolate Company. Marissa's and Jean-Luc's friend
Genevieve Channing Wentworth – Gemma's estranged mother
Judge Hartwell – State magistrate
Annette Ferris – County judge
Alex Kedderson – Attorney
Peg Thackery – Owner of Thackery's Pub
Denny Thackery – Son of Peg. Bartender and bookkeeper at his mother's pub
Duff Northcutt – Friend of Marissa
Billy Gafford – Antisocial guy living on the edge of town near Duff Northcutt
Natalie Henwick – A member of the book club and real estate agent
Lucinda Fenton – Marissa's next-door neighbor
Ginny Sue Maples – Luke's nurse
Radley Fisk – Drummer in the band Fortitude, a schoolteacher
Bosco Reynolds – Plays bass guitar for the band Fortitude, bartender at Duck & Rum
Theo Longhorn – Zeb's father
Rima Longhorn – Zeb's mother
Willow Longhorn – Zeb's younger sister

Trent Longhorn – Zeb's younger brother
Denise Coolidge – Dale's girlfriend who works at the Two Sisters' Food Mart
Jeff Tuttle – The medical examiner
Cheyenne Song – Veterinarian
Ebbie Lucas – Receptionist for Dr. Song, the veterinarian
Corkie Davenport – Dr. Song's tech nurse
Ansel Conover – Elnora's boyfriend
Enid Lloyd – Lianne's next-door neighbor
Aaron Barkley– Fleet's father
Harry Ashcomb – Pharmacist
Sam Wells – President of the bank and owner of the local radio station KYOT
Talia Davis / Lewis – One of Leia's friends who recently got married
Brandt Lewis – Man who married Talia
Birdie Sanger – Friend to Enid Lloyd
Inez LeMond – Runs Protect the Paws, a no-kill shelter for animals.
Tully Beacham – Fire chief
Dinah Underwood – Sister to Dharma and co-owner of Two Sisters' Food Mart
Dharma Kelly – Sister to Dinah and co-owner of Two Sisters' Food Mart. Mother to Denise Coolidge.
Cody Chato – Tribal police officer, works for Zeb
Jacob Culross – Tribal police officer, works for Zeb
Greta Todd – A recent high school graduate who plays the flute
Taylor Rainford – Leia's high school boyfriend
Dr. Margaret Kinsdale – Coyote Wells physician in general practice
David Border – The new bank president, replacing Sam Wells
Lucien Thorne – Commercial fishing boat captain
Joe Don Bowden – Local hot dog vendor
Ellen Emberley – Owner of The Crazy Daisy, a garden center next to Captain Jack's
Shaun Emberley – Gardener, brother of Ellen
Tiffany Ringgold – An old acquaintance from high school
O'Dell Owen – Manager of the airstrip
Darby Berwick – Owns the old shipyard
Kenny Painter – Manages the night shift at the casino on the Rez

Tina Ashcomb – Daughter of Harry. Tina works as a reporter for the county newspaper

Anna Kate Baccarat – Old friend from high school days

Laura Leigh Baccarat – Older sister of Anna Kate and a murder victim

Flanner DelRay – Military veteran who served in Afghanistan and now lives off the grid

Lucy Devereux – Nurse at Dr. Margaret Kinsdale's office

Don't miss these other exciting titles by bestselling author

Vickie McKeehan

The Pelican Pointe Series
PROMISE COVE
HIDDEN MOON BAY
DANCING TIDES
LIGHTHOUSE REEF
STARLIGHT DUNES
LAST CHANCE HARBOR
SEA GLASS COTTAGE
LAVENDER BEACH
SANDCASTLES UNDER THE CHRISTMAS MOON
BENEATH WINTER SAND
KEEPING CAPE SUMMER
A PELICAN POINTE CHRISTMAS
THE COAST ROAD HOME
THE BOATHOUSE

The Evil Secrets Trilogy
JUST EVIL Book One
DEEPER EVIL Book Two
ENDING EVIL Book Three
EVIL SECRETS TRILOGY BOXED SET

The Skye Cree Novels
THE BONES OF OTHERS
THE BONES WILL TELL
THE BOX OF BONES
HIS GARDEN OF BONES
TRUTH IN THE BONES
SEA OF BONES
FORGOTTEN BONES
DOWN AMONG THE BONES

The Indigo Brothers Trilogy
INDIGO FIRE
INDIGO HEAT
INDIGO JUSTICE
INDIGO BROTHERS TRILOGY BOXED SET

Coyote Wells Mysteries
MYSTIC FALLS
SHADOW CANYON
SPIRIT LAKE
FIRE MOUNTAIN
MOONLIGHT RIDGE

ABOUT THE AUTHOR

Vickie McKeehan's novels have consistently appeared on Amazon's Top 100 lists in Contemporary Romance, Romantic Suspense and Mystery / Thriller. She writes what she loves to read—heartwarming romance laced with suspense, heart-pounding thrillers, and riveting mysteries. Vickie loves to write about compelling and down-to-earth characters in settings that stay with her readers long after they've finished her books. She makes her home in Southern California.

Visit Vickie online at

www.vickiemckeehan.com
www.facebook.com/VickieMcKeehan
vickiemckeehan.wordpress.com/
www.twitter.com/VickieMcKeehan
www.instagram.com/vickie.mckeehan.author

Printed in Great Britain
by Amazon